Hooker to

Housewife

Also by Joy King

Dirty Little Secrets

Hooker to Housewife

Joy King

 St. Martin's Griffin ➤ New York

HOOKER TO HOUSEWIFE. Copyright © 2007 by Joy King. All rights reserved. Printed in the United States of America. For information, address St. Martin's Press, 175 Fifth Avenue, New York, N.Y. 10010.

www.stmartins.com

Library of Congress Cataloging-in-Publication Data

King, Joy, 1978–
    Hooker to housewife / Joy King.—1st ed.
        p.   cm.
    ISBN-13: 978-0-312-35408-4
    ISBN-10: 0-312-35408-8
    1. African Americans—Fiction.   2. Hollywood (Los Angeles, Calif.)—Fiction.   I. Title.

PS3611.I582H66 2007
813'.6—dc22

                                    2006051191

10 9

This book is dedicated
to all my industry chicks who
are putting in that overtime trying
to go from Hooker to Housewife.
I see you. I wish you the best of luck!

ACKNOWLEDGMENTS

Wow, I'm back again for part two. Where do I start? Of course, thank you to my family, I love you. I especially want to thank my mother, who is my biggest supporter. You're always willing and ready to read my stories and to give me your honest opinion—I do so appreciate that.

To my true friends, you know who you are, because I don't have that many (smile). I truly adore you.

Monique Patterson, I'm trying to hit one out of the ballpark this time. Only because of your expertise is it even possible for me to say that. My gift is highlighted because of your talent—thank you.

Much love to Marc Gerald and everybody at St. Martin's Press; Emily Drum—girl, I miss you!

To all the book clubs, vendors, and retailers, I greatly appreciate your giving a rookie in the game a chance to shine.

Finally, but most important, my readers—you're the best!

When I received tons of email from people who read *Dirty Little Secrets* it touched me in a way that's almost unexplainable. You embraced Tyler Blake as if you knew her personally, and that means I did something right when I wrote that character. For all of you who didn't get it—oh well. But seriously, hugs and kisses to everyone who supports my work, because if the readers don't embrace me, then I might as well put the pen down. For my previous booklovers and my new booklovers, thank you for joining me on yet another journey. So sit back and prepare yourself for what I hope will be the ultimate ride!

Hooker to Housewife

Sex Is the Key to . . . Money,
Power, and Respect

2000, Southside Chicago

"Chantal, time to get up," Mrs. Morgan said in her usual chipper voice. Chantal could never decide what annoyed her more, the sugary sweetness in her mother's voice or having to wake up early to attend school. She felt lucky knowing today was officially her last day in high school. After graduation Chantal had big plans and none of them included having to hear her mother tell her it was time to get up.

"Dear, you're going to be late, now you really should get up." Mrs. Morgan lightly tapped Chantal's shoulder under the blankets.

"Ma, I heard you," Chantal said shrugging her arm. "Now can you please leave my room? I don't need you standing over me when I get out of bed."

"Okay, but your breakfast will get cold if you don't hurry up."

"Please, don't wait for me. I ain't eating that fattening shit anyway. I have to watch my weight because I'm going to be a star, and my hips don't need to spread no further." Chantal mumbled under the covers.

"What did you say, dear? I couldn't quite hear you."

"I said I'll be out in a minute."

"Oh good, then I'll start fixing your plate."

After another five minutes Chantal finally pulled herself from under the covers and stepped out of bed. When her feet touched the floor the first thing she noticed was that she was in desperate need of a pedicure.

"Damn, I don't feel like polishing my toes. I'll have to go to the nail salon." Chantal smacked her lips and walked over to the dresser drawer and took out her wallet. She only had thirty dollars and that was barely enough to get her hair done for the graduation ceremony. "Ain't this some shit?" Chantal tossed her wallet on top of the dresser and grabbed what she needed before heading to the bathroom.

After a few minutes in the bathroom Chantal exited, dressed and ready to finish her last miserable day of high school. When she entered the kitchen she noticed her mother reading her daily chapter from the Bible. Chantal knew for a fact her mother had read the Bible front to back at least six times and never understood why she would start again from the beginning when she had finished. Her father, of course, was reading the classifieds in the local paper, looking for yet another job. He already had two but insisted on having a third part-time job.

"Daddy, you still looking for another job?" Chantal said as she sat down at the table. She observed the plate her mother had prepared for her. Pancakes with tons of butter dripping down the sides, greasy maple-smoked bacon, and eggs with cheese, but there was much more cheese than eggs. Chantal turned her face away from the food and picked up her orange juice and sipped on that. At only eighteen, Chantal had already envisioned what her life would be like in the near future, and it didn't consist of eating the plate of fat her mother placed in front of her. Although she grew up on what many would consider the wrong side of the tracks, Chantal still felt superior to everyone around her, including her docile parents. Chantal would often reflect on the biblical phrase her mother would quote about highly regarded leaders who did positive deeds to uplift the community: "Many are called, but few are chosen." Chantal derived her own meaning from the phrase; that many women wanted to be born beautiful, live a life of wealth and privilege, and marry the man of their dreams, but only a select few would seize all three. With Chantal's gleaming honey blonde hair, her sun-kissed bronze skin, flawless features, and a body no man could resist, there was no doubt in her mind that she was one of the few who were chosen. Chantal felt that no one, including her parents, understood her determination for reaching greatness. Instead of people viewing her attitude as confident, they called her stuck-up and arrogant. Chantal's parents would constantly tell her to be more humble, but she ignored them. Chantal had already made up her mind. No one would stop her from living her dreams.

"Well, a man gotta work and it's hard out here."

"I don't understand why you just don't get one good job that would pay all the bills instead of getting nickel-and-dimed at those other little jobs you got."

"Because nothing in this life is guaranteed. I like knowing that if one job lay me off then I have another to fall back on."

Chantal took in a deep breath and rolled her eyes. "With all these little jobs you got, I'm sure you can spare twenty dollars."

"What you need twenty dollars for?" he asked suspiciously.

"I need to get a pedicure."

"What in the world—is that the procedure for your feet?"

Chantal ogled her dad for a moment, not sure if he was serious with his question. "Yes."

"Well I'll be—you actually have to pay for that? I thought you were supposed to clean your own feet."

"Daddy, if you don't want to do it yourself then, yeah, you have to pay somebody to do it. It's a job. Ain't nothing for free."

"Sorry, but I can't help you with that one. Your mother needs some money for groceries." Her mother nodded "yes" while her head was still buried in the Bible. Although she was supposed to be reading, her ears were obviously still listening.

"We don't need no more food up in this house. I can't believe ya'll gon' have me walking around with jacked up toes because you want some more pork on the table."

"Now ain't nothing wrong with some good pork, Chantal."

"Oh please. I'll see ya later."

"Dear, you haven't touched your breakfast," her mother looked up and said.

"I'm running late and I don't want to miss the bus. Give it to Daddy—I'm sure he's still hungry, since he needs to give you money to buy more food." Chantal's parents looked at each other and she stared at them for a moment. She didn't understand how they could've produced her. Physically, she understood, because although both were in their fifties Chantal could still tell that at one time they had been a striking couple. Chantal's mother put her in mind of Diahann Carroll and her father was what many of her classmates labeled her: a mutt. He was a combination of African-American, Irish, Venezuelan, and Italian. None of that mattered to Chantal because when she looked in the mirror all she saw was a gorgeous, exotic-looking black girl.

Yes, their physical genes ran through Chantal's blood, but that's where the similarities ended. Her mother was a devout Christian who never raised her voice and her father was just plain clueless. Chantal wondered if the fact that her parents had had her later in life played a role in why they were so different from her. Chantal's mother had been told she couldn't have any children so when they conceived Chantal they called her their miracle child. When Chantal was born they spoiled her rotten. Not in a material-istic way because the Morgans didn't have the money to do so, which added to their guilt. But they spoiled Chantal by letting her say and do whatever she wanted. So although Mrs. Morgan was an avid Bible reader she must have missed the passage that said, "Spare the rod and spoil the child."

"Chantal, don't be that way. Here, take this twenty and go get your feet all pretty."

"Thank you, Daddy. I knew you wouldn't let me down." Chantal kissed her father on the forehead, but not before making sure the twenty was placed securely in her back pocket. Chantal's father just smiled in his customary fashion while Mrs. Morgan discreetly shook her head. Mrs. Morgan knew she and her husband had created a monster with Chantal but she felt it was much too late to do anything about it.

The Morgans had put Chantal on a pedestal since the day she was born. Mrs. Morgan couldn't believe that God had blessed one child with so much beauty. Wherever she took Chantal they were constantly stopped and told what a gorgeous little girl she was. By the time Chantal was ten years old she, too, knew just how beautiful she was and made it known.

When Chantal started elementary school, Mrs. Morgan took a part-time job cleaning houses to bring additional income into the home. One day, due to a school half day, Mrs. Morgan had to bring Chantal along for one of her cleaning assignments. She had to clean a mansion for an affluent white family in North Chicago. Chantal's eyes widened when they pulled up the long driveway leading to the opulent estate. "Ma, I ain't never seen no house like this before. It look like one of those castles I seen in my book."

"Well, it's big like a castle, too. Now you know I'm not supposed to have you with me so don't touch nothing, Chantal."

"I won't. I promise. You gonna clean this big old place all by yourself?"

"No. They have regular on-staff maids, but a couple of them are sick and they need me to do some light cleaning. We need the money so I couldn't turn the job down." By the time Mrs. Morgan finished her sentence Chantal had already made it to the door and rang the bell.

"Can I help you, little girl?" the butler asked when he opened the door.

"Excuse me, I'm here with my mother." Chantal brushed passed the man as if the house belonged to her.

"I'm sorry, sir, my daughter can get a bit excited. I'm Patricia," she said, extending her hand. The butler simply ignored her gesture and continued to stare directly into her eyes. Feeling embarrassed, Mrs. Morgan put her hand down. "I'm here to clean the house." The butler then turned and eyed Chantal. "Oh, I explained to the cleaning company that my daughter was out of school today and I would need to bring her with me on this assignment. They said it would be okay. I promise she won't be any trouble." The butler gave her an annoyed smirk and moved to the side, finally acknowledging that she was welcome to come in.

"You'll be cleaning the bedrooms upstairs. I'll escort you to the master suite." Mrs. Morgan and Chantal followed behind the snotty man. When they reached the master bedroom Chantal thought it looked more like a mini-mansion. The bedroom was twice as big as the entire house they lived in.

"One day I'll have a bedroom that looks exactly like this," Chantal stated proudly. Both her mother and the butler glanced at her simultaneously, but Chantal was oblivious to their glares.

"I'll be leaving you to your work. Let me know when you're done."

When the butler left, Mrs. Morgan stared at Chantal. "Chantal, you can't say things like that in front of the butler."

"Why not?"

"Because I'm here to do a job and that's not appropriate."

"You always tell me to be honest and I was telling the truth. One day I will have a bedroom like this and a house, too. That man should know it. Who knows, maybe he'll be working for me in the future."

"Oh, Chantal, such big dreams you have."

"They're not dreams. Look at these people," Chantal said as she pointed to several family photographs that decorated the room. "I'm more beautiful than all of them. If they can live like kings and queens, then so can I."

"It takes more than looks, honey. These people work very hard."

"Work hard doing what, Mama? They can't be working harder than you and we ain't living like this."

"Still, trust me this family worked very hard to get what they have."

"I bet you the only work the lady of this house is doing is on her back."

"Chantal, don't you say such things. Where did you learn that from?" Mrs. Morgan was stunned that her ten-year-old daughter was talking so grown.

"Mama, on my summer breaks you watch soap operas just like I do. All those white broads married to rich men don't do nothing but keep their hair, nails, and clothes tight. They go to bed looking like that and they step out the bed looking just as good. Obviously that's all men want, a woman who keeps herself looking pretty and ready to pleasure him in bed anytime he like."

"Chantal, that is television, it isn't real life. Plus, you have been blessed with God-given beauty and should never use it as a weapon. That's just evil."

"So you say. I call it using what you have to get what you want. I'm sure the Lord would understand. If he didn't want me to have it, he wouldn't have given it to me."

"Dear Lord, please heal my child," Mrs. Morgan said closing her eyes in a brief prayer. "You just make sure you're ready for church Sunday morning." Chantal rolled her eyes, already dreading their upcoming Sunday ritual. Mrs. Morgan could've had the pastor preach the entire sermon with his hand placed on Chantal's head and it still wouldn't have changed her heart.

That distant Monday morning, in the bedroom of a multimillionaire, Chantal had made it clear to her mother that living a life as a rich man's wife was her ultimate dream.

"Patricia, can you hear me?" Mr. Morgan asked for the third time. She had been so caught up in reminiscing about the past that she didn't hear her husband talking to her. It was seven years ago when she realized how jaded her daughter was and nothing had changed. Mrs. Morgan felt completely responsible for Chantal's thirst to live that life. She wondered if they had been more financially secure and provided her with more, maybe Chantal's attitude about the importance of material things wouldn't be so twisted.

"I'm sorry, honey, this scripture got me in deep thought. What did you say?"

"Here's the money for the groceries." He handed her four twenty-dollar bills. "I'm a little short of the hundred I promised, but you know Chantal did need the money." Mrs. Morgan looked down at the money and realized this was the story of their lives. Always sacrificing what they needed in order to give Chantal what she wanted.

As Chantal sat on the bus on her way to school she pulled out the new issue of *Vibe* magazine. The headline read, MEET THE KING OF NEW YORK. It had a full shot of one of the most handsome men Chantal had ever seen. When she looked inside to read the six-page article and photo layout her panties started to get moist at the thought of being married to a man with all that money, power, and respect. They showed snapshots of him with the mayor of New York and a couple of movie stars and supermodels. Chantal knew she was just as pretty, if not more so, than the women pictured with him. In Chantal's mind they just happened to get to the limelight faster than she did, but that was a small obstacle for a young woman as determined as Chantal. In a few days she would be a free woman and no one would stop her from achieving all her dreams.

Late Saturday afternoon Chantal returned home with her parents from her high school graduation. She laid her cap and gown on the kitchen table and headed to her bedroom. She returned ten minutes later and her parents were bewildered when they saw their only daughter standing in front of them with a suitcase and what appeared to be a bus ticket.

"Chantal, are you going on a trip?" Mr. Morgan asked with a perplexed look on his face.

"As a matter of fact I am."

"What is it, a graduation trip with some of your school friends?"

"Ma, I don't have no friends in school." Even though many had tried, Chantal refused to befriend any of her classmates; she kept to herself. She had the reputation as being the most beautiful girl in school but also the one with the nastiest attitude. Besides a couple of neighborhood girls Chantal kicked it with, she felt above everybody else. In Chantal's mind she already knew she was special and would live a lifestyle that most of them only fantasized about. The thought of putting her energy into befriending any of them seemed like a waste of her time.

"Then where are you going?"

"To a place where I can make all my dreams a reality."

"Where is that?" It was obvious to Chantal that her parents were dumbstruck.

"I'll let you know once I get there."

"But what about college? How will you support yourself? You don't have any money." Chantal just nodded as her parents continued to say what sounded like mumbo jumbo to her ears.

"Listen, I ain't going to no community college and I will find a way to support myself—it just won't be here in Southside Chicago."

"But, Chantal, if you stay here you'll have our support. That's fine if you don't want to go to school. We'll help you at whatever you decide to do," her dad pleaded.

Chantal chuckled for a minute. She didn't know whether to laugh at her father or pity him for being so naïve. "Daddy, with where I'm gonna go and what I'm gonna do your assistance won't be needed."

Mr. Morgan stood there completely confused, but Mrs. Morgan wasn't. She knew her daughter was up to no good and all they could do was pray that she wouldn't be eaten alive by the wolves she so desperately wanted to tangle with. Mrs. Morgan doubted they needed to worry about Chantal; instead their concerns should be for the prey Chantal was seeking out.

"You're my little girl; please don't leave us."

"Sorry, Daddy, but I have to go. The platinum streets are calling my name." Chantal picked up her suitcase and headed toward the front door. Mr. Morgan moved forward to stop his daughter.

"Cliff, let her go," Mrs. Morgan stated firmly.

"But she's our baby."

"No, she hasn't been our baby for a very long time."

"Chantal, please at least let me give you some money," he screamed out in his last attempt to make her stay.

"That's okay, Daddy, I'll be fine." Those were the last words Mr. Morgan heard before Chantal slammed the door.

Later on that evening when Mrs. Morgan was putting away the money she made from the previous day's work, it became crystal clear why Chantal had no need for the money her father had offered her. Chantal had stolen the very last penny of the $7,000 Mrs. Morgan had been saving up for the last few years, hoping Chantal would want to continue with some form of higher learning after high school. Mrs. Morgan was from the old school and, even though she had a checking and savings account at the bank, she always believed you were supposed to keep a secret stash at home. Unfortunately for her, no secrets were safe from Chantal.

ONE

Queen of New York

2007

The honey-blond bombshell strutted into the nail salon on Park Avenue like she owned New York City. All eyes turned to catch a glimpse of the cover girl beauty. She had the gorgeous face and impeccable style that made you ask yourself, *Where have I seen her before? Is she a model, actress, or singer? Is she famous?* No, she wasn't any of the above, but she was famous. Make that *infamous.*

Chantal Morgan did what many considered the impossible. She used her powers of persuasion to land the biggest mogul in the music industry. Andre Jackson was the Bill Gates of hip-hop, and Chantal was the femme fatale of industry chicks.

She didn't come by her fame the conventional way, but she worked the tools she had. Those tools were her lips, her ass, and her pussy. The deadly combination put her at the top of her game. For the average girl that would've been enough, but there was nothing average about Chantal Morgan and she assumed everyone else knew it.

Chantal couldn't fathom why after almost five years of her precious services she still hadn't walked down the aisle with Andre. What was it going to take, she'd quietly wondered. She had had his daughter, been through more drama with him than the law should allow, and still he refused to make her legitimate. Chantal's fame continued to come from being his baby mother and girlfriend. That was unacceptable for the self-proclaimed Queen Bitch.

She refused to remain in the ever-expanding group of celebrity baby mamas, which she considered beneath her. The frustration was building up and Chantal was exhausted from hitting the same brick wall. Maybe it's true what they say: "A man won't wife a ho."

Chantal sat at the nail salon getting Swarovski crystals on her gel-coated tips, admiring the ten-carat emerald-cut diamond sitting on her finger. It was a present from Andre for her twenty-fifth birthday. It was the third ring in two years but he still hadn't proposed. Every time she wanted to discuss getting engaged, it seemed he would immediately buy her a new bauble, as if that was supposed to keep her mouth shut. With Chantal being the materialistic slave that she was, it always worked. This ring, like the ones before it, was one more gift she could shamelessly flaunt in front of her equally shallow girlfriends. But when she was alone, with no phony cheerleaders to gas her up with false praises, Chantal had to admit that this situation was wearing on her psyche. She believed it was time for Andre to wife her. Not just say it, but do it.

"Pretty ring. You married? Husband must be rich," said the Chinese manicurist, as she meticulously created the design on Chantal's index finger.

"Not yet, but I'm working on it."

"Oh, he not ready to get married?"

"Not yet," Chantal retorted, smacking her lips.

"Oh, work harder," the Chinese lady said, shaking her head back and forth, as though Chantal was a disappointment.

Chantal said to herself, *I should have told the nosey bitch that I was engaged. Now she's looking at me like why am I wearing this big-ass rock and I can't get my man to commit. Come hell or high water, by end of this year I will be Mrs. Andre Jackson.*

After sitting under the dryer for a half hour, Chantal's $300 design was finally dry. She was being extra careful because she wanted her nails to stay in perfect form. Chantal had to be more on point than usual since she was escorting Andre to a red carpet movie premiere and wanted all eyes to be on her. With the dress she was picking up from Roberto Cavalli and with Marisa doing her hair and makeup, the original movie goddess herself, Dorothy Dandridge would have to make a grand entrance in order to shut her down. And since she was resting somewhere in royal diva heaven Chantal knew she had it all sewn up.

When Chantal opened the glass door and stepped outside, the cold air instantly sent chills down her spine. It was the middle of March and there is nothing like a New York winter. Even with her floor-length chinchilla coat she couldn't escape the harsh weather. Not being one to wait, especially for people who are supposed to serve her, Chantal became frustrated when the driver wasn't parked in front waiting as he was ordered to do.

"You have to be kidding me. Where is the dumb fuck? It's freezing outside and the hired help is nowhere to be seen!" Chantal muttered as she scanned the area for the car. Just then Chantal saw Carlos driving the black Rolls-Royce Phantom around the corner. She ran toward the vehicle in her black Gucci stiletto boots because it was too cold to wait for him to drive around a taxi that was blocking traffic. When she finally got in the car and slammed the door, the heat instantly warmed her and it felt so good she almost forgot to drill Carlos about where the hell he'd been. He gave her some lame excuse about the cops telling him to move out of the way. *Whatever,* she thought to herself, *he was probably cruising around the block trying to pick up some girls and frontin' like this is his whip.* Chantal knew the game. She used to be one of those girls chasing the guy in the fly ride because she assumed he had some paper.

"Go to the Roberto Cavalli boutique at 711 Madison Avenue," Chantal directed him, thinking to herself that as soon as she got home she was going to tell Andre to fire him.

As Carlos pulled up to the store she called the sales lady and told her to bring out her dress. She wasn't about to step out of the balmy car into the freezing cold. Chantal eyed the petite wannabe Eva Mendes–looking trick as she exited the store and ran toward the Phantom. The Cuban salesgirl gave Chantal a fake-ass grin and handed her the bag with the dress inside. As she waved good-bye and turned her back Chantal rolled her eyes and said under her breath, "That bitch doesn't think I know she was fucking Andre. Trying to act like she's so professional all the while she was swallowing my man's dick. Huh, that's why she's working at Roberto Cavalli, and I'm shopping here."

Those struggling days were long gone for Chantal now. She was finally living the good life. No more worrying about where her next dollar was coming from. She'd sealed that deal when she locked Andre down with their daughter. Melanie was a beautiful little girl and Chantal knew Andre was proud of her. People could say what they wanted, but Chantal knew if there was one thing she was good at besides sex, that was making some pretty babies. Ever since she was in high school, every guy would tell her they wanted her to be their baby mama. She reasoned that dudes always want the girl with the nice complexion and pretty hair, plus she had the body, too. She was constantly beating cats off with a baseball bat.

As Carlos opened her door, Chantal handed him her bags and walked into the lobby at the Trump World Tower. Andre had a penthouse in the building, and the fact she was laying her head there made her the envy of all women. Okay, maybe she wasn't laying her head there every night but the fact was she was the queen of that domain. When Chantal wasn't in Chicago, then she was in New York with Andre. She was still scheming to get him to move her and Melanie in permanently but until that happened she made sure to leave all her shit around for his hoochies to see.

On her elevator ride up, Chantal reflected back on one night when she came to town unexpectedly and thought she was about to catch a case. She had wanted to surprise Andre, so she caught a flight and arrived at his place in the early evening. When she opened the door she could hear some Sade playing but didn't think anything of it. Andre loved to listen to Sade when he was try-ing to relax. Chantal took her pumps off so he couldn't hear her feet on the marble floor. When she walked up the wraparound stairs she was the one who was surprised by intense breathing mixed with moaning. As she tiptoed closer to the bedroom door she heard a woman's voice saying, "Oh baby, you feel so good. Go deeper, deeper baby."

Then a male voice, which sounded like Andre, groaned, "This dick feel good to you, baby?"

"Yes, baby, I love my dick," the woman moaned.

"Your dick! Bitch, you've lost your damn mind!" Chantal roared as she pushed opened the door. They had candles lit with the soft music playing. Andre's ass was in the air about to come down and stroke the chick in her pussy once again. He looked up at Chantal like he was being introduced to the devil himself. There was so much rage across Chantal's face, Andre knew it was about to be on.

"What the fuck are you doing here? Your ass supposed to be in Chicago," Andre said.

"Yeah, that's what you thought. So what, you decided to dick down the next bitch because I'm not here? I'm gonna fuck this trick up and then I'm coming to get you."

The half-black, half-Filipina chick jumped out of the bed, putting her hands over her pint-size tits. Like Chantal gave a fuck about her body, she just wanted the trick out of her man's bed and his house.

"Chantal, calm the fuck down, you're acting real crazy right now."

"Oh, you haven't seen crazy yet!" Chantal barked while taking off her jacket and diamond hoop earrings, preparing for a brawl. She kept on her rings hoping to leave a signature mark on the girl's face. "You think I'm going to let you play me out with some cunt?"

"Ain't nobody playing you out. You wasn't even supposed to be here. Now calm down. This shit ain't funny."

"Andre, you better get this bitch out this house right now or I'm gonna fuck her up. Do you understand me?"

By this time the chick had tears rolling down her face. She didn't know what was going on. The distraught groupie was under the impression she would be making love and spending the night with superstar Andre Jackson. Well, not tonight, bitch. The Queen was now here and was claiming what was rightfully and undoubtedly hers. Andre was handing the frazzled woman her clothes, trying to apologize for the misunderstanding. Under his breath Chantal heard him call her Arisa. Arisa was looking scared and confused just the way Chantal wanted her to be. In the future she would think twice before bringing her bony ass to this crib. Just to make sure, while Andre was escorting Arisa out, Chantal snuck in a sucker punch to the woman's right cheek.

"That's my token to you. Think about that, bitch, when you crawl in your cold ass bed all alone," Chantal said with so much frost that even Andre got the shivers.

That was the type of bullshit Chantal had to deal with when it came to Andre. She knew he was screwing other women because Andre could not sleep in the bed alone. He needed to have a warm body next to him. With her living in Chicago, she damn sure wasn't cuddling up to him every night. But after that incident, Chantal made sure to leave everything from panties to lipstick to purses and clothes around the house. A bitch was gonna feel her presence.

The minute Chantal stepped foot in the front door, Marisa was anxious to make her into a glamour queen. Nobody could beat her face like Marisa. Yes, Chantal was naturally gorgeous, but when Marisa finished she would look flawless from head to toe. Chantal could never understand why Marisa would always have her looking like a dime piece but she herself strolled around looking like one-cent copper. Marisa wasn't a stunner, but damn if she just applied half her skills on her unruly hair and makeup-free face, she would at least be a nickel. But Chantal was no one's savior and she didn't have the time to make the suggestion. Plus, Marisa had access to mirrors and the eyes never lie. All that mattered was that she was the best and that's why Andre insisted that Chantal use her. Andre expected Chantal to look unblemished when she attended any event with him. That was fine with her; she liked to see the other women green with envy and the men drooling.

When Marisa finished dolling Chantal up, she slipped on her dress. She was divine. Her normally pale winter skin was luminous against the peach-colored dress, compliments of the beautiful golden tan from her and Andre's recent trip to Anguilla. Marisa pulled her wavy shoulder-length hair back to accentuate Chantal's perfectly featured face. The dress hugged every curve and made her ass look plump and round. The crystal-studded Jimmy Choos were the finishing touch.

"Chantal, you ready? It's time to go," Andre said impatiently.

"Just a minute, baby, I'm trying to tighten up my strap."

"Well, hurry up. I don't want to be late." Andre continued pacing back and forth in his gray wool three-piece Valentino suit and white cotton French cuff shirt. His black crocodile loafers and silver silk basket-weaved tie made his attire the perfect combination of playboy and New York City chic.

This was Andre's night to mingle with the Hollywood power-houses. He was determined to break in to acting. Hell, he had conquered the rest of the industry. Andre had his hands in everything. Music, sports, fashion—and now he wanted movies. Chantal loved it; that meant more photo ops for her. She grabbed her studded bag that matched the shoes and headed out the door.

When the stretch limo pulled up to the red carpet at the Ziegfeld Theater, all you heard was the paparazzi screaming for Andre Jackson. Chantal lived for these events. All the cameras flashing and people screaming her name—it gave her a rush, because she was a celebrity, too, in her own right. People wanted to grab at Chantal and take her picture. Some pathetic idiots even wanted her autograph all because she was with Andre. Chantal was his woman, so now all she needed to do was become his wife.

As they stepped out of the limo, Chantal smiled and gave her standard beauty pageant wave to all the cameras and fans. She was just as beautiful as any other celebrity walking the red carpet. This was the East Coast premiere for Halle Berry and Bruce Willis's new movie *Perfect Stranger*. Everyone from Denzel Washington to Julia Roberts was in attendance. The Hollywood elite were so different than their normal music industry peers. Everyone here looked refined; whereas the music industry set looked like brand new about to go broke money.

This crowd here was right up Chantal's alley; as for the other crowd, she had been there and done that, literally. Chantal had basically fucked every music bigwig and couldn't get any of them to sponsor her on a long-term basis. She was their trophy piece for a minute and then after they had twisted her back out and partied with her every which way, they traded her in for the next hot chick. Thank goodness she met Andre when she did, because Chantal Morgan had come one step from being a has-been in this town.

As they made there way to their seats, Andre stopped to chat with Tom Hanks and Harvey Weinstein. While he was doing that, Chantal checked out the competition in the room; Catherine Zeta-

Jones was looking gorgeous in a red Chloe dress. The new up-and-coming It Girl of Hollywood, Tyler Blake, had on an unbelievable white Zac Posen dress and, of course, the now divorced Jennifer Aniston had on her standard but beautiful black dress. Still, in Chantal's mind none of them could hold a candle to her.

By the time the movie ended Chantal was ready to get the hell out of there. She never liked sitting through a long movie, especially one that was borderline boring, and all movies were boring to Chantal unless it was one she was making in the privacy of her home. When Andre finally located their limo she just sat back and poured herself a glass of champagne. She was beginning to relax when Andre caught her eye with his devilish grin. Chantal could always tell when he was horny because his eyes would start dancing and he would give her a lustful half-smirk.

"Baby, why don't you come over here and kiss Daddy's dick?" Andre said.

Why not? If Chantal didn't, the next bitch would. She had no problem giving Andre head or whatever else he wanted anytime he pleased. She tried to fulfill every sexual fantasy he had and then some. The way these chicks were putting it out she had to stay on top of her game. Chantal gladly got down on her hands and knees in her new $10,000 dress and deep throated her man's penis and had him cumming before they reached the third stop light.

Seeing how aroused Andre was got Chantal all worked up, so she massaged his dick to get it back to a rock-hard position. Since she never wore panties, she simply lifted up her dress and straddled her man. Andre was grabbing at her dress trying to get a hold of her voluptuous breasts. Once he did he put his warm mouth around her erect nipple and squeezed the other breast, going back and forth. Andre was moaning in pleasure and they continued to fuck until the driver told them they had reached their destination. Even then they stayed in the limo for another fifteen minutes until both reached their climax.

Chantal had to throw it on Andre like that every so often so he wouldn't forget who had the best pussy out there. Everybody has a gift and seducing a man was Chantal's gift. She knew how to put it on her man like a professional. Sometimes she wondered if she was too good. Andre knew about her past for the most part, but at the same time she thought it bothered him a little when she screwed his brains out. She assumed it made him think that every man had gotten the complete mojo package like that and not just him. But what in the hell did Andre expect? Being the baddest bitch inside and outside of the bedroom used to be Chantal's livelihood. That's how she got him and that's how she planned on keeping him, too.

Promiscuous Girl

When Chantal met Andre in the spring of 2002 she was about to get evicted from her $7,500-a-month apartment on the Upper West Side; she could barely pay her electric bill. Times were hard. She had been dating this big time rapper and a superstar basketball player, and both were hitting her off lovely. She was pushing a drop-top Benz, traveling to all the hot spots, and chilling. By this time she was ready to lock one of the cats down and have a baby to guarantee some steady income. The problem was she was fucking them both raw and she couldn't take the chance of not knowing who the father was. She decided it was time to cut one of them off and reasoned the rapper had to go. Rappers make good money, but not that superstar NBA paper. Plus, the rapper already had a baby mama. He could never spend a holiday with Chantal and would constantly cancel at the last minute because his child's mother would call for some emergency regarding their snot-nosed kid.

Chantal never liked playing second fiddle and her NBA player was child-free and perfect for the taking.

When Chantal cut off her rapper friend, he wigged out. He went through all her belongings and found out that she was messing with Michael Mitchell. He whined, "You not dealing wit me no more for that punk-ass basketball nigga? Fuck that!"

When Breezy-B spotted Michael at a club he put her on blast like a scorned lover. He told Michael all the different positions he had dicked down Chantal and about the ménage à trois they did with this stripper chick who worked at Magic City in Atlanta. He just put all her business on Front Street.

Later that night Michael came over and cursed Chantal out. "You trick-ass bitch. You ain't nothing but a tired-ass ho. Take that contaminated pussy elsewhere. I don't want no part of it." After calling her all sorts of sluts and hoes, he then took the keys to the Benz and had the dealership people pick it up the next day. He took back every piece of jewelry he ever bought her and some that she didn't even think he gave her. To make matters worse, he snatched up the last bit of stash money that he would always put in her top drawer, too. Talk about being devastated: Chantal's cash cow checked out leaving her destitute.

The next day Chantal stayed in bed and cried her heart out. She had no man, no money, and no car. She didn't know what to do. She couldn't sell her jewelry because Michael took it all. She had no savings and no one to call for help. Chantal called Michael hundreds of times trying to get him to take her back, but he wasn't hearing it. She was so desperate she finally broke down and called the scorned rapper.

"Yo, please help me out. Because of that shit you told Michael, he ain't fucking with me no more. I'm dead-ass broke," she pleaded.

The bitch-ass rapper chuckled before saying, "I got you, shorty." Chantal let out a deep sigh of relief. "There's only one catch," he added.

"What's that?" she asked, figuring he wanted to get between her legs one more time, which she was more than willing to do under her humbling circumstances.

"I'll hit you off with some cash. You just have to let me and my five homeboys run a train on your trifling ass."

"You sick son of a bitch. I'm bad off but not that bad." Chantal slammed down the phone. By the time the second month rolled around the building manager was trying to put her out on the street.

Chantal's back was nailed against the wall and all her options were gone. She couldn't go back to Chicago because her parents were still pissed that she stole money from them and had never attended college, just to pursue what they considered the faulty glamorous hoochie-mama life. She had no friends that could put her up because they, too, were holding on to their last dime and wondering where the next one would come from.

One night while mourning over her predicament, Chantal's girlfriend Arlene called and told her Jay-Z was having a listening party and they should stop through. She was in no mood to go to an industry party, but Arlene said they could have a couple of drinks and unwind. It sounded good, especially because of the depressing mood Chantal was in. She put on some skintight jeans with a red, low-cut sweater and a pair of high heel boots. She brushed her hair back in a ponytail and spread red lip gloss across her luscious lips.

When they arrived at the Fiesta Lounge it was on and popping. Mad heads were holding court in the Euro-style spot. The décor had touches of red, exotic greenery, mixed with Asian accents to create a dynamic atmosphere. Chantal clicked her heels on the bamboo floors as she rushed the open bar and immediately had a shot of Hennessy. She was trying to forget about the shambles her life was in at the moment. Arlene was sitting on an ivory Barcelona chair, mingling with some A&R guy.

Chantal was downing her fourth drink when she heard a man say, "You are the prettiest thing I've ever seen."

Chantal slowly turned around and the deepest, most intense eyes were staring her in the face. Despite her buzz she knew that the eyes she was gazing into were those of the famous Andre Jackson. His videos were in rapid rotation on MTV and BET. He had endorsements out the ass and had just launched his own high-end clothing line.

"What did you say?" Chantal asked, starstruck.

"I said you are the prettiest thing I've ever seen. Why don't you come over to my table and share a bottle of champagne with me?"

"That's okay, I've already had too much to drink."

"Then why don't you come sit with me and keep me company?"

Chantal's head was starting to spin and sitting down sounded awfully nice, plus Andre was fine. She followed him to an elevated, glass-enclosed VIP area that overlooked the room. It had an unobstructed view of the stage so she could still observe the action, but then again there was no one in the spot that could give her better action than Andre Jackson.

"So what's your name, beautiful?"

"Chantal."

"I'm Andre Jackson."

"Oh, you trying to be funny. I know who you are; everybody knows who you are," Chantal said sarcastically.

"I apologize. I wasn't trying to be funny. I figured it would be rude not to formally introduce myself."

"No need to apologize. I'm enjoying being in your company," Chantal purred.

"Likewise. So what is your profession, Chantal?"

"I'm a model/actress," she answered knowing full well that was the job description every wannabe industry trick out there used instead of the title "well-paid hooker."

"How nice," Andre said, sounding amused since he hadn't

seen her in jack. "Would you like to be the lead in my next music video?" he asked, fully expecting she'd jump at the opportunity.

"Is it paying?"

"Of course, all jobs do, or at least they should," Andre said.

"No doubt then, just give me the day and time and I'm there," she said, giving Andre the answer he already expected.

He figured why not give her the part. If it wasn't her it would be some other groupie that sucked off the director for the role and they wouldn't be half as pretty as Chantal.

As Chantal sat back talking to Andre she considered that the sun might be shining bright for her again. Maybe all hope wasn't lost. If she could bag Andre Jackson then she, their kids, and grandkids would be set for life. So when he said the magic words, "Would you like to go home with me?" Chantal jumped at the opportunity. She quickly looked around for Arlene to tell her, but when she wasn't within reaching distance, Chantal was like, "Oh well."

All eyes in the club followed the fabulous-looking pair as they hit the exit. They couldn't help but wonder who the lucky beauty was leaving with the most eligible bachelor in New York. As they walked outside and the valet pulled Andre's red Ferrari to the front, they hopped in and sped off into the night.

Andre was zooming so fast on 208 North he almost missed the Summit Avenue exit. He eventually drove up to a long winding driveway that led to his fabulous mansion in Franklin Lakes, New Jersey. Over three and a half acres surrounded the architectural masterpiece situated on the crest of a hill. The stunning Tuscan-style estate had a gated entrance and a state-of-the-art security system. Chantal reflected back to the first mansion she ever laid eyes on in Chicago when she was ten years old. This was just the kind of home she envisioned herself luxuriating in.

When they entered the palace, Chantal was overwhelmed by the soaring mahogany ceilings, massive rooms, walls of glass, and marble, cherry, and limestone throughout. She followed Andre to the luxurious sunken living room that was enhanced by a television projection system, ashwood floors, and cherry-trimmed doors opening to a courtyard. She almost hesitated to sit down on the pristine plush white couches, because growing up in the Southside of Chicago, houses like this didn't exist. Even after hitting New York and fucking with top-notch ballers none of them was doing it like this. When Sheila E. sang "The Glamorous Life," this had to be it. Chantal sat back admiring how amazing Andre's digs were and how she could definitely imagine coming home to this every day.

While Chantal was scheming on how to make this her permanent residence, Andre was standing near the wet bar looking her up and down, imagining what her body was like underneath the tight jeans and revealing top. "Why don't you try a line of coke?" he offered, preparing her for the sex down.

She was a little taken aback because Chantal had smoked weed and popped a few pills but never fucked with the white girl. But hey, she was willing to try anything once. When she knelt down by the glass table and snorted three lines through a hundred dollar bill, Chantal felt like her nose was on fire. But then instantly her body started feeling warm and loose. A surge of sexiness came over her. She felt like she was a sex goddess or something. After snorting two more lines and having a glass of champagne, Chantal was wired.

"Baby, take off your clothes, so I can get a good look at you," Andre said, ready to fuck. Chantal couldn't drop her panties fast enough and he was impressed with the buxom beauty. He put coke on her breasts and down her stomach and snorted it and fucked her at the same time. The shit was crazy. Chantal felt like she was Paris Hilton starring in some porno movie.

Andre's tongue was down her throat and he was pounding on her so hard Chantal thought she would be on bed rest for the next three weeks. His dick was huge and he kept going deeper inside of her until Chantal thought her pussy would explode. Then he flipped her around and started hitting it from the back. He had his hands around her waist and was pushing her ass back to make his manhood go deeper and deeper. She had never felt this good in her life, and Andre was wondering if Chantal's pussy was the best he had ever had. She didn't know if it was the coke or the dick but she was open. They both reached their climax simultaneously and then passed out.

In the middle of the night, Andre woke up and carried Chantal upstairs to his bedroom. When she opened her eyes late that afternoon she found herself under what seemed to be a white fox fur blanket. She wondered if Andre had a fascination with white, because the whole décor in his bedroom reflected such. She then looked around, but Andre was nowhere to be seen. Chantal got out of the bed and stepped on the white marble floor. When she went in the bathroom she noticed a letter was on top of the sink.

> *Last night was unbelievable. I had to step out,*
> *but please don't leave. I'll be back shortly. Feel free to*
> *make yourself at home.*
> *Andre*

That was exactly what Chantal wanted to do, make herself at home. She had no intentions of going anywhere. Andre Jackson was the cream of the crop. She was never going to let him go. After reading the note six more times Chantal picked up the phone and called her girlfriend Arlene. When she answered the phone Chantal heard the grogginess in her voice. Since neither had a job it wasn't surprising to still be on shut-eye at three o'clock on a Wednesday afternoon.

"Arlene, wake up!" Chantal screamed through the phone.

"Chantal, is that you?"

"Yeah, it's me, wake up."

"Girl, what the fuck happened to you last night? I was looking for you for almost an hour, then someone said they thought they saw you leave with Andre Jackson. I was like, please, if my girl had lucked up and got with Andre Jackson she would be blowing my phone up bragging about the shit," Arlene said, laughing through her wooziness.

"I was too busy getting the best twist out of my life to pick up the phone and call you."

"So they were right. You left the party with Andre Jackson. Damn, Chantal, that's big. So what, you just now getting home?"

"You don't have caller ID?"

"Yeah, my shit said 'private' when you called."

"When I normally call you from my crib doesn't my name and number pop up?"

"Yeah, so what's your point?" Arlene snapped, still not putting two and two together.

"Bitch, stop smoking weed, your brain is slow. I'm still at Andre's house—no, make that *mansion*."

"You're fucking kidding me."

"Nope, I'm lounging in his king size, white fur bed. It's like the clouds are surrounding me. Yo, on the real Arlene, his crib is some other next level shit. You ain't never chilled in no place like this. It's like that shit you see on the movies but this is real life."

"Where that nigga at, while you talking all free with the tongue?"

"He had to step out, but he left me a note saying to make myself at home. I think he fell in love with the pussy last night. It's all good though, because I fell in love with the dick."

"He let you stay in his crib by yourself, he must be open. You must have put the classic X-rated move on him that we mastered."

"Damn sure did. That shit works every time. I put something extra in my move for Andre because he's special."

" 'Special' is an understatement. After that bullshit with the basketball player, Andre might be your last hope for the glamorous life we all reaching for. As soon as that nigga walk through

the door get down on your knees and swallow him up. You fuck
and suck him so good that even if his mind is telling him to send
you home, his body is begging you to stay. You feel me? You do
as I say and you'll be Erica Kane out this bitch," Arlene said,
point-blank.

Chantal listened intently like she was the go-to player on the
team, allocated by her coach to make the winning shot for the
NBA championship. She had nothing but the utmost respect for
Arlene. When Chantal had stepped on the scene, Arlene was already a seasoned veteran at the game. Even though she would give
all the other groupies shade, she instantly took a liking to Chantal,
primarily because she was a younger, prettier version of herself.
Seven years Chantal's senior, Arlene was the envy of all the up-
and-coming industry chicks. She was pregnant by the most sought
after R&B crooner on the airwaves. Arlene locked him down when
he was at the height of his music career. Unfortunately that height
lasted all of fifteen minutes. Traveling on private jets, sitting front
row at the Grammys, and luxuriating at five-star hotels came to a
halt by the time their son turned one. The once shining star left Arlene and the baby high and dry when the endless cash flow came
to a halt and Arlene had to take a job as a receptionist just to keep
food on the table. For months Arlene wondered why her man
bounced and left her and their son with nothing. She soon learned
that at the same time she was pregnant, he had another girl in LA
who was pregnant with his child, too. He decided to make it work
with her because, unlike Arlene, his other baby mother had a job
making great money and didn't need anything from him. She was
able to hold it down. That news crushed Arlene. Chantal was right
there being schooled through Arlene's tragedy.

One day when Chantal was at Arlene's apartment soaking up
another dose of her words of wisdom she said, "Chantal, watch
and learn from my mistakes. You don't want to end up struggling
the way I am."

"Arlene, it's not your fault that clown-ass baby father of yours bounced. You don't have anything to feel bad about. You were getting straight dough from that nigga and living good. So maybe right now you're on down time but it will all come full circle and you'll be right back on top."

"I appreciate your confidence in me, little mama, but let me tell you where I went wrong so you don't follow my path. I had a baby with a nigga that didn't have no established paper. The music artist is at the bottom of the totem pole when it comes to getting that money, unless they are consistently selling millions of records and they parlayed they shit into endorsements and other things. You fuck around and get knocked up by a one-hit wonder, you might as well had a baby with the local drug dealer."

"But the local drug dealer isn't going to have you on the scene at the hottest celebrity spots."

"Yeah, maybe not, but when the one-hit wonder's time is up neither is he. If you don't have no dough, it's all irrelevant. Past fame don't pay no bills." Chantal sat back, nodding her head, taking it all in. "You are a bad bitch, Chantal. Hands down one of, if not the, prettiest girls I've ever seen. Mad niggas is going to be checking for you. So just remember, when you decide to lock one of them down with a baby make sure he is at the top of his game. His paper needs to be so long that no matter what happens between you and him, he can never escape paying you those dollars." That was the best lesson Chantal ever learned regarding how the baby mama game worked.

Later that day when Andre came home, Chantal followed Arlene's advice to the "T." After screwing his brains out and snorting more coke, the two became inseparable. They hit a couple of rough patches, but Chantal was in it for the long haul. Andre paid her rent and continued to pay it and the rest of her bills until they moved in with each other for a brief time. He also let her keep his Benz so she had transportation until he bought her a car as a Christmas present. Andre picked up where Chantal's past money suppliers left off, but she had decided after that first night that Andre was a keeper.

THREE

Love Don't Live Here

Chantal awoke to the comfort of $1,500 Frette sheets, still dreaming about the incredible sex session she and Andre had had in the limo after the movie premiere, and the amazing night of lovemaking when they arrived home. She knew, after the fireworks their bodies ignited, that significant progress toward her goal had been made. Andre was warm, affectionate, and treated her with respect during the duration of her visit. Last night, they appeared to be the perfect couple. As she lay naked in bed, Chantal began making plans for the redecorating she would do once she moved in permanently. Andre did have exquisite taste, but she thought the place needed a woman's touch.

Although Chantal's preference was to live at the mansion in Jersey, Andre insisted that with all his business meetings in the city the penthouse was more convenient for everyday purposes. They would usually stay in Jersey on weekends or long holidays.

But Chantal had no doubt in her mind she would change all of that shortly. So when she stepped out of bed and opened the double French doors that were adjacent to the master bedroom, and heard him making flight arrangements for her depature, her bubble instantly popped. To Chantal's dismay, Andre was putting her back on a plane to Chicago.

"Why are you in such a rush for me to leave?" Chantal wanted to know as Andre was hanging up the phone.

"I have a lot of shit to take care of. Business is crazy right now."

"So crazy that you need for me to leave?"

"Yes," Andre said in an agitated voice.

"How long is this back and forth mess going to last? You need for me and your daughter to be closer to you. Why do you insist on having us way out in Chicago when you are here? It doesn't make any sense, Andre. Don't you think your daughter wants to be near her father?"

"I'm not in the mood for this bullshit, Chantal. I told you before that I'm not ready for this living together crap. Last time we tried it, you started wilding out on me."

"Yeah, because I caught your ass fucking around with mad bitches."

"See, that's what you get for looking. I told you not to be all up in my business and you wouldn't find anything. But being the nosey bitch that you are you can't let shit go."

"Fuck you, Andre, just fuck you. I don't have to deal with this." Chantal turned around and began gathering up her belongings as if she was going somewhere.

Andre walked toward the bedroom where Chantal was randomly picking up shit and tossing it in her luggage. When Chantal saw him standing in the doorway from the corner of her eye she met his glare. Andre looked at her in a vicious, almost hateful, way. His words were clear and defiant. "Chantal, you don't have anywhere to go. I make you. Without me, you're just that weed smoking, pill popping, coke snorting whore. Everybody who is somebody has fucked you, and the ones who haven't, heard about the pussy and chose to pass. So my suggestion to you is to get on the plane and take your ass back to Chicago. When I need you, I'll call you."

This was how Andre could get sometimes, cold and cruel. When he acted like this, Chantal knew he was trying to get rid of her so he could be with the next bitch. He would send her home pissed, and a couple of days after he fulfilled his urge with one of his jump-offs, he would call saying how sorry he was. This was a constant ritual. Chantal was hoping by now he would've outgrown it. But until he did she would have to hang tough. Chantal had started off as one of Andre's jump-offs, but she played her cards right and was able to stick around. She wasn't about to let one of these other tramps come along and take her place. Chantal would give him his space for now, because he would be back begging for what was between her legs soon.

The moment Chantal arrived at the Chicago O'Hare International Airport, the first thing she did was call her girl Shari. She needed someone to vent to and Shari was always there for her when she ranted about what an asshole Andre could be.

"Girl, what you doing?"

"On the phone with Michelle," Shari replied.

"Tell her you'll call her back, 'cause I need to talk," Chantal said.

"Hold on, I'll get right off," Shari said before clicking over to the other line.

Shari knew what time it was. Chantal always came first and all her other friends were put on pause when she needed her. Shari and Chantal used to be ho partners in crime, but unfortunately Shari hadn't found her long-term sugar daddy yet. Shari was almost as pretty as Chantal, so all hope wasn't lost. Sooner or later she would hook her man, but she needed to hurry up. Shari already had a six-year-old son by some has-been actor and he wasn't giving her a dime. She was in serious need of a sponsor and every day they were plotting on her next victim.

"Girl, I'm back. Michelle be getting on my damn nerves. She act like she doesn't know what 'I'll call you back means.' So, what's up?"

"Andre's motherfucking ass."

"What did he do now?" Shari asked in that "here we go again" tone.

"I know he got some new piece of ass he's fucking with because he rushed me out of New York the day after the movie premiere," Chantal complained.

"Girl, how was that?" Shari asked, more interested in that topic of conversation.

"Off the chain—all the Hollywood big shots were in attendance. I even met fine-ass Denzel Washington. If I wasn't with Andre that cat would be mine."

"Damn, Chantal, you can't have all the men."

"Says who?" They both burst out laughing.

"What you doing, because I'm coming to get you," Chantal said. She needed to talk to her best friend in person.

"Okay, I'll be ready." Shari hung up the phone and Chantal hopped in her new silver Porsche Cayenne and started listening to what she considered a classic CD, Usher's *Confessions*. Chantal said to herself, that Usher kept it real on this joint. As she listened to the introduction to "Confessions," she couldn't help but think to herself, *That's my girlfriend Tina he was all up in the Beverly Center with. Ha. Oh well, there is no baby so that payday is gone.*

When she pulled up to Shari's crib, her friend came running outside in some tight black pants with a bad-ass Dolce & Gabbana shearling coat.

"Bitch, you better work. Where the fuck did you get that coat?" Chantal gasped.

"Ain't this shit fly? Chris hooked me up."

"Chris, who the hell is Chris?" Chantal was curious to know.

"That football player I told you about."

"You still messing with him? It's been like six months. Are ya getting serious?"

"Well, he took me and Alex on a shopping spree and besides this coat he got me this tennis bracelet." Shari pulled up her sleeves to reveal a sparkling platinum and diamond bracelet that even made Chantal green with envy.

"So he's spending dough like that and time with your son?" Chantal stated sounding surprised.

"Yes. He said he wanted to be a father to Alex."

"You think he might be the one?"

"I'm hoping because I'm tired of running these streets. I'm ready for someone to wife me."

Chantal knew exactly what Shari was talking about. This ho game was no joke; these bitches were vultures. It was every hooker for herself. Chantal had played the game for so long she was beginning to believe the game was playing her. She had to get Andre to marry her soon because she wasn't about to let Shari beat her to the punch. Shari was her girl, but it was still about competition. She had put in too many years with Andre to let Shari and her new six-month fling upstage her. As Chantal was driving she glanced at Shari who was still admiring her new diamond tennis bracelet. Shari was stunning. She had that Gabrielle Union–type look, but far more beautiful. Her complexion was a perfect shade of brown and she had long jet-black straight hair that was all hers. She was tall and model slim with full C breasts.

Lucky for them they never attracted the same type of guys. If you were looking for that runway model look, then Shari was for you. If you wanted that drop dead gorgeous *Playboy* model look, then Chantal would be your choice. That was probably why they were best friends, because they were totally opposite physically but both had the love for the dollar in common.

Chantal turned the corner to West Armitage and pulled up to Charlie Trotter's restaurant. They were going to have an early dinner and a couple of drinks. They frequented the spot so often there was no need to make a reservation. Once they were sitting at their usual table in the corner, Chantal immediately began to vent. "I don't know what I'm gonna do about Andre. I'm trying to figure out exactly who he is creeping with. For some reason, I think this might be more of a relationship than just your casual jump-off."

"Why you say that?"

"Because he has been acting strange. Remember, I started as the jump-off. When he first started seeing me and got caught up he was going hot and heavy with that movie-star chick. Of course I shut that down when I got pregnant with Melanie, but I remember how he was giving her the runaround. Canceling dates, not picking up the phone, and just ducking her on a regular basis until he could no longer keep shit in the bag. I'm feeling like he is playing those same games with me."

"Have you said anything about it to him?"

"Not exactly, but I did ask him when he was going to have me and Melanie move back to New York to be with him."

"What did he say?" Shari asked.

"Nothing that I wanted to hear. That same bullshit about him not being ready. Girl, I thought we would be engaged by now."

"Me, too. You got about five crazy diamond rings and not one of them is the engagement ring. It's like, damn!"

"Tell me about it. This shit is getting so tired. I'm sick of my name being in the papers as his 'baby mother' or 'gal pal.' Do you know one paper actually called me the 'long-suffering girlfriend'? They talk about me like I'm fifty years old and at the end of my rope. This is some bullshit. But I feel stuck right now."

"Maybe you should dump him and find a new man. You're beautiful Chantal. There are a ton of guys that would love to wife you."

"But are they Andre Jackson? Hell no! You can't get no better than that. All the work and time I put into this relationship, you think I'm gonna let the next chick step in my shoes? I don't think so. I'm riding this out to the bitter end."

Poison

Andre Jackson seemed to be destined for greatness since the day he was born. His father was the lead singer of a legendary R&B group that stayed at the top of the charts throughout the late seventies and eighties. By the time Andre was seven years old he had accompanied his father on at least two worldwide tours. By the time he was thirteen, the word "virginity" was a distant memory and having one of the band member's groupies give him head was to be expected. Actually, by then Andre had a few groupies of his own. His father treated Andre more as a friend than a son. He would allow Andre to sit back and indulge in alcohol with the fellas and even smoke weed. Mr. Jackson reasoned he was making his son a man. During this time Andre began discovering his love of hip-hop music and perfecting his skills as a rap artist. In Andre's formative years, he had experienced and seen more than men twice his age. Witnessing women being degraded and degrading themselves on a regular basis gave him a warped view of relationships. He believed it was a woman's duty to please a man and a man's duty to please as many women as he liked. The only woman Andre respected was his mother.

Mrs. Jackson was the complete opposite of the groupies Andre was used to being around. He never understood how his mother and father even married since they were so different. She never indulged in the superstar musician lifestyle. Instead of attending glamorous parties she enjoyed tending to her huge garden or designing and sewing outfits for the group's backup dancers. She was extremely talented in her own right but preferred staying in the background instead of seeking the spotlight. As Andre got older he assumed that's why their marriage was able to survive all those years because, although she didn't condone her husband's hard partying lifestyle, she let him be and chose not to be a part of it. His mother didn't like Andre being exposed to the vulgar surroundings one could witness in the presence of her husband and his band, but Mr. Jackson was the king of his household and he decided where and what his son would see.

Being the son of a music icon definitely had its advantages and Andre made sure he got maximum usage out of it. He'd grown up around music royalty all his life and knew one day he would dominate the profession as his father had. But Andre also wanted to take over the one arena that would never open its doors to his father: Hollywood. Andre's father longed to break into films but during the height of his stardom the roles for black men were limited and the ones available were already occupied by a chosen few. Although his father had plenty of money and a successful career, not being embraced by the Hollywood elite had bruised his ego and left him with a chip on his shoulder.

In the early nineties, after more than ten prosperous years in the music industry, Mr. Jackson hung up his mike and retired. With the eruption of the hip-hop world he became his son's biggest fan. Andre catapulted to rap stardom damn near overnight. By the time Andre was twenty he already had two multiplatinum albums under his belt and a few Grammys and BET and MTV awards to go with it.

The same year Andre was about to break into superstardom his father passed away unexpectedly from lung cancer. Despite all the money he had, he always neglected his health. Going to the doctor for a yearly checkup was never on his to-do list. On his last night in the hospital before he died, Andre promised his father that not only would he be the biggest music entertainer in the world, but he would also become the movie star Hollywood never gave his father the opportunity to be.

The death of Andre's father hit him hard. Instead of facing the pain, he chose to escape it by focusing more on his booming career and delving deeper into the world of sex, drugs, and all-night partying. Before long the time seemed to run together and Andre couldn't differentiate between the days and nights. Andre's life was one endless party filled with little happiness. His mother prayed that her son would snap out of his destructive path but she'd been married to a man with the same stubborn streak and she was well aware that only Andre could make that change when and if he chose to. During that dark time in his life was when he met Chantal Morgan, the type of woman that was his mother's worst nightmare and that his father warned him about. Andre knew his dad was turning in his grave knowing he had become infected by a woman that his father would label "poison."

Andre didn't know what he was going to do about Chantal. Their minds were in two different places. All the stress she was putting on him about moving to New York and getting married was driving him crazy. He didn't think they were going to last this long and wouldn't have if it wasn't for Melanie. Andre's daughter was beautiful, just like her mother. He just prayed she didn't grow up to be a tramp like her mother. He wondered how he ever let Chantal trap him. *My dad used to always tell me don't keep company with a ho because you'll end up falling in love with a ho. You should fuck a ho, pay a ho, and send her home. Why didn't I do that with Chantal?* Andre questioned himself, shaking his head with disgust.

Something about Chantal just kept Andre coming back. He couldn't shake her. For one she was the most beautiful girl he had ever seen, and her body was perfect, plus she could suck a mean dick. But she had no substance. Everything was about money to Chantal. She had no ambition besides fucking, sucking, and spending his money. No matter how hard Andre tried, he couldn't get her to go to school or start any type of career. All Chantal wanted to do was sleep all day and party all night. She didn't even take care of their daughter. Chantal would leave Melanie with a nanny and run around, tearing the streets up with her girlfriends, getting high.

Andre came to the conclusion that all of that was about to change. Chantal was in for a rude awakening. He had big plans and most of them didn't include her. He was tired of dealing with her dead weight. He needed an official woman to settle down with and make a wife. One that his father would've approved of and his mother could respect. The places Andre was trying to go called for a certain caliber of lady and Chantal didn't fit the bill. It was time to start putting his plan in effect.

He was in deep thought, and the ringing phone shook him back into reality. "Hello," he said.

"What's up, baby? I was wondering what time you were picking me up."

"Um, give me about an hour."

"That's cool, where are we going?"

"My man Jay-Z is having a private party at his club 40/40. Supposed to be real nice, so wear something sexy."

"Okay, baby, I sure will," Arisa said before hanging up the phone.

Arisa was still hanging in there. After that crazy night when Chantal tried to kill her, Andre didn't think she would want to fuck with him anymore, but all it did was make him more enticing. Andre was digging the chick because she didn't give him no problems. She wasn't exactly wifey material, but she was definitely a keeper as one of his main jump-offs. Plus, she didn't mind getting freaky with hers. For his birthday Arisa actually brought two of her girlfriends and they gave Andre the show of his life. They ate each other out, finger popped one another and then started fighting over who was gonna blow him first. Andre loved that shit; he kept them freaks at his crib for three days straight. Taking turns dicking them down and watching them do each other.

Andre had to admit, though, that shit was getting a little old. He was ready to settle down and have a family, but his lifestyle was hard to shake. If he was going to settle down with a good woman that would mean no more coke, popping ecstasy or ménage à trois, and he wasn't sure if he was ready for all that. On another note he didn't want some ultraconservative woman who bored the hell out of him. Andre needed some spunk in his life, and one thing he could say about Chantal was that she had a lot of spunk.

Even if Andre did find someone new who he could wife, how would they deal with Chantal? She made it clear that she was willing to die for this relationship. Andre didn't even know if it was so much that Chantal was in love with him or if she just loved the life. She had been trying to lock down a baller forever and she felt like she'd hit the jackpot with him.

But Andre had to admit that when he first met Chantal he was so caught up. Nobody had ever put it on him like she did. She made him feel like he had the best dick in the world, which was an excellent ego booster. But the more he had her out there with him, the more he kept hearing stories of her past indiscretions. He soon realized that she basically was no more than a high-priced ho. But by that time he was already sprung. Andre refused to stop fucking with her. He figured he could keep her as his main jump-off and keep his relationship with Aubrey Price, his movie star girlfriend. Then Chantal dropped the news that she was pregnant and everything just spun out of control. Andre didn't have any kids and he knew Chantal would make him a beautiful baby; he also had to admit to himself that he was in love with her, or at least in extreme lust.

Andre decided to just go all out and try to make it work. He broke things off with Aubrey, and of course she was devastated. His mother couldn't believe that he had now made this known whore into his woman. Growing up on the road with his father and being exposed to scandalous women like Chantal on a regular basis, Mrs. Jackson didn't understand how her son had gotten sucked in by such an obvious tramp. She wasn't very fond of the movie star girlfriend he had been dating, either, and secretly hoped he would one day settle down and marry a nice girl, but when she met Chantal Morgan for the first time she was ready to call the movie star herself and beg her to make it work with her son. The only person who was happy about everything was Chantal. He moved her into the big house and she now felt like the Queen of Sheba. But Andre quickly became miserable. He bought the chick everything her heart desired but she still wasn't content. She wanted to tell him what to do and be in his business like they were husband and wife. The more Andre tried to explain to her that he wasn't ready for that, the more she pressured him. It was to the point that he seemed to be buying her a big-ass diamond every other month just to shut her up. And it did, because all Chantal really liked to do was show off in front of her friends. She got a kick out of flaunting every new piece of ice or wardrobe she got.

The more Andre gave her, the more she wanted. Once Melanie was born it got even worse. Andre reflected on the day he had wanted to punch Chantal in her mouth. He walked in unexpectedly while she and her girlfriends were running their mouths. Chantal was holding their daughter and boasted, "Ladies, I'm holding the million dollar baby."

Her girlfriends chimed in, "Yeah Chantal, Melanie is the million dollar baby, and you set for life."

"You silly bitches saying that shit like it's cute. There ain't no price tag on my daughter! And you, Chantal, have absolutely no substance," Andre told Chantal and her worthless group of friends. He was furious. Their mouths all hit the floor and eyes jumped out of their sockets as they got caught revealing their true one-dimensional selves.

"Baby, we were just kidding. It was a joke. We know that Melanie is worth more than that," Chantal said, giving what she considered an apology.

"If that was supposed to be an apology, you sound even more jaded," Andre said, as he grabbed his daughter and left the room.

Even with all that, he was still willing to stay with her. Andre would have continued to stay with Chantal and given her everything except for the official ring, which was the one prize she wanted most. Because of that, their relationship was different. She was making the issue bigger and bigger, even using Melanie as pawn. He was becoming more and more stressed because he didn't know how to rectify the situation. Andre wanted to be a father to Melanie and still wanted to be with Chantal, too, but not as her husband. He was perfectly content with her being his baby mama.

It was evident to Andre that Chantal had another objective and was determined to see it through. She would never accept him getting married to another woman and still see her, too. Chantal had ego for days and felt no other woman even deserved to breathe the same air as her. She stomached him fucking around with random bitches, but it was a whole other thing for him to get in a full-fledged relationship. At the end of the day, as long as she was the official girlfriend she thought all the other chicks were just irrelevant sexual peons. She was willing to deal with that because she figured Andre had no real attachment to them, but he was now ready to find "the one." Andre decided to keep all this to himself, because there was no telling what Chantal would do if she knew he was planning on settling down with someone besides her. When the time was right Andre would discuss it with her and make her understand. Until then, he would just continue to dabble with his sidepieces.

Changing the Game

When Andre's driver pulled up to Arisa's apartment building on 125th Street, he contemplated moving her out of the sleazy neighborhood and upgrading her to a more upscale location. Arisa lived in the seedy part of Harlem and although this was only Andre's second time coming to pick her up, the area made him feel uneasy. But then again he really didn't want to make that type of investment in this chick. It would be nothing for him to put her in a $2,000-a-month studio, but then that would lead him to getting her a two bedroom, and then a car and bunch of other shit that he didn't want to be responsible for. It wasn't about the money; it would be about what all that stood for—some sort of commitment. She would be dependent on him on a regular basis. She would count on him to pay her bills every month and if something was late he would have to hear her nagging voice asking him to fix it. Nah, Andre decided he didn't need that headache; Chantal was enough. He would just continue hitting Arisa off with money and add a little extra. Then suggest to her that maybe she should find a better area to live in. That way it's all on her and none of the responsibility would fall on him.

Arisa finally came down, looking sexy in a black fitted jumpsuit; her long black hair was sweeping down her back. She was a very pretty girl but she nowhere compared to Chantal's beauty. But Arisa was a good fuck and a great party girl. Andre actually met her when he was on his man Nelly's video set. She caught his eye because he remembered seeing her in *XXL* magazine in the eye candy section. She was what he would call a "hofesional." But Andre needed that in his life right now. He had other jump-offs that had their own money and careers but they would always put pressure on him to leave Chantal. Arisa never dared part her lips and make such a suggestion. Even after Chantal had sucker punched her she didn't have a bad word to say about her. Arisa was just happy to be able to tell her friends that she knew Andre and she wasn't going to let running off at the mouth jeopardize that.

"Hi baby. How do I look?" Arisa asked before entering the car.

"You look beautiful. I can't wait to get you out of that outfit later on tonight."

"If you like, I could call one of my girlfriends and have her meet us later." That was why Andre dug Arisa, because she was always out to please him and he loved that. *Maybe a ménage à trois is what I need to get my mind off of all this other bullshit,* Andre thought to himself.

When Andre and Arisa stepped into 40/40 they went directly upstairs to one of the private rooms. Andre really didn't like to be seen out with other women but this was supposed to be some real down low shit and he wasn't in the mood to be alone. It was already a little crowded and the champagne was flowing. Jay and Kanye were shooting pool, while a group of lovely ladies cheered them on. Lebron James was in the corner talking to some hot chick and a few other basketball players he didn't really recognize were holding court on the couch.

As Andre was about to pour Arisa a glass of champagne he saw T-Roc walk in with some Victoria's Secret model. On his way to sit down, he stopped by, said hello, and gave Andre a pound. T-Roc gave Arisa a long hard stare and turned back to Andre and smiled. Andre didn't think too much of it and continued pouring Arisa's drink. He thought it was nice being there, relaxing with no press to bother him and no one to answer to. Chantal would've been bored as hell at this sort of function. Her new thing was Hollywood. If it wasn't something that was dealing with a photo op then she'd rather be at home. Still, Andre was beginning to miss Chantal. He had hit below the belt with his comments before she left. Tomorrow he would call and apologize, before stopping by Cartier and having them send her the diamond watch she told him she loved. That would put a smile on her face. But tonight it was all about the sex show Arisa and her girlfriend would be putting on for him. As his eyes scanned the room, Andre thought maybe they wouldn't have to call her girlfriend after all because the shorty in the corner was looking right. Yeah, that's when Andre decided he needed some new ass to break in.

Chantal was in a deep sleep when she heard the phone ringing. She looked over at the clock and it was two in the morning. *Who in the hell would be calling me at this time of night?* Chantal thought to herself. Her caller ID showed a New York number. In an evil-ass voice she said, "Hello."

"Chantal I'm sorry to call you so late but I had to talk to you." She didn't recognize the woman's voice on the other end, maybe because of the loud music blasting in the back.

"Who is this?" Chantal asked, frustrated.

"It's me, Arlene."

"Arlene?" she repeated sounding annoyed.

"Yeah," she said so the loud music wouldn't drown out her voice.

"Girl, what's up? I know it must be some hellafied shit to be calling this late." Although Chantal and Arlene were still tight, they didn't talk that often. After Chantal became serious with Andre she had no time to run the streets with Arlene. The women went in two different directions. Chantal became Andre's arm piece and even though Arlene never found a permanent replacement sponsor, she managed to sleep her way to a high-ranking position at a major record label. With both having busy schedules, they would speak every couple of months. Since they'd had their routine powwow a few weeks ago, this call meant trouble.

"I'm at this party at 40/40 and Andre is here, Chantal." Chantal knew what she was about to tell her. That sorry son of a bitch was with somebody. She immediately rose up in the bed and turned on her night light. She had to mentally prepare herself for the break off Arlene was about to spit at her.

"Andre is there? Well, did you say hello?" Chantal knew Andre didn't say hello; he didn't even know Arlene like that. He could see Arlene standing next to Chantal and not recognize her face. Chantal was just trying to downplay the fact she was calling her about some shady shit regarding her man.

"No, I didn't speak; I don't think Andre knows me like that," Arlene replied.

"Oh, so what's up?"

"Girl, I'm going to just come right out and tell you."

"Yeah, that would be wise."

"Andre is here with some girl," she blurted out.

"Is it just the two of them?" Chantal calmly asked.

"When they came in, it was just the two of them, but now some other girl has joined them."

"Do you know who the chick is that he came with?" Chantal was curious.

"At first I didn't, but then I asked a friend of mine, and he said some video chick."

"Not a video hofessional!" Chantal screamed. At first she was trying to act calm, but she could no longer contain her anger. "What's the bitch's name?"

"Arisa. Do you know her?"

"Arisa!" Chantal howled into the phone. Luckily Melanie's bedroom was way down the hall because she felt like she could've woken up the whole neighborhood with that one. "Is she half-black, half-Filipina?"

"Yeah, you know her?"

"Yeah, I know exactly who she is. I can't believe that mother-fucker is still screwing that bitch. He is at a party with that hofessional Arisa, has he lost his damn mind? Andre has gone too far. It's one thing to fuck these tricks behind closed doors, but he has the nerve to take it to the streets. Talk about a slap in the face."

"I know, girl, that's why I had to put you on alert. Remember I played this game before. I know how these bitches getting down. This was your warning. We know these niggas fuck around but taking this bitch out on some public shit is a no-no. It's time for you to put your dog back on a leash."

"I appreciate that Arlene, good looking out. I'll speak to you later."

Chantal reasoned it was time to take Andre back to school. He had forgotten that she, too, started off as a player, but gave all that up when she got him. Hell, she didn't have to play those games anymore because Andre could give her everything that she wanted. But now he was so comfortable he was starting to treat her like a bum bitch. Yeah, Chantal may be known as a party girl with a past reputation of being a high-priced ho, but that was the past. Now she was Chantal Morgan, his girlfriend and the mother of his child. There are privileges that come with that, but he was playing her out right now like she was just some other ho that he didn't give a fuck about. Chantal was about to smack Andre back to reality and make him see exactly what was at stake.

After hanging up with Arlene, Chantal called Shari. Her answering machine came on. Right when she was about to hit her on her cell she remembered Shari told her she was spending the night with her football player man. So Chantal called her back at home and left an emergency message saying to call her ASAP. One thing about Shari, she don't care where she is; she calls first thing in the morning to check all messages. She believes that someone may call about some paper and she never liked to keep money waiting.

Chantal could barely sleep that night. All she kept seeing was Andre putting his dick in Arisa. She knew how the game worked and never thought for a second that Andre was true to her, but to sport Arisa in front of cats that they chilled with was too much. She wasn't even a top shelf trick, just some struggling hofessional. Chantal had done her background check on the chick after she caught him dicking her down the first time. After her research she had Arisa stashed in the "nobody" file. Now, Andre had her out there and she instantly became somebody.

See, a man can fuck with a random bitch and make her a celebrity overnight, but it was different for a woman. In order for Chantal to show Andre up and put his ass back in place, she had to let him know he was replaceable. That meant fucking with the right nigga, which meant dealing with someone equal or above him. The only cat out here right now that was on top of his game like that and wasn't already taken was T-Roc.

T-Roc had it together. He was young and had conquered just about everything, just like Andre. They were enemies on the low. Not that they ever had any beef; both of them were too powerful to entertain that, but they were in constant competition trying to be first to the finish line. He was the perfect man to fuck Andre's head up with. See, women are judged on their looks and men are judged on their power and pockets. Chantal was about to take Andre's power away from him and T-Roc would be the one to make it happen.

Chantal first met T-Roc when she started dating Andre. She had been one of the models for his fashion spread and he tried to kick it with her. By that time she was deep into Andre and trying to lock him down, so dealing with T-Roc was out of the question. Every now and then when she would see him at an industry party, he would tell her if she ever wanted to know how life was with a real baller to give him a call. Chantal never thought she would have to place that call but it was time to pull out the big guns.

Early the next morning Chantal's phone rang and true to form it was Shari.

"What's going on, girl? Your message said it was an emergency."

"It is. I need for you to call your friend who works at Def Jam and get T-Roc's number for me."

Chantal heard Shari taking a deep breath before saying, "T-Roc? What do you want T-Roc's number for?"

"Shari, I'm not in the mood for your twenty-one questions. Just get the damn number from your friend and call me back. Do it now," Chantal said, as she slammed the phone down, anxious to put her plan in action. Within five seconds of hanging up on Shari, Chantal's phone rang again. She didn't even look at the caller ID because she assumed Shari was calling her back with some dumb-ass question. She picked up the phone and abruptly said, "What?" But it wasn't Shari—it was Andre.

"Who did you think was calling you answering the phone like that?"

"Oh, I thought you were Shari. She wanted to have breakfast this morning and I told her I was still asleep. I thought she was calling to try and convince me one more time. You know I'm not a morning person." As Chantal was talking she looked at the clock and saw it was nine thirty in the morning. *Andre must have sent his ho home early,* she thought.

"Baby, I wanted to apologize for the other day. I didn't mean anything I said. I've been so stressed with business and I took out my frustrations on you. I have a surprise coming for you today, just a little something to let you know how sorry I am."

"You didn't have to do that, baby." *I already know how sorry your black ass is.*

"I wanted to. I hope you like it."

"I'm sure I will. You have excellent taste."

"Call me after you get it."

"Okay baby, I love you."

"I love you, too," Andre said feeling relieved they were back on good terms.

Chantal hung up her phone. For a brief second she felt bad for the torture she was about to put Andre through, but that feeling didn't last. If she truly wanted to be Mrs. Andre Jackson then she had to go through with her plan. Her conversation with Arlene last night was a wake-up call. Andre was obviously comfortable with having her tucked away in Chicago while he ran the streets in New York. It was clear that he had no intentions of marrying her. Andre was perfectly content with their current arrangement. When he wanted Chantal at his side he would fly her in, or if he wanted to appear like the father of the year he would bring her and Melanie to well-orchestrated photo ops. Then he could dismiss them and resume to his bad-boy partying ways. Andre had been running the show for so long, she didn't realize how bad things had gotten. It was crunch time and Chantal needed to make her move.

Sweetest Revenge

It took Shari a couple of days to track down her friend at Def Jam, but Chantal knew she would, and Shari came through with T-Roc's digits.

"Girl, I went through hell getting this number for you," Shari complained. "I had to promise the fat fuck dinner in order to get the damn digits."

"Honey bunny, I definitely owe you but this is an emergency. I need to get my plan up and popping because I'm already having second thoughts."

The day Andre called to apologize, Chantal got a special delivery courtesy of Cartier. Andre purchased the diamond watch she'd been eyeing for over a month. He attached a card saying, "To my beautiful diamond, I'll always love you." Chantal immediately called him expressing how much she loved the watch and him.

She basically deaded her plan until she got the second phone

call from the concierge, whom Chantal promised to tip hand-
somely if he'd go check on Andre for her. He told her that when he
went to the penthouse and knocked on the door some girl who fit
the description of Arisa answered, butt-naked. He said she seemed
giggly and high. When he asked to see Mr. Jackson she let him in
and Andre was sitting on the couch and another naked girl was on
her hands and knees sucking him off. Andre asked him what he
wanted and the concierge made some excuse saying the car service
he ordered was here to pick him up. Andre looked at him and said,
"I don't use no damn car service. I got my own car and personal
driver. Now get out, can't you see I'm in the middle of something."

Chantal was livid to say the least, but it just reinforced that she
was making the right decision to put her plan into effect. Andre
had some nerve, she reasoned. One minute he was calling and
apologizing, sending her a $25,000 watch, the next thing he was in
his penthouse participating in yet another ménage à trois with
Arisa. Chantal had had enough and was too through. When she
finished with Andre, he would be so shook he'd be rushing her
down the aisle, Chantal rationalized.

Later on that night while Melanie was asleep, Chantal was lying in her bed munching on popcorn and watching *America's Next
Top Model*. "Where does Tyra find these chicks at? I can go to New
York and walk down Sixth Avenue to find twenty hotter ladies
than these trollops. Tyra isn't fooling anybody; she just doesn't
want a real fly bitch taking her shine so she makes sure she only
picks whack-ass chicks," Chantal said with disgust. As the show
was going off, Chantal looked at her clock and thought it was a
perfect time to call T-Roc.

She had already practiced what to say, so she started dialing his
number. An intense, agitated voice answered, "What?" Chantal put
her sweet innocent tone on and asked to speak to T-Roc. He didn't
seem impressed by her Marilyn Monroe imitation and huffed,
"This is T-Roc—who the fuck is this?"

She took a deep breath and said, "It's me, Chantal Morgan."

There was a long pause on the phone and the silence was driving her crazy. She could tell he was trying to put a face to the name, so she decided to give him a little help. "A few years back I was the lead model for the launch of your women's clothing line."

Still not a word, then he blurted out with cautionary excitement, "Andre's Chantal?"

"Yeah, that's me." The agitated voice was now a distant memory and the infamously smooth playboy T-Roc instantly took over.

"How did you get my number?" he asked.

"Through a friend. Why? Do you have a problem with me calling you?"

"Of course not, I'm just a little surprised. I actually ran into Andre the other night at 40/40," he said sarcastically, so Chantal knew he must have seen him with that hoochie, Arisa.

"That's nice, but I didn't call to talk about Andre. I was actually trying to get back on the modeling scene and thought you could help."

" 'Modeling scene,' " he said jokingly. "From what I understand you're getting taken care of lovely. Why are you trying to get back into modeling?"

"I'm becoming restless, and I want to do something of my own. How about it, T-Roc? You think you can hook me up with something?"

"I might. Let's sit down and talk about it."

"That sounds like a plan. When and where?"

"I'm headed to LA tomorrow, so how about meeting there on Friday?"

"That'll work."

"Okay, cool, I'll be in touch with all the arrangements. I look forward to seeing you Chantal." And with that T-Roc hung up the phone.

The plan is all coming together nicely, Chantal thought. She decided not to even inform Andre that she would be in LA. He'd find out the news just like everybody else. That was just the first step, but she believed her plan would work out perfectly. By this time next week, Andre would be having second thoughts about their arrangement. Chantal went to sleep that night going over what she titled "Operation: Get Hitched," at least a hundred times. She tossed and turned with the hope that this would finally seal the deal.

T-Roc was feeling intrigued after his conversation with Chantal. He analyzed why she was tracking him down after all these years. Yeah, he had seen her a few times at some industry parties, but it was always a quick hello and good-bye. Something told him she was up to more than just getting her modeling back on track. Whatever it was, it definitely had something to do with Andre, and that was fine with him. T-Roc never really liked the cat, and if Chantal was using him to infuriate Andre then by all means she could use him. Plus, Chantal was one of the prettiest pieces of ass he had ever laid eyes on; it would be his pleasure to help her get over her man.

Right when T-Roc was about to call it a night and hit the off switch on his flat panel plasma, a face that he hadn't seen up close and personal in a long time flashed across the screen. He couldn't help but rewind the commercial in order to view the image once again. Then he hit pause so he could stare at the object of his affection. Through all the catastrophes she had endured, the innocence that attracted T-Roc to her so many years ago was still intact. He stepped out of bed and walked to the screen, running the tip of his finger over the outline of her lips as he said, "Tyler Blake, the one who got away." He couldn't believe how far she'd come in such a brief amount of time. There was Tyler, the new face of Revlon cosmetics, giving that over-the-shoulder smile that would melt any man's heart. T-Roc never got over the fact that Tyler had never been completely his. During their brief affair, T-Roc had not planned to become so completely enamored with the young beauty. He was the one used to loving them and leaving them at his convenience. When Tyler broke off their relationship, it had come as a complete shock. He didn't believe for a minute that she would be able to walk away. As the time passed, he later learned that she had a baby with someone else. For the first time in his life a woman had actually devastated him. Now there she was on his screen as if he could reach right through and touch and feel her again.

As T-Roc reminisced about the past he'd shared with Tyler, he hoped that his trip to LA would be the beginning of a new start for them. After placing several phone calls to people in the know, he tracked down Tyler's whereabouts. He had everything planned out and the call from Chantal was just an unexpected and added twist. Now when he saw Tyler again for the first time in many years he wouldn't be solo. He would be accompanied by a gorgeous woman that would hopefully pique her interest. It had always been T-Roc's belief that if you want to ruffle the feathers of a gorgeous woman, then put another one in her face. He trusted that belief would work on Tyler.

Friday morning Chantal was on her way to LA. T-Roc's assistant called with her flight schedule and hotel accommodations. It was a first class American Airlines flight and she was staying in a suite at the *L'Ermitage* Beverly Hills. "T-Roc sure has a lot of class," she said after hearing the setup.

She called Andre before she left and told him she would be spending a day at the spa with Shari. Chantal then informed Melanie's nanny if Andre called to tell him she was still out with Shari. He would think that they went shopping and had dinner after the spa so he wouldn't call back until later in the evening. By the time Andre finally got Chantal on the phone her plan would be in full swing.

When Chantal arrived at LAX, T-Roc had a limo waiting to pick her up. She handed her Louis Vuitton luggage to the driver and immediately called Shari to make sure she had her story straight if Andre decided to track her down and call Shari when she didn't pick up her cell. Shari was on the same page, so Chantal hung up and placed a call to her friend at *In Touch* magazine.

After getting rid of Arisa and the other video hofessional Andre had met at 40/40, he could finally relax. He thought to himself, *Those chicks were not trying to leave. It's like damn, we've fucked, sucked, and everything else so it's time to get yo ass outta here. Women always overstay their welcome, and they wonder why rich powerful men call escort services. They're not paying for the pussy; they're paying for the pussy to leave.*

Andre had to finally break that down to Arisa and the other chick, whose name he couldn't even remember. They were under the misguided impression that their pussy was so good he wanted to move them in. After the twentieth hint and they still hadn't left Andre went hard and told the tricks to get the fuck out. Then Arisa broke down crying and saying she thought he cared about her, then the other one started talking about she hoped he didn't think she was a ho. This was too much and he was ready for them to go. Andre turned the charm back on because he didn't want them leaving his crib all upset and disheveled. After they finally calmed down, he handed them a few hundred dollars and told them to have a nice lunch on him.

Times like that made Andre reconsider keeping Chantal around on a more permanent basis. At least she knew his moods and would give him his space when he demanded it. Yeah, she might bitch a little bit, but she had way too much pride and ego to break down and start crying and begging to stay. The rest of the chicks he dealt with always seemed so desperate and eager to hold on, when in actuality they needed to let go.

When the limo pulled up to L'Ermitage, Chantal's cell started ringing. It was Andre. That was one call she wasn't picking up. He was probably trying to check on her in between his workouts with them hoes. Chantal was on a mission and a phone call from Andre wasn't going to interrupt that. When she opened the door to her suite, the room was full of beautiful pink roses and white orchids. There was a card lying on the bed. It was from T-Roc telling her to meet him at Mr. Chow's for dinner. She had a few hours to burn so she decided to get a massage and a fresh manicure and pedicure.

While getting a massage Chantal went over her plan again and again. This had to work—too much depended on it. She closed her eyes and a smile crossed her face. Yeah, this was definitely going to work.

As Chantal was getting dressed she debated on what look to go for. She needed sexy and classy mixed in one. She opted for her silk Gucci skinny pants, with a nude mussola oversize top with chiffon inserts. The finishing touches were gold sandals with yellow enamel snake heads and the gold teju small frame bag with enamel detail to match. She let her honey blond hair cascade down her shoulders and added some Oh Baby lip gloss that went perfectly with her bronzed complexion. She gave herself the once-over in the full-length mirror and headed out the door.

When the driver pulled up in front of Mr. Chow's, Chantal had butterflies in her stomach. Her plan was now fully in motion and there was no turning back. When she entered the restaurant, T-Roc was already at the table. She walked toward him and by the way his eyes lit up and mouth dropped she knew she looked like a million bucks. He quickly tried to pull it together as he stood up and greeted her with a kiss on her cheek. After giving her the lingering once-over one more time he finally said, "You look absolutely gorgeous."

Chantal smiled slightly and blushed as though she didn't already know that. It seemed to have worked, because T-Roc apologized for making her feel uncomfortable. As the waiter poured her a glass of 1995 Krug, T-Roc was in deep thought. Chantal knew he was still trying to figure out exactly what this was about. She decided to interrupt his contemplations and put him at ease.

"I can't believe I'm having dinner with the super famous T-Roc. What a lucky girl I am," Chantal said flirtatiously.

"Oh, is that what this is about? You're getting bored with one mega-star and you want to try another?"

"No, this is business—although, I find you very attractive. And there is no doubt you are a star, which is why I want you to assist me with my career."

With a sarcastic tone in his voice, he said, "Pretty girl, I'm not a manager for bored baby mamas. So what career are you speaking of?"

"Cute, T-Roc, but I want to get back into modeling and maybe branch off to acting or something."

"That's interesting because I'm trying to break into this acting game. I'm actually politicking for a role in that movie *Angel* that Tyler Blake is starring in."

"Tyler Blake is starring in her own movie?" Chantal knew Tyler was up-and-coming on the acting scene, but she had no idea she had stepped her game up to being an actual star of her own movie. Chantal was immediately enthralled.

"Yeah, it's the new movie William Donovan is directing. He is determined to make her a superstar."

"Wow, that's big."

"It is. You know I have a little history with Tyler. We go way back, before she became the next big thing in Hollywood."

T-Roc definitely was holding Chantal's attention for other reasons now. If Tyler Blake was really doing it like that, then maybe she should use him to try to break into this whole acting game if, heaven forbid, things didn't work out with Andre. There was big money in movies and maybe T-Roc could show her the way. If she didn't become Mrs. Andre Jackson, then being a movie star was an excellent fallback career.

"What type of history is that?" Chantal asked, trying to seem interested but not too interested.

"Let's just say I was the first person to introduce her to this whole industry life. We definitely have some unfinished business, and I'm hoping we can catch up while doing this movie."

Chantal knew this meant T-Roc obviously had had some sort of relationship with Tyler, but she couldn't figure just how far it had gone. Whatever it was, he definitely hadn't gotten her totally out of his system. Her relationship with T-Roc could turn out to be more lucrative than what she'd originally planned. Besides using him to make Andre jealous in an attempt to get him to marry her, T-Roc could make her a star if all else failed.

After finishing up their dinner, T-Roc and Chantal walked out of the restaurant and headed to White Lotus. As soon as they hit the pavement Chantal grabbed T-Roc's hand and planted a kiss on his cheek. He gave her a quizzical look, but instead of questioning her, he grabbed her face and put his tongue down her throat with a passionate kiss. Chantal's plan couldn't have worked out more perfectly. After doing some club hopping, they eventually ended up at Chantal's hotel room. Chantal couldn't help but be extremely attracted to T-Roc but she had decided beforehand they wouldn't have sex. T-Roc would surely rub it in Andre's face and his ego would never allow him to forgive Chantal, but it was imperative that he stayed the night. She was hoping the sleeping pill she slipped in his drink at the club would have him knocked out before he was able to get it up.

As they kissed and T-Roc fondled her breasts, Chantal told him that she wanted to get more comfortable. She went in the bathroom took off her clothes and came out in a pink lace La Perla bra and panty set. T-Roc couldn't contain himself. If he didn't pass out pretty soon, she might have to give him some.

"Damn baby, I knew you were fine but I didn't know you had all that going on." T-Roc began kissing Chantal's stomach until he worked his way up to her breasts. He was squeezing her buttocks as he licked her nipples. She had to admit she was getting turned on and wanted to feel his manhood inside of her. T-Roc lay on his back on the bed and Chantal sat on top of his chest as they passionately kissed. And just when he unclipped her bra, he passed out like a newborn baby. Chantal felt relieved and disappointed at the same time. He had got her pussy wet and she was ready to fuck, but that wasn't part of her plan, so it worked out perfectly.

The next morning Chantal got up bright and early and called room service. She ordered every breakfast item on the menu. T-Roc was still knocked out cold but she knew he would wake up shortly. Chantal hoped he wouldn't ask her a million and one questions about his condition, but she had her answers prepared just in case. As she ate her French toast she heard T-Roc trying to snap out of his drug-induced sleep. She picked up the newspaper and looked at it as though in deep thought. She finally heard T-Roc mumble, "Where the hell am I?" Chantal took a deep breath and got her acting chops in order.

"Baby, how did you sleep last night?" she said in a concerned voice. T-Roc looked at Chantal like she was a martian and blinked his eyes a couple of times to make sure his vision wasn't playing tricks on him.

"Chantal, what the fuck happened last night? I feel like shit."

"Baby, I don't know, maybe you had too much to drink. One minute we were kissing and about to make love and the next you were sleeping like a baby."

"Oh fuck," T-Roc moaned. "I have the worst fucking headache."

Chantal offered him a glass of orange juice but he opted for bottled water. She sat on the bed next to T-Roc and gently rubbed his back. He still had on his silk Prada shirt because she wanted to make sure he knew they didn't have sex. As he struggled to get his thoughts together, Chantal offered him some food, but that was the last thing on his mind. This episode had left him frazzled.

T-Roc finally let out a deep sigh and said, "I did have a lot to drink last night. I need to stop partying so hard."

Chantal innocently chimed in, "You're right. Me, too."

With that T-Roc looked at his watch and said he had a mass of work he needed to get done today. He asked Chantal if they could hook up later on and of course she accepted. Originally this was basically where the plan was supposed to end, but now Chantal wanted T-Roc for even bigger reasons. She wanted him to make her a star.

When T-Roc left Chantal's hotel suite he knew the vibe was all wrong. He had been around the block enough times to know when someone was up to no good. T-Roc opted to brush it off because he needed Chantal as his sidekick tonight. He also knew whatever game she was playing would eventually be revealed. They always were.

SEVEN

Scheming

Andre was driving himself crazy wondering where in the hell Chantal was. He couldn't get her on the phone all day or night, yesterday or this morning. *This shit is crazy*, he thought to himself. He knew she couldn't still be holding a grudge because of all the garbage he was spitting to her, especially after the Cartier watch he sent that she loved. Chantal was never one to hold a grudge as long as he kept the gifts and the money flowing.

When Andre spoke to Shari last night she told him that Chantal had just dropped her off and was on her way home. When he called her, Chantal's cell phone kept going straight to voice mail and the nanny wasn't picking up the house phone. When he called Shari back, she told him that Chantal had probably gotten home and gone straight to sleep. The entire story was sounding suspect. Andre thought maybe he should catch a flight to Chicago and see what was really good.

Chantal called Shari to see if she spoke to Andre and how the conversation went. To her surprise he called her not once, not twice, but five times. *Obviously Andre is irate. Good for him,* Chantal thought. This was all part of the lesson she was teaching him. Chantal still had her cell turned off and wasn't planning on turning it back on until she was about to leave LA. After she spoke to Shari she called home to speak to the nanny. The nanny told Chantal that Melanie was doing fine and Chantal explained that the next time Andre called to pick up the phone and tell him she left early that morning to run some errands. Chantal would be home the next evening, and hoped by then shit would've hit the roof.

T-Roc was on his way to pick Chantal up but she had no idea where they were going. She opted to play it safe and put on some Paper Denim jeans and a hot pink, low-cut Missoni top. Her floral print Salvatore Ferragamo heels were the finishing touch.

"So where are we going tonight, T-Roc?" Chantal asked as they sat back in the limo.

"To an acquaintance's house for an intimate dinner," T-Roc said nonchalantly. T-Roc hadn't said more than two words since Chantal had gotten in the car and she didn't know if he was upset about last night or if something else was engrossing him. After what seemed to be a long ride they finally pulled up to a beautiful beach house. When the driver opened the door, Chantal realized they were in Malibu. Right before they were about to walk through the front door, T-Roc informed her that this was William Donovan's home. Chantal couldn't believe her luck. She was about to have dinner with the superstar actor-turned-director, William Donovan. Through her many conquests, he was one man that always seemed out of reach. She would finally have the opportunity to seal the deal.

The maid greeted them at the door. She escorted T-Roc and Chantal to a huge room with Art Deco furniture. Each wall had a fifty-five-inch XBR plasma WEGA high-definition television and each flat screen had something different playing so you could roam freely and watch whatever interested you. What interested Chantal was rubbing elbows with William Donovan, although she noted his layout was top notch.

As Chantal surveyed the room looking for her prey, her eyes zoomed in on a woman in a gorgeous peach-colored negligee-style dress. She admired how nicely the outfit complemented the woman's beautiful body and wondered who she was. As the woman's face turned toward the gentleman she was talking to, Chantal realized it was Tyler Blake. Her hair was pulled back in an elegant bun and she looked flawless. William Donovan walked toward Tyler and handed her a glass of champagne and kissed her on the mouth. *Could they be a couple?* Chantal thought to herself. She knew he was married but that didn't mean anything in this business. Chantal couldn't help but feel a twinge of jealousy seeing Tyler Blake stand there looking like a movie star with William Donovan eating out of the palm of her hand.

Although Chantal and Tyler never ran in the same circles per se, Chantal knew exactly who she was. She was another out-of-towner who came to New York with big city dreams. Tyler quickly got snatched up by music producer Brian McCall and didn't have to be on the scene fucking this one and that one for a big break. After having a son together they eventually broke up, but by then she was straight and moved on to bigger and better things. Knowing the egos of men in the entertainment industry, Chantal couldn't help pondering that it must kill Brian to see Tyler doing so well without him. Yeah, Tyler Blake was definitely Chantal's inspiration. She had kicked Brian to the curb and didn't look back. Chantal didn't know if she was ready to leave Andre, but she damn sure was about to show him that she could hold it down with him or without him.

"Hey baby, would you like a glass of champagne?" Chantal was so deep in thought, she barely heard T-Roc ask her the question.

"Oh, thanks," Chantal replied while reaching for the glass.

"This is a pretty happening party, wouldn't you say?" T-Roc said with a big grin on his face.

"Damn sure is, these Hollywood bigwigs sure have class." Chantal knew that T-Roc wanted to be a part of this world and she was hoping he would bring her along for the ride.

"Let's go say hello to William Donovan." T-Roc grabbed Chantal's arm and pulled her toward the side of the room where William Donovan was standing. Chantal knew the real reason T-Roc wanted to talk to William Donovan: Tyler Blake was standing with him. T-Roc was not fooling anybody.

T-Roc reached out his hand to shake William Donovan's hand.

"I'm glad you could make it," William said.

"I wouldn't miss one of your parties for nothing in the world. Let me introduce you to a friend of mine, Chantal Morgan."

"It's a pleasure to meet you, Mr. Donovan," Chantal said nervously.

"Call me William, Mr. Donovan is for my father." He gave a slight laugh and Chantal felt herself blushing. William then introduced Chantal and T-Roc to what he referred to as his star, Tyler Blake. Tyler smiled graciously and acted like she didn't even remember T-Roc. Chantal could tell T-Roc was offended.

Tyler looked amazing. Chantal remembered her being a beautiful girl, but now she was unbelievably gorgeous. That was what Hollywood money did for you. They chatted with them for about twenty minutes as T-Roc went on campaigning for a part in William's movie *Angel*. William casually told T-Roc that he was about to start auditioning young men to play Tyler's love interest and if he was serious, he would schedule him an audition. T-Roc assured him that he was dead serious and William told him to call him Monday. It didn't seem to Chantal that William was taking T-Roc's interest in the big screen seriously, but from the spark in T-Roc's eyes, Chantal knew otherwise. And something about the way he gazed at Tyler told her he was truly smitten with the woman.

As T-Roc was walking away he couldn't help but be excited about the audition. He knew this was the type of role that could launch his acting career. But more important, it could open the doors to a relationship with Tyler. He laughed to himself at how she acted as though she didn't remember him or their brief but intense fling. It was all good though because she was in the big leagues now and you have to play the game. T-Roc was hoping they would play the game together.

"That so-called history you shared with Tyler Blake must have been awfully intense," Chantal said in a bid to be nosy.

"Don't go worrying about matters that don't concern you," T-Roc replied as they got in the car.

"I think it does concern me."

"Why is that?" he asked, sounding half-interested in what her answer would be.

"Isn't Tyler the reason you brought me to this shindig? I know it isn't because you love my company. You thought her seeing you with a beautiful woman would spark all sorts of jealous feelings and she would beg you to come back to her. Well, T-Roc, I hate to burst your bubble but it's going to take more than a pretty face, even one as gorgeous as mine, to make that happen. Tyler is in the big leagues; she's playing footsie with fucking William Donovan. Your only chance at getting between those legs again is to snatch that role in her movie, so good luck because you're going to need it." T-Roc knew Chantal was right, and it pissed him the hell off.

Early the next morning when Chantal woke up she was still fantasizing about her evening at William Donovan's house. When they left the party, T-Roc had dropped her off at the hotel and didn't even try to make a move. He claimed he had to catch an early flight back to New York so he needed to get some rest. After she had stated her opinion, T-Roc seemed preoccupied; she assumed he was scheming on how to secure his role in the movie and bagging Tyler Blake at the same time. They briefly discussed getting her some modeling work and he gave her a kiss on the cheek and said they would speak tomorrow. Chantal felt more than a twinge of jealously knowing T-Roc was fantasizing about another woman. She was almost tempted to invite him up to her hotel room so she could bless him with the skills that at one time made her the most sought-after vixen in the music industry. But this was a business trip and Chantal refused to lose focus on her ultimate goal. Maybe in the future, if Andre continued to dog her out, she would get naked and take a dance with the infamous T-Roc. Chantal didn't have time to dwell any further on that because her flight was leaving in a couple of hours and she had to make some stops and calls to make sure her initial reason for the trip was still in effect.

Shari was coming out of church with Alex when her cell started going off. "Damn, I just turned this shit back on and it's already blasting," she said to her six-year-old son, as if he were one of her girlfriends.

"Where the fuck is Chantal?" Andre screamed before Shari could even get out a proper hello. It was now Sunday afternoon and Andre was livid that he hadn't spoke to Chantal in three days. Shari tried to pretend as though he and Chantal must be playing phone tag, but Andre wasn't buying it. Right when Andre was about to go postal on Shari, his other line beeped and it was Chantal.

"Hi, Andre," Chantal said in a low sweet voice.

"Where the fuck have you been? I've been calling you nonstop since Friday and haven't been able to get you on the phone. So what the fuck is up?"

"Well, Andre, I've had a lot on my mind. There were some things I needed to sort out." Chantal was mentally preparing Andre for the bullshit that was coming his way. She had to plant the seed of distress so when shit hit the fan he would reflect on this conversation for answers.

"Sort what out? You had to get missing for damn near three

days to do some thinking? That shit don't sound right. You need to have a better explanation than that, or you gonna have a problem in the medical sense."

"Baby, we can talk about it later when I get home. Right now I have to go." Before Andre could say another word he heard the phone click.

"That fucking bitch!" Andre screamed as he walked upstairs to his bedroom. Andre couldn't believe that Chantal was putting him through these mind-playing games. *What in the hell did Chantal mean by when she gets home? I know she wasn't gone this whole weekend. Maybe she went away to a spa or something. But what in the hell could be on her mind? She don't do shit. She doesn't have a job. Melanie's nanny takes care of all the domestic duties. What the fuck could she possibly be stressed out about?* Andre felt like hopping on a plane and beating the shit out of Chantal just for having him so worried about her whereabouts, but he had way too much to do. He decided to see what was going on in her head later.

As Chantal sat on the plane buckling her seat belt in preparation for landing, she couldn't help but feel fear and excitement about the results of her plan. She wasn't sure of the final result but it had to work out perfectly. She closed her eyes and hoped for the best.

Seeing Tyler again had had a heavier impact on T-Roc than he'd anticipated. Tyler looked damn near flawless and even though they didn't engage in a conversation, her aura seemed so much more mature. Time had passed and of course she was older, but the confidence Tyler exuded was almost intimidating—even to a self-assured man like T-Roc. He was more determined than ever to win her back and had no doubt auditioning for *Angel* was the way to start.

EIGHT

The Pleasure Principle

Tyler Blake was feeling on top of the world. She was the new It Girl of Hollywood, which was no small feat. With her newfound success came tons of perks, but it also came with constant scrutiny. William had basically made her a star overnight. After he convinced Albert Moore to let her be the star of his upcoming movie *Angel*, there was a full-fledged publicity blitz to make her the most sought after young actress in Hollywood. At first she got small parts in major motion pictures with stars like Tom Cruise, Will Smith, and Leo DiCaprio. That led to the job as the new face for the Revlon cosmetics ad campaign. She was now sharing screen time with her idol, Halle Berry. All her dreams were coming true and she had William Donovan to thank for all of it.

"Good morning, Ms. Blake," the secretary smiled as Tyler walked toward William's office. Tyler never waited to see William, as so many other people had to. It was well known but discreetly discussed that she was William's love interest. The fact that he was married only added to the gossip and curiosity of how serious their relationship was. She hadn't meant to fall in love with William—it had just happened. It was almost an incestuous relationship because in a lot of ways William was like a father figure to her. William discovered Tyler at an acting workshop in New York City and soon after brought her to Hollywood. He literally spent every day and night molding her into a Hollywood starlet. Their relationship quickly went from mentor-student, to falling in love. Although William wasn't ready to leave his wife, Tyler knew that he was in love with her and eventually they would be husband and wife. Until then she decided to remain loyal to him, because no other man could compare.

No man had ever made Tyler feel like William did. He was warm and compassionate but strong and powerful. He could melt her heart with charm or turn cold as ice if he needed to handle business. She admired his skills inside and outside the office. In bed he had those same attributes. When he wanted to, he was the most gentle and caring lover. But he also could be rough and passionate if that was what she was in the mood for. Although close to fifty, William's body was flawless and his stamina was incredible. To add icing on the cake, his oral skills would keep her having orgasm after orgasm. For the first time in Tyler's life she felt that she was truly in love.

"Hi, baby," William said as he gave Tyler a long passionate kiss.

"William, I haven't even closed the door yet; people can see what we're doing," she said, feeling perturbed that he always wanted to display open affection in spite of his married status.

"So what? Like everyone doesn't know that you're my lady and I'm your man. You make me so proud I have to show you off."

"You're so silly. I know you may feel like my man, but it makes me feel uncomfortable when everyone is in our business," Tyler complained.

"Get used to it, baby, this is Hollywood. When people stop caring about your business is when you should start feeling uncomfortable." William definitely had a point there. One minute you can't get rid of the paparazzi and you scream for some privacy. The day you finally get it means your career is all but dead in this business. The fact that people were interested in what Tyler was doing meant that she was a hot commodity, which was what you had to be in order to stay on top. Look at Jennifer Lopez: every time her stock starts to plummet she gets married, and it works. Instantly her romance is front page news. This business is cutthroat and if you want to stay on top you have to do what you have to do. More and more, William was teaching Tyler that.

William cut right to the point of their meeting. "Listen, we need to find your love interest for *Angel*. You had no chemistry with anyone you've tested with. We've run through all of our potential candidates."

"Why don't you play the role?" Tyler laughed as she put her hands around William's waist and started to unzip his pants. William grabbed her hands with force and pulled Tyler back in front of his desk. When it came time for business, William had no tolerance for fun and games. Tyler knew to back off and get serious.

"Listen, this is serious. This project has already been delayed because we haven't found the right actor for the part. I'll be damned if this movie falls apart because of this shit. Time is up, and we need our Damian."

"Do you have any other actors in mind? We've met with every young hot black and Hispanic actor out and none of them worked," Tyler questioned.

"Yeah, well maybe we should go with an unknown."

"But baby, this is the first movie I'm headlining, do you really think we should get an unknown? I really think we should get an established actor." Tyler observed William getting that twinkle in his eyes when he felt he had a bright idea.

"How about T-Roc? The other night at my party he showed a genuine interest in auditioning for the part. He is unknown in the

movie world but he is a superstar in the music and fashion industry. He has a ton of endorsements and is known worldwide. He is
the right age and has the appropriate attitude for the part."

"You mean arrogant and egotistical? What if he can't give that
off on the screen? It's one thing to have those characteristics; it's
another to deliver it in a movie."

"True indeed, but the only way to know is to get him in here for
a screen test."

"Didn't you tell him to call you, William?"

"Yeah, but he has his hands in so many pots he might've forgotten."

"If he has forgotten, then maybe he isn't that interested. We
shouldn't waste our time with someone who isn't going to be committed to the project and, more importantly, the role."

"I hear everything that you're saying but I have a good feeling
about this." William immediately got on the phone and called
T-Roc's manager. As Tyler sat down on the leather couch listening
to the conversation, she started having flashbacks to her tumul-
tuous relationship with the quintessential male chauvinist. When
Tyler had first come to New York, she had had the biggest crush on
T-Roc. He was the King of New York and she had wanted to be his
Queen, if just for the night. He charmed her right into his bed but
Tyler soon realized that all that glitters is definitely not gold. Her
love triangle with him and his superstar basketball player cousin
Ian Addison sent her life into a tailspin. She vowed after that to
never speak to T-Roc again. Now four years later he was back.
When Tyler saw him the other night at William's party she felt so
uncomfortable. She could feel him undressing her with his bedroom eyes. Although he had a beautiful woman on his arm he still
had to lust after her. One woman was never enough for T-Roc. The
woman that got him to make her his wife, God bless her.

When William hung up the phone he immediately seemed re-
juvenated by his conversation. "T-Roc is a go. His manager, Craig

Silverman, is setting up the screen test for the day after tomorrow. Plus he informed me that he just got Andre Jackson as a client and he is eager to break into the movie business, too. He is going to speak to him about auditioning also."

"Wow, this is good."

"Fuck 'good,' this is great. These two guys are the biggest commodities outside of the Hollywood scene. This would be the perfect opportunity to introduce them to the movie industry."

"Baby, we don't know if they are good yet."

"Well, my little princess, you better hope so because if neither one of them work, this movie could be prolonged indefinitely."

Shari and Chantal were in the living room watching *Access Hollywood* when footage of Chantal and T-Roc walking hand and hand and then kissing as they came out of Mr. Chow's splashed across the screen. The headline was, IS THIS SUPERSTAR T-ROC'S NEW LOVE INTEREST? They went on to show the couple coming out of White Lotus and then returning to Chantal's hotel and T-Roc leaving early the next afternoon. The next clip was of them entering William Donovan's house for the party they attended in Malibu. Correspondent Shaun Robinson went on to identify Chantal Morgan as part-time model and the mother of music mogul Andre Jackson's young daughter. They even showed the picture of Chantal she had given her media pal of when she did the ad for T-Roc's clothing line. The picture was from four years ago and they were trying to insinuate that the relationship had been going on since then. The whole episode was too juicy for words. They immediately cut to a recent picture of Andre and Chantal from the Halle Berry and Bruce Willis movie premiere and then wondered if she was Andre's girl or T-Roc's. It was all delicious.

Chantal glanced over at Shari, who just stared at the television speechless. She was so entranced by what Shaun Robinson was saying that it didn't seem to dawn on her that they were talking about Chantal and she was sitting right in front of her face. Chantal's cell and home phone instantly started ringing. She needed to gather her thoughts together and get her story straight before she spoke to anyone. Chantal's media contact already gave her the heads-up that the explosive story was hitting, but Chantal never believed anything until she saw it for herself. Shaun Robinson ended her segment by saying that the inside story would be on this week's front covers of both *Us Weekly* and *In Touch*. Shari was still glued to the TV and right when she was about to spill her thoughts, the name "T-Roc" came across Chantal's cell. This was one call Chantal couldn't avoid because she needed to stay on his good side for many reasons.

"Hello," Chantal purred in an innocent yet frazzled voice. Before she could go any further with lying about how shocked and embarrassed she was for what she just heard on *Access Hollywood*, T-Roc cut her off.

"You sneaky little bitch. It all makes sense now."

"What are you talking about?" Chantal gasped as though she was taken aback by his insult.

"Save the bullshit, Chantal. Actually I'm impressed. You must have gone through a lot of trouble and scheming to set this up. I hope it was worth it, because Andre is going to be one pissed motherfucker. I'm sure this whole charade was for his benefit, so whatever you're after I hope you get it." Before Chantal could explain herself with another lie, T-Roc hung up the phone. Shari was on her cell and as soon as she saw Chantal hang up she told whomever she was talking to she would call them back.

"Girl, what the fuck is going on? I knew you was scheming, but this is on some next level shit. How in the fuck did you pull this off?"

"Andre left me no choice but to go hard. After T-Roc made my flight arrangements and I knew where we would be going while in LA, I called in my media contact and got shit popping."

"You are the shit, Chantal. Only you and J-Lo can scheme up some mess like this. But girl I hope in your will you left me your jewelry collection because Andre is going to kill you."

"Oh well, his ass fucked around first and second with that damn Arisa bitch. He deserves everything he gets and then some."

"All that's cool, but you knew that Andre was a dog before you had his baby and became his girl. If memory serves me correctly he was already taken when you moved in for the kill and locked him down with Melanie."

"Sweetheart, don't hate the player, hate the game. Yeah, I might have sealed the deal with Andre and broke up his little Hollywood romance by getting pregnant but many bitches have tried and failed before me and after me, you being one."

"I have never fucked or tried to fuck Andre."

"Darling, I'm not talking specifically about Andre. I'm talking about women in general who try to tie a man down by getting pregnant and having a baby. A lot of women fuck around and have a baby with a nigga who they think is a baller and he ain't got shit, example you. You had a baby with some half-ass actor who probably hasn't seen a residual check in two years. You just knew he was going to be the next Mekhi Phifer and tried to lock him down. Everybody doesn't get it right, so don't be mad at me because I did."

"Ain't nobody mad at you, Chantal. I'll give you your props for landing Andre, but you're not satisfied with that. Being his baby mother isn't enough for you. You are determined to be his wife."

"Damn right. Why in the hell should I settle? All the work I put in, if he is going to wife anybody it's going to be me."

"Well, if you pull off that you are truly the baddest reformed industry ho out here. You and I both know the deal and as the saying goes, 'A man is not gonna wife a ho,' reformed or otherwise. But then again, Chantal, you're not the average bitch. You might be the exception to the rule."

"That's my plan." With that, Chantal picked up the phone to deal with Andre.

All Chantal heard was screaming over the phone. She couldn't decipher what was being said because Andre's voice was so loud and he was talking so fast. Her heart was pounding because she did manage to catch words like "whore," "slut," "dick lover," and did she let T-Roc fuck her in the ass. It was all to be expected. Chantal knew Andre and this was phase one of their argument, but phase two was going to be a little different this time. Instead of begging for his forgiveness, Chantal would simply tell Andre why she did what she did and that he was right, they shouldn't be together. After he cursed her out for ten minutes straight, Chantal finally took a minute to interject as he was catching his breath.

In a calm voice Chantal said, "Andre, I know all about your recent ménage à trois with Arisa. Not only did you fuck her and some other chick, but you had the nerve to take them to a private party at 40/40 where you knew all of my friends would be. You then had the nerve to keep those tricks at our apartment for at least two days, all while you're sending me a $25,000 watch as some bitch was probably sucking you off. To make matters worse I have to get bombarded with phone calls letting me know about you and your video hofessional. To say I was devastated would be an understatement."

"So, what, you go to LA and fuck my enemy and have it splashed across all the networks and paper? That's how you get back at me?"

"I wasn't trying to get back at you. I just needed to get away and feel wanted by someone who cared about me."

"Oh, so T-Roc cares about you? Bitch, please. You just another ho that he fucked."

"Unfortunately for me we never had sex. He was too much of a gentleman for that. Unlike you, he doesn't run up in everything that has a pulse. T-Roc prefers to wine and dine you and treat you like a lady before getting you in the bed."

"Well, when I meet a lady that is what I'll do," Andre shot back.

"Well, that's cool. Good luck."

Just when Chantal was about to hang up the phone, she heard Andre blurt out, "I know you're not checking for that nigga on some serious type shit?"

"Why wouldn't I be? He's the hottest nigga out."

"Chantal, I swear on everything I love, if you fuck that nigga, start having your moms make funeral arrangements because you're a dead bitch."

"Andre, fuck you. I'm tired of this bullshit. All you do is fuck around with twenty million tricks and expect me to watch from the sidelines. You're no type of father to Melanie and no type of boyfriend to me. Yeah, I know I've made mistakes in the past but I was trying to do the right thing and be a family. But you don't want that—you rather run the street with this bitch and the third. Good for you but not for me. This relationship is over, Andre, and I wish you luck and happiness in life, but it's time for me to do me. Thanks for the ride." Chantal then hung up the phone and had the biggest grin on her face, as though she were the cat who just swallowed the canary.

Shari stood up and started applauding for her. "Like I said, you are that bitch. Chantal, that was brilliant. You've never played that hand with Andre before." As Shari was talking, Chantal's home phone kept ringing and the caller ID showed it was Andre. She didn't bother to pick it up. It was time for Andre to suffer a little.

Chantal couldn't help but express her true feelings to Shari that she so often kept to herself. "Nobody but God knows this and now you, but I've spent many nights crying my heart out over Andre. Yeah, everybody thinks I'm this cold, calculating gold digger, but I hurt like everybody else. It never gets any easier. Every time I catch Andre cheating it breaks my heart. All the diamonds in the world can't heal that pain and it never will. But it was time for me to play hardball because at the end of the day, Andre is the only man I want to be with. I want him to be my husband and I want to be his wife."

T-Roc didn't appreciate Chantal using him as a pawn for whatever game she was playing with Andre, especially since he didn't even have the opportunity to make love to the bronzed beauty. That wasn't entirely her fault since he somewhat gave her the cold shoulder after making a long overdue reconnection with Tyler Blake. After all these years he still hadn't gotten the delectable Tyler out of his system. She was the one woman he was unable to fully conquer. After their nasty breakup he wasn't sure he would ever have the chance to redeem himself. Now with the movie *Angel* he finally believed this was the break he had been waiting for. Tyler seemed to be happy with William Donovan, but T-Roc figured he was much too old for a young, vibrant Hollywood starlet like Tyler. She needed a man like himself to share the spotlight with. T-Roc envisioned them being a dynamic pair that brought a hot new, sexy aura to the Golden City.

As T-Roc finished up his drink before his private jet landed in LA, he couldn't help but feel anxious. Not only did he want the girl, but he also wanted the part as Damian. To triumph over both would be more than just another notch on his belt. This would be the start of a new chapter in his life.

After her blowup with Andre, Chantal was more than happy to escort Shari to a private party her boyfriend Chris was having at a swanky lounge. She hadn't spoken to Andre in almost a week and was feeling quite neglected. She was hoping that maybe one of Chris's Chicago Bear teammates could give her a little tender love and care until Andre got his act together.

"Shari, what street is this club on again?" Chantal asked, growing tired of circling the same block for the fifth time. Shari dug in her purse searching for the gold foil invite.

"The spot is called Reserve. It's on 858 West Lake Street," Shari said, starting to feel anxious herself and ready to get out of the car.

"What's the cross street, because we've been driving up and down Lake for a minute now."

Shari toyed with the invite, hoping that additional information was available. To her relief it was. "The cross is Peoria Street," she told Chantal.

When Chantal made a right and saw all the cars lined up waiting for valet parking they both let out an audible sigh.

"Girl, this shit looks like it's hot. You see all these Benz, Beamers, and a couple of Maybachs. I might find me a cute little side-piece up in here," Chantal boasted.

"All right, hot mama, you already a little shaky with Andre, don't cause a full fledge earthquake." The heavenly pair stepped out of Chantal's alpine white BMW 650i convertible and strutted into Reserve. When they entered the posh lounge there were two rows of candles reflecting off the gleaming custom glass red tiles behind the marble bar. The setting complimented Chantal's radiant crimson Nicole Miller dress.

"Lead me to where they're popping bottles," Chantal said as her hips glided to Beyoncé's new track.

"Follow me. I see Chris and I know they popping bottles," Shari said, guiding Chantal toward her boyfriend. Chantal immediately began sizing up the cloud of people that were in a roped-off section.

"I thought this was a private party?" Chantal asked.

"It is," Shari stated, wondering what warranted Chantal's question.

"Then why does he have this section roped off like he in a regular club and he need his own private VIP area?"

"Girl, that's Chris for you. See all this out here," Shari said, pointing to their surrounding area. "This is the VIP area. Behind that velvet rope is what Chris would call the 'VVIP section.' He's a little extra with his."

"Whatever floats his boat," Chantal said as they walked up on Chris and his posse of friends. Chantal observed that there weren't a mob of groupies occupying the section, which pleased her. "I'm glad I don't have to share space with a gang of bitches," she whispered in Shari's ear.

"Hi, baby," Shari said as Chris greeted her with a kiss on the cheek. "This is my friend, Chantal."

"It's nice to finally meet you. Shari always talks about her running partner, Chantal."

"I hope all good things," Chantal said.

"Of course, it's all good. If I didn't know better I would say you were Shari's idol," Chris said, smiling at Shari.

"Calm it down, Chris, you don't need to pump Chantal's ego any more than what it already is. This girl is damn near a legend in our old neighborhood—ain't that right, Chantal?"

"Stop making me blush, Shari. You know how I can't stand a lot of attention." Both girls laughed as if sharing an inside joke. Both knew that attention was all that Chantal craved.

"Enough of this, you ladies grab a glass and make yourself comfortable," Chris said, leading the ladies to the leather couches. Chantal and Shari giggled as countless women in their tightest jeans and most curve-defying dresses tried to finagle their way into the exclusive area. But neither the security nor the high rollers chilling in the VVIP area was having it. One disgruntled beauty finally managed to break through after screaming that she was the wife of one of the NFL players. The bouncer still wasn't budging until her husband finally came up for air from an intense conversation with another player and ran to her rescue. After about an hour, one confident man decided to take his chances and approach Chantal.

"Would I be too forward if I said you're absolutely stunning?" the tall, broad-shouldered man asked.

"Of course not—it's the truth," she said with a slight smile. The man couldn't tell if she was serious or joking but decided to have a seat next to her nevertheless. Chantal didn't object since she was somewhat attracted to the well-built man with the most perfect teeth she had ever seen.

"So what's your name, beautiful?"

"Chantal, but you can stop with all the beauty comments; you've covered that."

"I'm sorry. It's just rare to meet a woman that looks like you."

"I know, but still enough already. Don't waste my time, or yours for that matter, telling me things that I already know. You may only have a couple of minutes to make a good impression, so be a little bit more original and step up your conversation game."

Staying true to form, the man continued on with his champagne campaign but soon realized he was no closer to reaching his goal. Chantal was at first responsive to the handsome athlete but was now giving him shade. After she and Shari finished up the bottle he purchased, Chantal lost all interest. She barely even noticed when he took his business elsewhere.

"You ladies enjoying yourself?" Chris asked as he approached the two women.

"Yeah, this party is nice, baby. I'm getting a little tired though. But I wanted to wait for you so we could leave together," Shari said.

"Oh, baby, if you're tired you should head home. I'm not sure what time I'm leaving this spot. We trying to party all night."

"All night? I wanted to spend some time with you."

"I tell you what, go home get some rest and tomorrow it's all about you. We'll get a bite to eat, do a little shopping, and then have a romantic evening, just the two of us," Chris said as he ran his fingers through Shari's tousled hair.

"Okay, baby, call me in the morning," Shari said as she kissed Chris good-bye. As the ladies exited the club, Shari couldn't help but feel a tad disappointed that she wasn't going home with Chris. Chantal could tell that her friend wasn't thrilled about leaving her man.

"Shari, snap out of it, he said he'll see you tomorrow."

"I know, but you saw all those chicks in there. Any one of them would love to get their hands on a chipped up nigga like Chris."

"True, but honey he seems to be all caught up in you."

"You think so, Chantal?"

"Girl, yeah, and he spend paper on you and little Alex. You got that in the bag. Even if he do fuck one of those hoochies, that is all it would be. They ain't getting nothing out of the deal but some dick, so who really gives a fuck?"

"I hear you, but I really dig him, Chantal. I don't want to share him with a bunch of random bitches," Shari somberly admitted.

"I know, baby girl, but that's the double-edged sword to this game we're in. You can't expect to be with a man who has money and fame and expect to be the only one. It don't work like that. You just make sure that the relationship is worth your time. That means getting compensated with that dough. See, we ain't like those other silly bitches running around bragging that we fucked so-and-so and ain't got nothing to show for it. It's okay to catch feelings, but just keep it in check. The bottom line is get that paper because you never know when shit will hit the fan."

"Is that last statement for me or are you speaking about your relationship with Andre?" Shari's statement caught Chantal off guard.

"Shari, what in the world are you talking about?"

"You're going on about it being part of the game for men to cheat and stacking paper because things might hit the fan. I mean, Chantal, if there's one thing you make clear, you don't want Andre sleeping with other women. You be the first one ready to beat a bitch ass over Andre but you're telling me that I should overlook it with Chris. That doesn't make sense."

"Girl, when has love ever made sense? Do as I say, not as I do. I made the mistake of really falling in love with Andre's whoring ass so I've become territorial. Call me greedy. I want it all; money, power, and respect, but achieving two out of three ain't bad."

NINE

Mesmerized

As Tyler sat in the studio waiting for T-Roc to arrive for his screen test, she felt extremely nervous. She couldn't tell if it was the normal nervousness she got each time the camera started rolling or if it was because she was looking forward to seeing him. But it didn't matter because T-Roc obviously had a girlfriend. It had been splashed on the TV and tabloids nonstop that he was now dating Andre's ex—talk about scandalous. The moment Tyler finished her thought, T-Roc was walking toward her looking stylish as ever in a cream linen pantsuit. The fabric highlighted the muscled definition of his sculptured frame. His perfect mouth of whites greeted the jumpy Tyler.

"Tyler, it's a pleasure to see you again," T-Roc said, extending his arm for a handshake. Tyler was thrown off by his professional attitude. She didn't think he would pull her close for a passionate kiss but she definitely did not expect a business-as-usual handshake.

"It's nice to see you again, too," Tyler replied with an on-edge grin. T-Roc held her hand in a tight grasp until he noticed William beside him.

"I'm glad you all are getting to know one another," William said, unaware of the fact T-Roc and Tyler had history. "Everything is set up, we just need the two of you to stand over this way and give us the performance of a lifetime," he stated in his "let's get down to business" tone as he led them to the other side of the stage. "Do you have any questions before we begin?" he asked, directing his questions toward T-Roc.

"No, I'm good, just ready to make it happen." T-Roc came across as totally confident and at ease to be a rookie, which somewhat intimidated Tyler. But then again he was overly confident with everything he did in life. That was, no doubt, one of the reasons he was so successful.

As they began the scene Tyler stumbled on her lines and realized if anyone was nervous, it was her. She eventually got into the flow of the character and the chemistry between T-Roc and Tyler was undeniable. He seemed like a veteran, spitting out the intense lines of Damian. When it was time for him to forcefully grab Tyler, he put his arm around her waist and with a quick jolt pulled her up close as they stood looking deep into each other's eyes for what seemed like forever. He then planted a passionate kiss on Tyler. T-Roc's lips were still soft and his kiss seductive. Her body felt a twinge and T-Roc obviously felt the electricity because he pulled her closer and kissed Tyler even harder.

"Cut," Tyler heard William say, applauding, letting T-Roc know he could now stop. With great reluctance T-Roc released Tyler from his embrace and gave her the "undressing her with his eyes" stare she was familiar with.

"That was excellent," William cheered. "If I didn't know better

I would think the two of you were in love," William joked with a hearty laugh.

"Well, it would be easy to fall in love with a woman as intense as the character Angel," T-Roc retorted, making both Tyler and William feel uneasy.

"My sentiments exactly," William said, trying to break the awkwardness of the moment. Tyler stood quiet, letting the men thaw out the frozen vibe.

"Well, T-Roc, you were terrific. We have one more actor to audition and then we will make our decision. You should be hearing from us in the next couple of days."

"Thank you so much for the opportunity, William. I know I'm the right guy for the part," T-Roc added, with his arrogance shining through. "It was a pleasure working with you, Ms. Blake, and I hope to be doing more soon." Tyler gave T-Roc a courtesy smile and stood there watching with William as he exited the building.

"That's an arrogant son of a bitch, but he can act. The two of you definitely have chemistry and he is the best Damian I've seen thus far. What do you think?" William asked, making Tyler feel uncomfortable for some reason.

"He's good, but we still have one other actor to audition. Let's see what happens before speculating any further."

"Speaking of audition, here comes Mr. Jackson now," William blurted out as he walked toward superstar number two, Andre Jackson.

Andre always believed that Chantal was the most beautiful woman he had ever seen, until he laid eyes on Tyler Blake. She was the epitome of beauty, sexiness, and innocence all in one. Her entire face and body glowed. As William and Tyler walked toward him, his heart actually started beating faster; it was love at first sight. Andre never believed in that until that very moment.

"Tyler, this is Andre Jackson," William said, introducing the two.

"Hi, it's a pleasure. I love your music and your clothes," Tyler said, feeling herself go red in the face.

"The pleasure is all mine. I hear you're the new It Girl of Hollywood. Congratulations, that's big!"

"Yeah, and a little overrated. We won't know exactly what I'll be until this movie is complete and the box office receipts are counted."

"You have to excuse Tyler; she's a bit insecure about her overnight success. I have no doubt this movie will do great things for her career and the audience will embrace her as the new hot young leading lady."

"William, you're embarrassing me."

"No need to be embarrassed, I'm putting my money on William Donovan. Being the mega-star he is, I'm sure he can spot another one in the making," Andre chimed in.

"Well, enough of this small talk, let's get down to work. Are you ready, Andre?" William commanded, back in business mode.

"As much as I'll ever be."

"Okay, give me a few minutes and we'll be ready to rumble," William said jokingly as he walked off. "Don't be nervous; just treat it as if you're having a confrontation with your girlfriend."

"Actually I'm single," Andre said, wanting Tyler to know that he was very much available.

"Okay, then *ex-girlfriend*."

"That will work," Andre agreed.

Andre Jackson completed his scene with the same ease as T-Roc. They both exuded a confidence and street edge that brought the character of Damian to life and gave him creditability. It also complemented the vulnerable but complex character of Angel. The decision of who should play the part was literally a toss-up. Either one of them could fill the shoes and do a magnificent job. After Andre left, it was up to Tyler and William to discuss who should be cast in the role of Damian.

"Tyler, what do you think? Both of them are excellent. It really comes down to who you feel most comfortable with."

"Me? You're saying the decision is mine?"

"As a director I could work with either one of them. You had chemistry with both and their name value is equal. You're the one that will be working with them on an everyday basis for the next few months. So only you know who can bring out the most from your character Angel."

"I have to think this over—this is a huge decision. You're asking me to decide the fate of two men's acting careers."

"Well, you don't have much time; I need to know tomorrow morning. Go home get some rest and we'll talk in the a.m." William kissed Tyler on her forehead and headed out. The thought of deciding between T-Roc and Andre was enough to make her decide to stop at the liquor store on the way home for a bottle of champagne and at her favorite bakery for two pieces of cake that gave Magnolia a run for their money.

"Girl, have you spoken to Andre?" Shari asked Chantal as they sat outside by the pool on a beautiful spring day.

"Not since he left for LA a few days ago."

"What, he had to handle some business there?"

"I don't know," Chantal said with a huff. "Andre doesn't really discuss things like that with me, but I have a feeling it has to do with him trying to break into the movies. I think Andre doesn't want to share his ambitions for being a movie star with me because if he doesn't catch his big break, he doesn't want to come off as a failure."

"Girl, if Andre became the next Denzel Washington that would be incredible. I could see you on E! getting interviewed by Joan Rivers as you walk down the red carpet."

"Um, I heard Joan Rivers isn't doing that anymore. I believe she switched to the TV Guide Channel."

"Stop it! E! isn't E! without Ms. Rivers. They can keep the daughter, but the mama is fierce."

"Yeah, but I'm sure someone can catch us coming down the red carpet in all my glory," Chantal bragged.

"Well, you better get your shit back tight with Andre or you won't be walking down any red carpet."

"So, you think? I'm trying to work my shit out like Tyler Blake so I won't need Andre at all but for my monthly child support check."

"Bitch, please. You pop all that shit about having a career as an actress, but your lazy ass don't even like to get out of bed before two in the afternoon. How the fuck are you going to be an actress if you not willing to show up on time to the set?"

"Shit, for the type of money they pay I'll pop me some uppers and stay the fuck up."

"You know how this game work; they not hitting you off with no real paper when you first get started. You are going to be an extra on the set, sitting around damn near all day and night barely making enough money to buy yourself a decent meal. You remember how whack that shit was when you did those video shoots. Them directors wasn't trying to pay them chicks no money. Most of the tricks were so happy to be there, scheming on a permanent sponsor that they were more than happy to take a couple dollars."

"Hold up, that was never me. I came on the video scene clocking real paper from them directors."

"Yeah, because you were fucking them." Chantal and Shari both burst out laughing.

"You do have a point there. I guess that's what I have to do to skip all that struggling in the movie business, too. Hell, I'd deep throat a powerful director for a coveted leading lady role."

"On the real, you would give up your dreams of being Mrs. Andre Jackson if you had the chance to be a movie star?" Shari asked, already knowing the answer.

"You my girl so I'm not going to even front. I could give a damn about being a movie star if I marry Andre. I would love to be a Hollywood wife. I much rather be a slave to one super-rich man than to have to lie on my back for a slew of them. Been there done that, and quite honestly my back is wore the fuck out. I'll leave all that hard work to Tyler Blake. Let her keep working her shit out while I luxuriate on my man's dime."

"Ain't that bitch working her shit out though? Did you see her in the new Revlon ad? She's trying to be the next Halle Berry."

"Yeah, she is definitely doing her thing. I saw her at William Donovan's party in Malibu looking incredible. I believe they're doing the tango in the bedroom because he was all into her."

"I wouldn't be surprised with his fine ass. I don't know how that wife of his ever landed him. She look like his mama."

"Well, you know how that go. She was taking care of him when he didn't have a pot to piss in or a window to throw it out of. Marrying her was his way of saying thank you. Hell, he still able to get prime pussy from bad-ass bitches and keep the little woman at home with the kids."

"Yeah, at least she got him to marry her unlike the rest of us bitches who spend the next twenty years being baby mamas. Things have definitely changed." Shari sighed.

"You ain't never lied. The best you can hope for is a baby daddy with some long paper who is willing to take care of his child. These men today act like they petrified to walk down the aisle. It's too many young cats that are making millions. The thought of settling down with one bitch is out of the question. Then when your shit is super tight like Halle Berry who has looks, fame and money they be so intimidated they try to dog you out to bolster their ego. You can't win for losing. I'm starting to believe men only want to marry women that have the qualities of being a doormat, and like to keep their dime pieces on the side," Chantal reasoned.

"Girl, you're depressing me. Maybe I need to throw on a prairie skirt and some bifocals to land me a husband. Then once he's mine, take his credit card and go to New York and tear Fifth

Avenue up. He gon be like, 'Where my wife at?' all while I'm floss-
ing in the Big Apple."

"Shari, you are crazy, but I feel you. I don't know what these
men are looking for in a wife. Hell, I'm still trying to figure out
how goofy looking La La landed Carmelo Anthony."

"La La, who's that?" Shari asked puzzled.

"You know that MTV vj—you didn't hear about her engagement to Carmelo Anthony?"

"Bitch, stop playing. You really think he's going to marry that
chick?"

"I don't know, but he's young and dumb. A bitch definitely
ain't turned him out yet so she might make it down that aisle. If I
would've met Andre when he was twenty and still wet behind the
ears we would definitely be married and probably working on
baby number four by now."

"Honestly, Chantal, do you think Andre was ever wet behind
the ears? I think he came out his mama's womb prowling for
pussy."

"Girl, I wouldn't be surprised," Chantal laughed. "Shit, I came
out sniffing for that money. Let's stop thinking about a husband for
a minute and go to the club tonight and shake our asses."

"That's what I'm talking 'bout. I had so much fun at Chris's
party a few weeks ago. We hadn't hung out like that in a minute.
I'm definitely up to doing it again," Shari squealed as she and
Chantal did their pinkie shake.

After gulping down half the bottle of champagne and devouring
both pieces of cake, Tyler was no closer to making her decision
about who should play Damian. Both men were actually incredible
and could dominate the role. Part of her wanted to automatically
reject T-Roc because she remembered promising her ex-boyfriend
Ian that she would stay away from his cousin since he was partly

responsible for Ian throwing her down the stairs, which in turn caused her to lose the baby. Making the reckless decision to date two cousins was a mistake that still troubled Tyler. After Ian learned of her deception Tyler felt responsible for the aftermath, but resented T-Roc even more since he was the one who revealed their brief affair. Tyler knew T-Roc did it to be spiteful because his ego couldn't believe that she chose his cousin over him. T-Roc's ultimate payback had changed the course of all three of their lives forever. But Ian was now married with a child and had moved on; there was no real reason to keep that promise. But Tyler couldn't help but bear in mind how deceitful and conniving T-Roc could be and she doubted he had changed. She questioned if it was fair to let their past relationship stand in the way of him getting his dream role. Tyler decided that it wouldn't be. T-Roc deserved the opportunity to break in to acting just as much as she did. *Fair is fair,* Tyler said to herself falling asleep.

When she closed her eyes and went to sleep all she dreamed of was Andre making passionate love to her. She hadn't realized that he'd left such a lasting effect on her. She had no choice but to choose him for the part because she couldn't take the chance of not seeing him again.

First thing in the morning Tyler headed to William's office to give him her decision. After her dream last night she was a hundred percent sure that she was making the right choice. As Tyler was entering the building she ran smack into William.

"Talk about right on time," William teased.

Tyler laughed before saying, "I don't believe in coincidences; I believe you're stalking me." William gave Tyler his movie-star grin before grabbing her hand as they headed to the elevator. As William and Tyler stood in the elevator she couldn't help but think that this was the first time since meeting William that she was actually dreaming about another man. Tyler had gotten so caught up in William that she was sure he was the one, even though he was married. Now she started feeling that he wasn't and an overwhelming sense of guilt flooded her. The only reason she carried on an affair with a married man was because she knew they belonged together, but the knowledge that he wasn't divorced made what they were doing repulsive. She felt it was definitely time for her to do some serious soul searching.

"So Tyler, who is going to play Damian? T-Roc or Andre Jackson?" William asked as soon as they reached his office. He was anxious to get his movie project moving forward.

"I struggled with my decision all last night, but I came to the conclusion that Andre Jackson is the right man for the part," Tyler proclaimed.

"Excellent choice. I thought you were leaning towards T-Roc, but I'm glad you decided on Andre. He seems a little more grounded than T-Roc. Well, I better put the call in to Craig Silverman and get this movie in motion," William said with great enthusiasm.

While Tyler sat in the chair watching William place the phone call, she couldn't help but surmise that William wouldn't be so excited if he knew the reason behind her decision. Tyler couldn't stop thinking about Andre.

"I just got off the phone with Craig. It's a done deal. Our lawyers are sending over the paperwork and once Andre Jackson signs them, we start shooting. Tyler, I have an excellent feeling about this. You definitely made the right choice!" Tyler couldn't help but feel she made the right choice, too.

"Oh baby, I'm about to cum," Arisa screamed out as Andre pounded her from the back. He began to feel a little disgusted for some odd reason. When he finally busted a nut, he immediately pulled out and took off his condom and walked to the bathroom and shut the door. Andre turned on the faucet and splashed cold water on his perfectly chiseled coffee-colored face. As he stared in the mirror he felt like a loser because he had settled and fucked Arisa instead of being with the woman who had been on his mind for the last couple of days. The whole time he was fucking Arisa he wished that he was making love to Tyler. She was just the type of woman that he wanted to have as a wife, although he had to admit to himself that he didn't even know her. She could be a psycho for all he knew. But something about her was pulling him in, and he welcomed it.

"Baby, the phone is ringing," Arisa said as she stood by the door. Arisa was getting way too comfortable for Andre's taste. Although the door was closed she felt she had the right to open it and tell Andre his phone was ringing. It never crossed her mind that maybe he didn't want to be interrupted or bothered with her for that matter.

"Thanks," Andre said as he brushed passed Arisa toward his cordless. "Hello," he trilled, aggravated by Arisa's acting too comfortable in his space.

"Andre, I have great news," Craig said, unable to contain his excitement. "You got the part!"

"What?" Andre wanted to make sure he heard Craig correctly before savoring his excitement.

"You heard me, you got the part of Damian. The call just came in from William Donovan and he is having his lawyers send the paperwork over ASAP. They want to start shooting immediately. So pack your bags, you're headed for Hollywood."

Andre was too stunned to speak. He had no idea how badly he had wanted the part until that very moment. Never in a million years did he believe he would get the role. He had decided that he would have to track down Tyler Blake some other way because he had already made up his mind that she would be his. Now they would be on set together just about every day, working side by side. Andre walked toward his closet and without delay began packing his clothes.

"Baby, where are you going?" Arisa asked, looking and feeling confused as to how one minute Andre had his dick thrust inside of her and then he was packing his shit up like he didn't even know she was there.

"I have to go out of town for a while," Andre snapped, put off by the fact Arisa was questioning him.

"Can I come?" Arisa asked in a seductive voice, as though she wasn't catching the shade from Andre.

"Can you come?" Andre stood and looked at Arisa for a second to get a reading on her face. In his mind she had to be joking because if she was serious, it was his sign that it was time to cut her loose. She had now overstepped her position if, even for a moment, she thought she was coming along.

"Yeah, I want to come with you. When you get finished handling whatever you have to do, at least you know you have somebody waiting for you," Arisa explained as though she was his girl.

"Arisa, understand something. If I want my woman waiting for me after I handle my business then that's what will happen. But you're damn sure not my wife, you not even my girl, so step back and play your position or you might find yourself without a position at all."

"Andre, you don't have to be cruel. If you want your space that's all you have to say. I just figured with all the drama going on between you and Chantal you might want some company, or at least someone to talk to."

"What, are you a shrink now?" Andre said sarcastically. He saw the tears starting to swell up in Arisa's eyes and right before they began to fall, Andre checked himself and opted for another approach. "Listen, Arisa, you're a sweet girl but I think you're putting more into this relationship than what it is. I think it's time for us to put it to rest."

"What, what are you talking about? Andre, I love you, I do." Those were the words Andre dreaded to hear. He quietly wondered if the chick honestly thought that he would take a hofessional seriously. But sadly it seemed like she did.

"Arisa, don't say that, because I don't love you."

"That's okay. I have enough love for both of us. I just want to make you happy, Andre." Andre realized he had an unstable woman on his hand and deliberated that it was pointless to have any sort of meaningful conversation with her.

"Arisa, I really have to catch this flight—we'll talk about this when I get back," Andre said, while handing Arisa her clothes.

"Okay, well when will that be?"

"I'll call you tonight and let you know. But, baby, I really have to go. Get dressed and I'll call you a car service." As Arisa was about to leave, Andre gave her a wad of cash and a kiss on her forehead. He figured it was the least he could do since he knew he would never see her again. He made a notation in his mind to immediately call his assistant and have his cell number changed.

As days began to turn to weeks, Chantal was grateful she had Shari. She wouldn't know what to do if she didn't have her best friend to keep her occupied, since Andre had all but vanished on her. If it wasn't for the quick, two-second calls to speak to Melanie, Chantal wouldn't know if Andre was dead or alive. His aloofness was breaking Chantal's spirit. Partying with Shari did numb the pain but it did little to stop it.

"Girl, we had a ball last night," Shari said as she talked to Chantal on the phone. "There was some fine-ass niggas up in the spot, too. Remember that one guy grabbed my arm when they took it back a minute and played 'Lean Back.' He came up and asked me to dance and I told him we gangsters and gangsters don't dance, we boogie," Shari announced proudly.

"Yeah, and I looked at you and said bitch you ain't no damn gangster. Yo silly ass thought you was Rémy Martin up in that spot," Chantal mocked.

"I know, but that line is so hot, I was dying to say it to somebody."

"Well, next time say it in the privacy of your home. I'm sure Alex won't think you sound crazy."

"Okaaaay, next topic, so what's up with Mr. Hollywood?"

"Girl, I have not heard from Andre, but I'm not stressing. He's probably trying to play hard to get. He'll be back, he always is."

"Well, yeah, but don't let him stay away too long, I heard those LA chicks are 'bout it 'bout it," Shari warned.

"I won't. I am going to call him later on today to see what's up. I do miss him, but I can't seem too anxious or I'll ruin my plan."

"I feel you. I have to run some errands and then I'm hooking up with Chris for a late lunch but keep me posted. I can't wait to see how this drama unfolds."

"You and Chris are really going strong. I told you that nigga was digging you."

"Yeah, that's my baby. I have a feeling he might be popping the question soon."

"What! Why you say that?"

"I didn't want to say anything, but the other day while Chris and I were shopping at Oakbrook Center he took me into Tiffany to try on rings."

"Why didn't you tell me?" Chantal screamed, overwhelmed by her friend's news.

"I didn't want to jinx anything. I'm not even sure if he's going to ask me to marry him but we did specifically look at engagement rings. When I asked him why he wanted me to pick out a ring, he said that just in case he wanted to pop the question in the near future, he would know which ring to get for me."

"That sounds like a proposal to me, or close enough to it."

"I want to think so, but you never know. The last thing I want to do is set myself up for a major letdown. But I'm hoping he's the one, Chantal."

"Me, too, Shari, you deserve to be happy. Chris seems like a really good guy. He would make a great brother-in-law. Plus, if they ever make it to the Super Bowl, we'll have prime seats."

"You're a mess. I'll talk to you later."

After Shari hung up the phone, Chantal continued to think about her best friend's possible engagement news and admitted to herself that she was disappointed Andre hadn't called. She fully expected him to be at her front doorstep by now, begging for her forgiveness. Chantal wondered if maybe she had taken it too far, but Andre had left her no choice. The clock was ticking and she had to make major moves. Chantal dismissed her skepticism and figured that as soon as Andre had some free time, he would call.

The Truth Hurts

Andre woke up to butterflies in his stomach. Never did he imagine being so excited about seeing Tyler again. Today was their first day of shooting and all his scenes were with her. He'd been holed up in his Beverly Hills mansion going over and over the script for the last few days and was more nervous about seeing Tyler than actually starring in his first movie. After devouring his omelet and washing it down with a glass of orange juice, Andre walked outside where his driver was waiting to take him to the studio. He sat back and closed his eyes as the Maybach cruised down the highway. He kept seeing visions of Tyler Blake and imagining the two of them in an intimate embrace. For the first time in over twenty years Andre Jackson felt like a love-struck adolescent, and when "So Sick" by Ne-Yo came on the radio it just heightened the feelings of it all.

Tyler couldn't believe she was going to be face-to-face with Andre Jackson again. He was more than her leading man; he was a love interest. No matter how hard she tried she couldn't forget how she was immediately drawn to him when they first met on the soundstage. And then when he gently held her hand for an intimate scene while auditioning for the role, it was as if an electrical shock had surged up her arm. With that level of familiarity Tyler felt as if they had known each other in a previous lifetime. She had even dreamed of him when making love to William. Tyler had been waiting for this day for over three weeks and it took all of her self-control to contain her enthusiasm. As she sat in her trailer on the closed set, she heard a knock at the door. "Who is it?" Tyler asked, agitated that someone was disturbing the vivid erotic images she was having of Andre.

"It's William, open your door."

"Sorry about that. You know what a privacy nut I am," Tyler said as she opened the door.

"Come on out. Andre is here and I want to briefly go over some things before we get started."

Tyler followed William to the meeting area. When she neared Andre, they instantly locked eyes.

"It's so nice to see you again," Andre said in a monotone voice, disguising the fact that he wanted to rip off her cream-colored jersey dress and take her on the couch, not caring who watched.

"You, too," Tyler said graciously, while imagining Andre being the father of her second child.

As William went over a few script changes and seemed to ramble on and on, Andre and Tyler tuned everything out, each absorbed with their own sordid thoughts of lovemaking. Both wondered if the other could feel the attraction or, better yet, could the other people on set feel the intense yearning between the two. While Tyler hoped it would remain a secret, Andre wanted everyone to know that he wanted Tyler; he just prayed she felt the same way.

———

T-Roc sat in his office going over some last minute revisions for an upcoming press conference to introduce his new men's cologne, when *Access Hollywood* came on announcing breaking news. At first T-Roc ignored the commentator until he heard the name Tyler Blake and *Angel* in the same sentence. He turned up the volume and listened intently to the report.

"We are the first to report that the new highly anticipated movie *Angel* starring Hollywood starlet Tyler Blake and directed by Oscar-winner William Donovan has found its leading man. It will be played by someone new to the Hollywood big screen, but a superstar in his own right, Andre Jackson. They began shooting yesterday on a closed set in LA. . . ."

As the report continued, showing pictures of Tyler and Andre coming and going on the set, T-Roc picked up one of his prized Grammys and threw it at the TV screen. Needless to say the flat screen broke and T-Roc embarked on one of his infamous tantrums.

"Rebecca, get Craig Silverman on the phone now!" T-Roc screamed to his assistant. He couldn't believe that Andre had gotten the part and he had to find out by tuning in to a tabloid show.

"Craig is on line one," Rebecca echoed.

"How the fuck did Andre get that part, and why the fuck didn't you tell me? I had to find out by watching fucking *Access Hollywood*. The type of money you make off me, I should know when you have to shit, you fucking asshole!"

"T-Roc, calm down."

"Don't tell me to calm down, you fat fuck. That part was supposed to be mine, what happened?"

"Honestly, I don't know. They felt Andre was better for the part. I'm sorry, but I just found out a few days ago and I wasn't able to get in touch with you to break the news. But listen, there are a lot more movie roles out there for you. I get offers across my desk every day. We'll find the right project."

"Fuck you, Craig. You're a lying fuck. You've known for more than a few days about this shit. If it wasn't for you, Andre probably wouldn't have even auditioned for the part. You're fired, you piece of shit."

"T-Roc, you can't do that, we go way back. I've helped you make millions and millions of dollars. You can't end not only our business relationship but our friendship over this small incident."

"Oh, yes the fuck I can. You better be lucky that I'm only firing you, instead of sending my man over there to make sure you end up in intensive care." T-Roc slammed the phone down, full of contempt. He couldn't decide whether he was more pissed because he missed out on an incredible breakout role or the fact that Andre beat him out for the part. Either way, he was determined to find a way to even the score.

When Chantal first heard the news that Andre had gotten the starring role of Damian in the movie *Angel*, she was furious. It wasn't that she didn't want to see Andre fulfill his dream of being an actor, but the fact that he was starring opposite Tyler Blake rubbed her the wrong way. To make matters worse, Andre didn't even call to share the news; she heard it on *Access Hollywood* like all the other common folks. Andre was sending a clear sign that she wasn't a priority and maybe not even a thought. The reality of that was sinking in and beginning to totally chip away at Chantal's confidence.

"Girl, I can't believe Andre is starring with Tyler Blake in the movie *Angel*," Shari said as they walked through the lush gardens and flowing fountains at the outdoor Oakbrook shopping center.

"You can't." Chantal stopped, paused, and looked at Shari before continuing. "You're my partner in crime, so I'm going to keep it real with you. Shari, I'm shook right now. The thought of Andre and Tyler filming a movie together is too much. That's the one bitch that can take my man. I'm just hoping that William Donovan will be watching them so hard that there won't be an opportunity for any hanky-panky," she said as they entered Braxton Seafood Grill.

"I know that's right. You need to get on a plane and track your man down. Dial that number to American Airlines," Shari said, while handing Chantal her cell phone.

"I don't know if hopping on a plane to see him will be enough. He hasn't called me, Shari. He's got me in that 'I'm not fucking with you' box. After all we've been through I never thought it would come to that."

"Chantal, it's not like you to be so pessimistic."

"I know, Shari, but this is my life, and for the first time I believe I've truly fucked it up. Andre is in LA right now shooting a movie with motherfucking Tyler Blake. She's gorgeous, Shari, I can't deny that. But besides being gorgeous she has an amazing career."

"Chantal, you're the most beautiful girl I know, and most people don't know but you also have an incredible heart. Andre loves you and some Halle Berry wannabe isn't going to change that."

"I'm glad you're so optimistic, because right now I'm an emotional wreck."

"I guess being in love with a wonderful man will do that to you," Shari said, as she affectionately stroked Chantal's arm. "It'll be okay, Chantal. You've been through worse than this. You're like a cat; you have nine lives and then some." They laughed and talked about how it would all work out while nibbling on crab cakes and drinking red wine. For a brief moment Chantal felt there was hope that she would win Andre back.

"Okay, everybody, let's take a break," William bellowed to the cast and crew. It was the second week of shooting and Andre was nailing every scene. It was obvious that the right decision was made by casting him; he was a natural talent. His scenes with Tyler were electric, even William had to admit that. In the back of his mind he hoped it was only acting at its best, but he, too, had had a couple of electric performances with actresses and both times they had been having heated affairs. William was determined not to let that happen with Tyler and Andre; he was watching both like a hawk. Andre made his way to his trailer and William followed Tyler to hers.

"Baby, you're doing amazing work out there, I'm so proud of you," William said, giving Tyler a wet kiss on the mouth. Normally, Tyler welcomed William's seductive kisses, but at the moment she was too busy watching the familiar-looking beautiful woman walking toward Andre's trailer.

"What has you so preoccupied?" William asked curiously.

"This woman just walked into Andre's trailer. I hope she's not a fan. I thought this was a closed set."

"Oh, that must be his girlfriend. The guard called me right before the break and I gave her clearance."

"I thought you insisted on no guests," Tyler said, her jealousy beginning to shine through.

"She is the mother of his child, for heaven's sake. I wouldn't exactly call her a guest."

"You're right. I just know how you like for everyone to stay focused." Tyler was hoping that William couldn't sense the immense jealousy that was enveloping her mind. To make sure, she began undressing for a quick lovemaking session.

"Chantal, what are you doing here?" Andre asked, irritated that she had showed up unannounced.

"Andre, I haven't spoken to you in over two weeks. You can't ignore me forever, and what about Melanie?"

"I've spoken to Melanie several times and she's doing just fine. I plan to send for her when I have a couple of days off."

"You mean send for us?"

"No, I mean send for Melanie."

"Andre, if you're still upset with me because of my T-Roc episode, nothing happened. I haven't even spoken to him."

"Well, that's too bad for you, because honestly I don't care, Chantal." All the color left Chantal's face. She couldn't believe what she was hearing. Andre was so distant and cold. He was different than his normal "I just want to get rid of you for a few days" type cold. It was as if he was indifferent to whatever she said or did. Chantal was flustered and turned to desperation. While Andre's back was turned away from her she quickly undressed and stood there in her red lace bra and G-string panties, determined to seduce Andre. But when Andre faced her, he only saw her actions for the desperation they were.

"Chantal, put your clothes back on," Andre said with pity while handing her the silk blouse and pants she just took off. Chantal stood there, embarrassment choking her up.

"What you mean, put my clothes on? You've never been able to resist me; we have more lust for one another than any two people I know."

"You're right, sex has never been our problem and you're certainly one of the most beautiful women I've ever met, but this shit is getting old. It takes more than great sex to make a relationship last." Chantal wasn't listening to anything Andre was saying. Only one thing kept replaying in her mind.

"I'm one of the most beautiful women you've ever met. You always use to say that I was the most beautiful. Who's taken my place, Andre, Tyler Blake?"

"What are you talking about, Chantal? You're tripping right now."

"No, I'm not. I know you, Andre, and something is different. But before you start planning a future with little Miss Tyler, she's taken. William Donovan will never let you get close enough to his prized possession. So you need to concentrate on the family you have right now."

"I don't know what you're talking about. My relationship with

Tyler is strictly professional and I don't have any other sort of interest in her. But that doesn't change the fact that I don't want to have anything to do with you. So please get your shit and get out of here. Now!"

Andre was cringing inside. Upon Chantal's exit he grabbed the tray of food that had just been delivered and threw it at the door. The sound of the plate and glass breaking sounded like a miniature explosion and his lunch was now wall decoration. Andre knew that Chantal was right. He did have it bad for Tyler and was afraid that nothing was going to come of it. He couldn't get a read on her and she seemed very happy with William. Andre couldn't fathom the thought of not getting what he wanted. He stared out his blinds to view Tyler's trailer, which was directly across from his. He pondered what the beauty was doing at that very moment.

"Oh, Tyler, I'm about to cum," William moaned as he gave one final thrust. He fell back on the chair breathing intensely. "Making love to you makes me feel like I'm twenty-one again," William said, admiring his protégee.

Tyler giggled. She knew she made William feel young and alive but it sounded amusing coming from the normally uptight businessman.

"Is that right? So you're using me to hold on to the fountain of youth?" Tyler asked half-jokingly.

"Not exactly 'hold on to.' But having you in my life makes me remember the times, all the wonderful ones in my youth. You give me this newfound energy. It's like a rebirth."

William felt he was paying Tyler a compliment by telling her she was the reason for his optimistic outlook on his life, but she saw it a little differently. To Tyler it sounded like a man having a midlife crisis. Not wanting to grow up and discovering endless adolescence through a woman half his age. It might not have bothered her so much if she shared in his newfound bliss for life, but

Tyler wasn't feeling it. The bliss she longed for seemed so out of reach but yet within touching distance.

After getting dressed, Tyler stood by the window gazing out the blinds. The bliss she longed for was only a few feet away but with William next to her it appeared like it was in a whole other country. In the trailer across from her she saw Andre staring out the opposite window. Their eyes locked and they communicated through their stares. When William touched Tyler's shoulder to get her out of her trance, she turned away briefly to acknowledge him. When she turned back around, Andre's eyes were no longer there to fulfill her hunger.

After her dreadful encounter with Andre, Chantal immediately caught the next flight back to Chicago. Part of her wanted to break down and bathe in her tears but her anger was more powerful. Chantal knew that the clock was done ticking and she was closer than ever to losing what mattered to her the most. For the first time in her life, she didn't know how to compete. Although Andre denied it, she could look in his eyes and tell that he had it bad for Tyler, just by the way he said her name. It was almost as though she was too precious for Chantal to speak her name. But Chantal had been around the block enough times to know that no woman was that perfect, including the divine Tyler Blake. She was determined to dig deeper into Tyler's closet and pull out a skeleton, maybe even two or three, and she knew exactly where to start.

T-Roc was still reeling over the fact that Andre had stolen the part of Damian from him. Not only did he blame Andre but he also held Tyler responsible. His gut instinct told him that she was behind the decision to cast Andre. T-Roc sat at his desk, replaying the day one of his workers brought Tyler to his office for the first time and she was so young and fresh, just the type of girl he knew he could take advantage of. He soon learned that Tyler wasn't as sweet and innocent as she appeared. After he put it on her he thought she would fall in love like so many of his prior conquests, but he soon labeled her an ice princess. After that fateful night T-Roc had made it his mission to conquer her mind, body, and soul. Unfortunately, that failed after the disastrous episode with his cousin Ian, and now once again his opportunity was halted by Andre. As T-Roc racked his brain for a solution, the phone rang, jarring his thoughts.

"T-Roc, you have a call."

"Didn't I tell you I didn't want to be disturbed?"

"Yes, sir, but the woman said it was an emergency and you would want to speak to her."

"Well, who the hell is it?"

"Chantal Morgan."

"Oh yeah, put her through. What up, Chantal?"

"T-Roc, I'm not going to even bullshit you. This is too important, so I'm cutting right to it," Chantal wailed, without even as much as a hello. "I'm sure you know Andre got the part in the movie *Angel* that you so desperately wanted. But that isn't enough for him, now he wants Tyler Blake to be his leading lady on screen and off. That can't happen and I need for you to make sure it doesn't."

"What can I do?" T-Roc asked, amused by her demand.

"You told me you have a history with Tyler. I'm sure you know about some of her trifling secrets that she would prefer to keep in the past. I'm asking you to fill me in so I can tell Andre and he can stop thinking about having any sort of romantic involvement with her."

"That didn't stop him from dealing with you, Chantal dear," T-Roc said mockingly.

"Andre knew what he was dealing with when he first started fucking around with me. But this Tyler bitch got him dazed like she's some angel that has landed in his lap. I know that look he had in his eyes when I mentioned her name. I've never seen him look at me that way. The only other person I've seen him get that gleam for is our daughter Melanie. That's a problem, T-Roc. I've put too much time and effort in this relationship to let some Hollywood starlet steal him away from me."

"Chantal, don't you think you're overreacting? From what I understand Tyler and William Donovan are very much in love, even though he is married."

"Exactly. How long do you think that relationship will last? Eventually Tyler will get tired of playing the mistress and Andre will be right there to comfort her. Oh hell no, not with my man. I want this shit deaded before it even has a chance to start. So what's the 411 on that chick, T-Roc?"

"Even if I did have some unflattering information about Tyler, why would I tell you, Chantal?"

"Because I know Tyler Blake's type; they appear to be all angelic but she's probably more ruthless than both of us combined. Those are the ones who are really dangerous. With that said, she has probably fucked you in the ass a couple of times. I'm sure the pain is still fresh in your mind. I can help you blow her spot up, which will devastate Andre, and you always find great pleasure in that."

T-Roc tapped his fingers on the desk listening to Chantal babble on about the demise of Tyler Blake. He found Chantal's amateur plan so juvenile and wondered if falling in love did that to you, put your scheming ideas on a childish level. "Listen, Chantal, I understand your concern, but waving some of Tyler's dirty panties in Andre's face isn't going to get you the platinum ring. You're going to have to step your game up a lot higher than that. I'll do some brainstorming and see what I can come up with."

"So that means you'll help me?" Chantal warbled with an ounce of hope in her voice.

"Let's just say I'm going to help myself, which in turn so happens to help you, too. Or better yet you can take a trip to New York and we can brainstorm together."

Chantal quickly pondered T-Roc's invitation. Two devious minds collaborating together were much more powerful than one. Plus Chantal was lonely. After her embarrassing encounter with Andre, being in the company of T-Roc would be fun. "I'll be there first thing in the morning. See you soon."

T-Roc hung up the phone with a grin on his face. He immediately began contemplating his next move. If what Chantal said was true then he knew exactly how to get the part he felt he so rightfully deserved back. If Andre had it bad for Tyler, then all he had to do was get them in a compromising position and bring it to the attention of William. William would no doubt flip out and fire Andre for coming anywhere near his precious Tyler. That would leave William no choice but to cast T-Roc, and he would get the part and eventually get the girl. Even though he had his game plan mapped out and doubted Chantal could come up with anything better, it couldn't hurt having a woman's input, particularly from one as manipulative as Chantal. On top of that, T-Roc always enjoyed the company of beautiful woman and especially a feisty one like Chantal.

When Chantal's flight landed at JFK, she was pleasantly surprised that T-Roc had his driver waiting for her.

"I'll be taking you to the Four Seasons hotel. T-Roc reserved a room for you there."

"Sounds good to me," Chantal replied. Chantal had made her own reservations at a midtown hotel but why would she turn down a free one at the Four Seasons? After checking in to her room and relaxing for a while, Chantal thought it was time to place a call to T-Roc.

"Hello," she heard him.

"Hello to you. I've been in New York for almost three hours. I must say I'm surprised you haven't called me yet. Especially since you had me picked up and got this beautiful suite for me. I have to admit, you really are a class act."

"How can I give you anything less? I mean you are Andre Jackson's girl, I'm sorry, I mean *ex*."

"T-Roc, don't try ruining what was starting off as a very pleasant day. And the reason I made this little trip is so we could make sure the 'ex' part is deleted."

"But of course. I apologize. How about we meet for lunch, say in the hotel restaurant in about an hour?"

"Perfect." Chantal took the time she had to take a quick shower and freshen up. She was anxious to hear if T-Roc had come up with any sort of plan to divide Tyler and Andre and then conquer her nemesis.

After stepping into a red wrap dress, brushing her hair and dabbing on some lip gloss, an hour had sneaked up on her. Chantal made her way downstairs and when she stepped off the elevator she saw T-Roc coming in. Chantal didn't know if it was because she had been sexually deprived for the last few weeks or if she was just thirsty, but T-Roc reminded her of a tall, delicious root beer float gliding through the hotel lobby. His smooth brown skin glistened against the off-white shirt and slacks he was wearing. The fist-size rock in his ear was so clear it was blinding her, even though they were on opposite sides of the lobby. Chantal slowly strutted toward T-Roc, wanting to take her time so she could continue to size him up.

"T-Roc, as always it's a pleasure to see you."

"Stop with the formalities, we're old friends."

"If you say so." After they were seated and ordered their food, Chantal didn't waste any time quizzing T-Roc. "So what's your plan?"

"Excuse me?"

"What is your plan to get that thorn in my side out of Andre's life?"

"Oh, you must be speaking of Tyler. Can we at least wait until our drinks get here before we start discussing business?"

"Here comes the waiter now. Drink up, so we can get down to it."

"Get down to what?" T-Roc asked in a flirtatious tone. Chantal simply smiled letting him know she welcomed it. "Let's toast, to great minds thinking alike." Chantal raised her glass of champagne and their glasses clicked.

Five glasses of champagne later Chantal found herself savoring every stroke as T-Roc filled her insides. She pulled him in deeper, wanting to feel each thrust. How Chantal went from sitting across from T-Roc at the table sharing crème brûlée to him twisting her out in her hotel suite was still a bit blurry for Chantal. She somewhat remembered them tonguing each other down on the elevator ride up as his fingers made their way up her dress to the insides of her thong panties. Now here they were in a full fledged sexual embrace and she was loving every minute of it. T-Roc was laying down the pipe with the same finesse he used to charm the world.

"Ah, T-Roc, fuck me harder! I want to feel every inch of you." The provocative pleading in Chantal's voice made his dick even harder. T-Roc lifted his upper body from Chantal's clenches wanting to see the pleasure in her eyes as he went deeper and deeper. Her warm juices were drenching his dick and T-Roc was about to explode.

"Damn, baby you feel so good."

"So do you. Oh gosh, I'm almost there," Chantal sighed. T-Roc kept hitting that delicate spot over and over and Chantal could feel herself building up to the ultimate release. Before she knew it she was lost in her orgasm; her screams of ecstasy were only drowned out by the groans of T-Roc cumming. They both exhaled after their intense sex session.

When the nostalgia of the moment wore off, Chantal immediately regretted two things. First, having sex with T-Roc with no protection. They were both so tipsy neither thought twice about wrapping it up. Second, that she had sex with him at all. It was true T-Roc had given her the sexual healing she was in desperate need of, but no matter how shaky her relationship was with Andre, he could never find out she had slept with his enemy.

"You were incredible, Chantal. I understand why Andre keeps you around."

"Speaking of Andre, he can never find out about this, T-Roc," Chantal said seriously.

"I got you. Your secret is safe with me. I have no intentions of destroying your plans of locking Andre down."

"Wonderful. I mean, what's wrong with mixing a little business with pleasure as long as it stays between the two of us?"

"My sentiments exactly. Now enough talking. Get back over here." T-Roc pulled Chantal closer to him and they were at it again. Chantal couldn't get enough of T-Roc but even in the midst of getting twisted out, Chantal was calculating how she could get one up on T-Roc. She didn't trust him or his promise to keep their sexual encounter a secret.

T-Roc finally left a few hours later. They both fell asleep after going at it, but T-Roc made it clear before he left that he'd be back later on that night. Chantal didn't mind; she enjoyed his company. She also hoped to use it as an opportunity to get the leverage she needed on T-Roc. Not wasting any time she placed a phone call to her girlfriend Arlene. Chantal tapped her fingers impatiently, willing her friend to pick up the phone.

"Hello."

"Arlene, girl, I'm glad you answered."

"Chantal, is that you?"

"Yes, the one and only."

"I haven't spoken to you since I called about Andre being in 40/40 with that video chick. I hope that girl didn't fuck things up for ya."

"Honey, I got much bigger problems than that silly hofessional Arisa."

"Like what?"

"We'll get into that another time. Right now I need your assistance with something else. Do you still talk to that chick Tina?"

"Uptown Tina?"

"Yeah, her."

"We still cool. I speak to her every now and then. We get our hair done at the same spot."

"Is she and her sisters still the same?"

"You talking about her little sisters, the hot-ass twins Rosalyn and Merita?"

"Uh-huh, that's them. How old are they now?"

"Sixteen going on thirty-five. You know them grown-ass little girls been fucking since they was ten. Why you asking about them no good hoes?"

"I haven't seen them since they were twelve. Do they still look the same? They were fast, but they were some real pretty girls and well developed to be so young."

"They still pretty and got even more body, so they really out of control now. Tina told me they little asses be tricking and everything. But because they so young minded they be fucking for bullshit like sneakers and tennis skirts. By the time they get eighteen they'll be so used up they won't even be able to make no paper selling their worn-out pussy."

"Well, today is their lucky day. I need you to locate the twins and let them know they can make enough money to buy sneakers for the rest of the year."

For the next hour Chantal sat by the phone waiting for the call from Arlene to see if she'd gotten in touch with the twins. Right when she was about to leave her room to get some fresh air the phone rang.

"Girl, Tina finally tracked down the hot boxes. They were hanging out in front of Juelz Santana's new soda shop trying to pick up some potential customers. When Tina informed them about a possible gig to make some loot they hurried they fast asses home to see what was up."

"Tell them to stay right there. I'm on my way."

By the time T-Roc called Chantal later that evening she had everything in place. She was meeting him at Destino on Fiftieth Street and First Avenue. He offered to pick her up, but Chantal had to neatly tie up all the loose ends so her plan would go off without a hitch. When she arrived T-Roc was already seated, drinking a glass of wine. The Italian hotspot was packed with some of New York's most popular celebrities. Both Katie Couric and Dan Rather were dining there but at tables on opposite sides of the room, of course.

"Chantal, you look beautiful as usual."

"It must be the glow I got from the amazing sex we had earlier today."

"We haven't even eaten our dinner and I'm ready to go." Every few minutes Chantal would casually glance down at her watch. At exactly eight-thirty her gift to T-Roc arrived. When Rosalyn and Merita paraded through the door, the Puerto Rican hotties had cleaned up even better than she expected. Chantal knew that T-Roc had seen his share of gorgeous women and for the girls to catch his eye, their hair, attire and all around look had to be extra tight. T-Roc could spot quality and if it was cheap he would immediately be turned off no matter how pretty the face and phat the ass. Chantal spent all afternoon doing her best to smooth out the rough edges on the twins, but luckily because they were so young their faces weren't reflecting the wear and tear they were inflicting upon their bodies.

Normally the twins wore their long black hair in pony tails and their gear consisted of tight jeans and sneakers. That look was cool for the thugs in Harlem but they had to step it up several notches to shine on the ritzy East Side. Chantal was able to squeeze them in at the hair salon she frequented whenever in town. The salon had the twins' hair bouncing and shining like they were about to shoot a Pantene commercial. Of course both received an immaculate French manicure and pedicure. And to highlight their voluptuous bodies Chantal pulled out her platinum to drape them in designer duds by Louis Vuitton. If Chantal hadn't revamped them herself she would've sworn they were the wives of some foreign elite businessmen.

Chantal had already made arrangements to have the host seat the ladies at a table near theirs. It cost Chantal a pretty penny since the restaurant stayed packed, but the investment would be well worth it if all went as planned. T-Roc was too busy enjoying his meatballs that he hadn't noticed Rosalyn and Merita but Chantal knew when he did. He stopped his fork in midair when he caught a glimpse of the beauties. They had the sexy polished look that would instantly get T-Roc's dick hard. Their tailor-fitted dresses accentuated every curve perfectly. With just the right touch of makeup anybody, including their own mama, would swear that the two teenagers were at least of the legal age to drink.

"T-Roc, what has you so in awe?" Chantal questioned, as if in the dark. She then purposely turned in the direction of the twins. "Oh, now I see what has you all worked up. They are stunning if I say so myself."

T-Roc eyed Chantal, trying to get a read on her comment. "Chantal, I didn't know you were also into girls."

"I'm not. But I like to watch."

"What do you mean?"

"It turns me on to watch a man that I've had sex with be intimate with another woman. It makes my pussy extra wet." T-Roc felt his third leg standing straight up ready to walk out the restaurant and fuck the shit out of Chantal.

"You got me so aroused right now, I'm ready to go."

"But what about those two lovely women sitting over there? I would love to watch you put your big cock down their throats."

"Damn, so would I. But we don't even know them. They are probably waiting on their boyfriends or something."

"You won't know unless you ask."

"What? You want me to go over to their table and ask them to have a ménage with me and let you watch? You trying to get me slapped up in here?" T-Roc was looking at Chantal like she was crazy.

"Come on, you're T-Roc. When have you ever been scared to get turned down by a woman?"

"I didn't say I was scared. I just don't think this is the appropriate place to make that sort of proposition." Right on beat, the twins turned around toward their table and gave a modest smile as if they were shy.

"Did you see that? They probably recognized you and have a crush on you like every other woman in this city." Chantal was stroking T-Roc's ego enough to get him open to her idea.

"They did smile at me, didn't they?"

"Sure did. You should go over there and introduce yourself."

"Nah, I wouldn't feel comfortable doing that. Maybe you should go," T-Roc finally said, hoping Chantal would've made the suggestion.

"Me? Why me?"

"You're a female and you could get a better read on them. You know, to see if they would be down for something like that. Just in case they're not, I don't believe they would be as offended by the suggestion coming from you as they would if it came from me." If T-Roc only knew that the same girls he was nervous to approach would suck him off right here in the middle of the restaurant for a few dollars. "Offended" was nowhere in their vocabulary.

"Okay, I'll go over there. But if I convince them to come back to the hotel with us then you better fuck the shit out of them and make it worth my time."

"If you can make this pop off, I promise it will be worth all of our time." Chantal smiled and walked over to the girls' table. They already had a couple of drinks so they were ready to put on the show of their life. Chantal pretended to be having an intense con-

versation with the women, when in all actuality she was compli-
menting them on how good they looked. They had rehearsed
everything so many times it made no sense to go over it again. After fifteen minutes Chantal came back to the table with an overwhelmed look on her face like she had just brokered the deal of a
lifetime.

"What did they say?" he asked anxiously. During the fifteen
minutes Chantal was at their table, T-Roc had imagined twisting
out the beauties in every position and watching Chantal finger herself as she watched. Chantal had put the idea in his head and now
he couldn't get it out.

"They live in Spain and have been in New York for a few days
visiting family, but they leave tomorrow."

"Damn, so they not interested," T-Roc said as he slumped over.

"Let me finish. They've never been with a black man before and
find you extremely attractive." T-Roc straightened back up and his
eyes started sparkling.

"Does this mean it's a go?"

"Damn sure is. With a little convincing on my part they bit the
bullet. I told them we are married and celebrating our wedding an-
niversary. I explained that we needed a boost in our boring marriage and it has always been my fantasy to watch my husband
make love to a set of gorgeous twins. So they think they're doing
me a favor and helping save my crumbling marriage."

"You're a genius, Chantal." T-Roc lifted Chantal's chin and
placed a wet kiss on her lips, as if she had given him the best news
he ever heard.

"They actually have a car service waiting out front for them so
they're going to follow us back to the hotel."

"That's cool. So are you ready to bounce?"

"Let's go."

T-Roc and Chantal left the restaurant and the twins followed
discreetly behind them. On the drive back to the hotel, T-Roc had
his hands all over Chantal. The thought of her watching him twist

out two women was turning him on more than he ever thought possible. He had never had a woman make such a request of him and he was looking forward to obliging.

"Should we wait for the women to get out the car so we can go up together?"

"No, I already gave them the room number. I'm trying to keep this as hush-hush as possible. We definitely don't want this hitting page six." During their elevator ride up Chantal kept going over every detail in her mind, wanting no hiccups. When they entered the room, T-Roc immediately started kissing Chantal passionately and exploring her body with his hands. "Wait," Chantal hissed.

"What's wrong? The ladies will be up here any minute now and I thought we could have a little fun before they arrived."

"That's cute but I want to save all my energy for when I'm viewing the show you're about to put on for me." Chantal reached over and gave T-Roc a teasing kiss. "Now, why don't you go take a quick shower so when the women get here you can get right to it?"

"I'll be back in a few but I want you sitting right over there in your birthday suit when I come back." Chantal nodded her head, letting T-Roc know she would do as he wished.

About five minutes later Chantal heard a light knock at the door. "Hi ladies, are you ready?"

"You know it, mami, we got you."

"Remember don't say too much. Just take off your clothes and start going at him right off the jump." Chantal wanted the girls to be mute because if they said more than a few words, it would be easy for T-Roc to catch on to their ignorance and juvenile age.

"I can't believe we about to fuck T-Roc. Ain't nobody on the block gon' believe this shit," Rosalyn said to her sister as they undressed.

"Oh, make sure you leave on your heels." Chantal knew if you wanted to instantly get a man ready to knock boots, just dangle a naked chick with a banging body in some stiletto heels in his face.

Chantal used the extra few minutes she had to check the teddy bear sitting on top of the dresser directly facing the bed.

By the time T-Roc emerged from the bathroom with water still dripping from his chiseled body, his rock hard tool led him straight toward the scrumptious eye candies. He was so caught up in the rapture that he totally forgot that Chantal was supposed to be sitting butt naked in the chair he had assigned her to only ten minutes ago. Once T-Roc hit the bed the twins began their award-winning performance and had his full attention. Chantal was able to fall back and let the teddy bear she purchased from the spy shop in the Village record T-Roc's sex escapade with the underage delinquents.

After two hours of watching the twins perform sex acts that she hadn't even mastered, Chantal was ready to call it a night. T-Roc wasn't even a match for the well-experienced duo. They licked and sucked every hole on his entire body and some that she didn't even think T-Roc knew existed. He took turns fucking each girl as the other pleasured herself. The sisters were so in tune with one another that they would actually cum at the same time. They more than earned the fifteen hundred apiece Chantal was giving them. She was so satisfied with their performance she decided to throw in an extra thousand as a bonus.

All three had come multiple times and eventually passed out. Chantal let T-Roc sleep but soon woke the twins, thanked them, paid them, and sent them on their way. Now that she had her own version of an R. Kelly tape on T-Roc, she no longer had any use for the hot boxes and wanted them out of her face. She sat down on the bed, beside a peaceful, sleeping T-Roc and couldn't help but smile. He was probably dreaming about the fuck fest he just had, unaware that his moments of satisfaction cost him what he cherished most—power. T-Roc's fate now rested in the hands of Chantal.

ELEVEN

Forbidden Fruit

Working so closely with Andre for the past month, Tyler was able to see a side of him that the music videos and commercials never captured—a warm, loving, and gentle man. On the occasions when they were on long breaks between takes he would talk about his daughter and his whole face would light up. Tyler would speak about how painful it was to be away from her son, Christian, and Andre genuinely seemed to care and understand. Soon, Tyler realized, she had fallen deeper in love with Andre. Being near him and unable to express her feelings of desire was the cause of sleepless nights. Initially she was hoping that maybe it was all a schoolgirl crush that would pass, but after the jealous rage her mind went into when she saw Chantal going into his trailer, she realized it was much more than that. Tyler desperately wanted to share her thoughts with someone, hoping that maybe a voice of reason would put her back on the straight and narrow. As she drove to

West Hollywood to meet her friend Chrissie for dinner at Dan Tana's, Tyler prayed she could finally divulge her secrets to someone she considered a true confidant. Tired of keeping all her emotions bottled up, Tyler felt Chrissie was the only person trustworthy enough to share such privileged information with. When Tyler entered the celeb-favored restaurant, Chrissie was already seated at a private table in the back.

"Tyler, you really look fabulous. I just saw you a few weeks ago, but it seems you keep looking better and better," Chrissie squealed as she hugged Tyler.

"Sweetheart, it's Hollywood. I don't know if it's something they put in the water or just the magnificent way they pamper you, but they do things a lot different out here."

"Well, whatever it is, keep it up," Chrissie encouraged while giving Tyler a high five. "So how's the movie coming along? I can't believe my best friend is like this movie star. Not only that, but you were able to get me the job as the publicist for the whole project. You obviously have major clout."

"Well, it helps to be sleeping with the director," she laughed. "But of course, who else would I want for the job," Tyler said with a sly smile. "I have to admit not only did I want you because you're the best damn publicist in the business, but also for my own selfish reasons."

"Reasons like what?" Chrissie asked curiously.

"Just in case a scandal breaks, you'll try extra hard to clean it up."

"What type of scandal are you referring to? Because if you're speaking of you and William, no one is going to dare touch that story; everyone knows that it is off limits."

"Actually, I'm speaking of something else. Nothing has happened yet, but I'm afraid that I won't be able to control my feelings much longer."

"I'm confused. Explain to me exactly what you are talking about."

"You have to first promise that this stays between the two of us."

"That goes without saying," Chrissie said, sounding offended. "Promise, Chrissie."

"Fine, I promise. Now what is this top secret information?"

"It's been building up for a while, but I'm starting to develop strong feelings for Andre," Tyler admitted, feeling like a huge weight had been lifted off her shoulders.

"What! You can't be serious. I thought you were head over heels for William."

"I thought so, too, and now I feel awful for causing all that unnecessary strain on his marriage. But I can no longer deny the feelings I have for Andre. Every time I'm around him all I want to do is reach out and embrace him with a long, lingering kiss."

"Tyler, dear, that sounds like lust to me. Maybe you should jump his bones and get him out of your system, but do it discreetly, of course. No, I take that back, don't have sex with him."

"This is more than about sex, Chrissie. I want to be with him."

"Like a relationship?" she asked, surprised.

"Exactly, if he'll have me. I think he's incredible and I would love to see what could happen between us."

"Besides William setting you both on fire."

"Chrissie, that's sick. William doesn't have a violent bone in his body."

"Everyone has a violent streak when pushed, and having a torrid affair with your costar right under William's nose might be the one thing that completely sets him off. All I'm saying is that you need to really think about this before you just jump in head first."

"I know you're right, and honestly I wish I didn't have all these feelings for Andre, but I can't seem to fight them. The harder I try to forget about him the worse it becomes."

"Well, working so closely with him every day isn't exactly making it any easier."

"Tell me about it. But I might be fantasizing over nothing. I believe he is in a relationship with his baby mother. I can't quite get a read on the two of them. When I first met him he casually told me he was single, but the other day I saw her going into his trailer."

"Tyler, let it go. You don't need to be bothered with no baby mama drama. You're a movie star now. You're so beyond such petty relationships."

"You don't call being involved with the director of my movie, who just so happens to be married, petty?"

"First of all, William is crazy about you and I know he will leave his wife; it's just a matter of time. Second of all, being in a relationship with him is a lot more respectable than the sloppy mess you will have with Andre Jackson and his baby mama. Trust me on that."

"I hear everything you're saying, but once again I've fucked up. Even if William did leave his wife, which I doubt, you go out how you came in. I should've never got involved with a married man. So if William did leave his wife he would probably eventually leave me, too, for somebody else. It's called karma—you can't escape it."

"I don't know what to tell you. All I can say is that whatever you decide to do, be careful. William will be out for blood if you leave him for another man, especially the actor he hired." Tyler knew that Chrissie was right but she wasn't thinking with her head right now. She was too focused on the tingles you get in your stomach when you first fall in love.

After Tyler finished her dinner with Chrissie, she checked her voice messages on her way home. To her surprise she had a message marked "urgent" from what sounded like William's assistant. She said there was an emergency meeting on the studio lot at eight o'clock. Tyler thought that was odd and wondered why William didn't call her himself. She figured he was probably hectic and when William got in business mode he had no time for anyone. It was pouring outside and Tyler did a quick U-turn in the middle of the street to head back toward the studio. When she arrived, the lot seemed damn near deserted. Tyler dreaded getting out of the car since it had been pouring rain for the last hour and she had no umbrella. Plus, she wore a negligee-style dress to dinner with Chrissie and knew she would get drenched in the almost-nothing fabric. As Tyler dashed across the parking lot in her five-inch Giuseppe Zanotti heels, her chiffon dress clung to her body as the rain saturated her. When Tyler reached the entry, it was locked and she banged for what seemed forever. Finally the door opened and Andre was standing in front of her.

After leaving New York, Chantal sat by the phone for a week straight hoping to hear some encouraging news from T-Roc. She figured that if anyone could put a halt to the possible pairing of Tyler and Andre it was him. It was an open secret in the music industry that T-Roc was as devious as they come. That's why Chantal found it necessary to obtain some security, which she now had with the kiddie porn tape T-Roc had made, unbeknownst to him. If he behaved himself he would never have to know that the delectable underage twins he bedded could send him to Rikers Island for a few years. Chantal hoped she'd never have to use her arsenal but the protection was warranted given T-Roc's reputation.

He was the same man that discreetly bought up the majority share of stock for a boutique label just so he could then turn around and terminate the newly appointed president who he felt had slighted him on a deal. To bring further insult to injury, T-Roc somehow managed to find a loophole in the president's contract so he was unable to get any payoff or benefits. The fired executive had to put his brand-new house back on the market since he used a substantial part of his signing bonus for the purchase and would be unable to pay the mortgage, or buy furniture for that matter. It was revealed that T-Roc was the mastermind behind the scheme, when he personally came to give the president the boot. The guy was so angry he tried to physically attack T-Roc. That was the wrong move. T-Roc's well-paid bodyguards beat him over the head with the champagne bottles he was popping to toast the signing of a much sought-after artist. Thus, Chantal assumed that keeping the star-crossed lovers apart would be a walk in the park for diabolical T-Roc.

"So, what's the deal with you and Andre? From what you just told me about you all's last encounter it ain't looking too good," Shari reasoned.

"That's an understatement, but I have a secret weapon."

"What's that, are you pregnant?"

"I wish, but you can't get pregnant if you're not fucking. Andre hasn't touched me in months. My pussy so thirsty right now I'm considering selling it on eBay to the highest bidder." Chantal put on her game face hard because she didn't even want her best friend to know she had did the nasty with the devil himself, T-Roc. She figured it was better for Shari to know that not only was she not getting any sex from Andre, but to think not from anybody else, either.

"You so damn silly. But what is this secret weapon you're talking about?"

"Someone who hates Andre almost as much as I hate Tyler."

"Not T-Roc," Shari said with a deep huff.

"You know it. If anyone can make it happen, it's him."

"Why do you insist on dancing with the devil? T-Roc is bad news, Chantal. I'm surprised he's still fucking with you after that *Access Hollywood* fiasco."

"T-Roc respects the moves one makes to win the game. If anything, he probably admires the fact that I had the balls to implement my plan."

"Or maybe he just likes to embarrass Andre and if using you can make it happen then why not?"

"Honestly, Shari, I don't care what the reasons are. I just want

Tyler Blake away from Andre. Whatever T-Roc has to do to make that happen is okay with me."

"I know you have all this confidence in T-Roc, but what if whatever plan he has doesn't work, then what?"

"Why you think I'm spilling my guts out to you, dumb ass? You're my backup plan. I'm hoping you can help me come up with some sort of scheme to get my man back just in case T-Roc comes up short."

"Well, Miss Thang, I don't know what to tell you. I ain't never been good at that scheming shit. That was always your specialty. But you better come up with something quick because you 'bout to be cut," Shari said while using her two fingers as scissors to make a snipping motion.

Chantal sat on her living room couch, taking deep breaths. She felt so helpless and didn't know what to do. Losing Andre wasn't an option, but figuring out how to keep him seemed so far out of reach. She knew she couldn't trust T-Roc as far as she could see him and Chantal always said she couldn't see that well. So putting all her eggs in that basket seemed like a guaranteed letdown.

"I don't know how I'm going to get myself out of this bullshit."

"Chantal, I know you don't want to hear this, but maybe it's time for you to bow out gracefully and let Andre go. Concentrate on being a good mother to Melanie and find yourself another baller. Andre is not the only one."

Chantal stared at Shari, not wanting to believe what she just heard. For Shari to tell Chantal to give up must have meant that she didn't see a way for her to win. That was devastating for Chantal since Shari always thought she was untouchable. Now her biggest cheerleader was basically telling her to put a fork in it.

"I can't do that. You're asking me to give up on everything I've worked so hard for. If Andre and I broke up and I got another man, he would do the same bullshit to me. At least with Andre we have a daughter together and we have history. I'm not trying to make new history with someone else. Relationships are so much work and I just don't have the patience."

"I feel you, but you may not have a choice. Listen, Chris is waiting for me. I'm meeting him for dinner and then I'm going to spend the night at his place. I'll call you tomorrow and, sweetie, try to get some rest. You have to stay strong no matter what happens."

After Shari left, Chantal walked to her kitchen, pulled out two bottles of Dom Pérignon and decided she would drink her sorrows away. She knew there would come a time she would have to pull it together, but tonight she just wanted to cry a river.

"Tyler, you're soaking wet. Come inside," Andre said as he gently pulled her in from the rain. Andre couldn't help but notice that he could see Tyler's hardened nipples through the pink dress she was wearing. He instantly became aroused by the sight and turned his head, trying to ignore the seductive image.

"It's pouring outside, that rain came from nowhere," Tyler said as she squeezed the excess water from her hair and pulled it back in a bun. "So where is everybody?"

"I don't know. I guess we're the first people here." Andre walked back toward the stage.

"Do you have any idea what this emergency meeting is all about?"

"I have none. I got a message from William's assistant telling me to be here by eight. I'm sure everyone will be here soon. They probably got held up because of the bad weather."

"I'm going to call William just to see where he is," Tyler said, while dialing his number. "Damn, my phone isn't getting any reception in this place. What time is it anyway?"

"Almost eight thirty," Andre replied, looking down at his watch, still not wanting to make eye contact with her. Both were feeling uneasy partly due to the peculiar circumstances surrounding the meeting but primarily because they were alone and it was hard to deny their mutual attraction. Tyler walked toward the front of the stage and sat in the chair with her arms wrapped around her shoulders trying to keep herself warm, although she was wishing that Andre's body would function as her blanket. As Tyler began daydreaming about the two of them lying naked by a fireplace, making love, she heard what sounded like a loud explosion but was actually thunder and lightning. In the next second the studio lights went out and Tyler could barely see a thing.

"Tyler, are you okay?" she heard Andre ask.

"Yeah, but I can't see anything."

"Just sit tight. I'm going to try and locate the toolbox they keep on the other side of the wall. There might be a flashlight inside." Andre slowly walked toward the wall, trying not to trip, with only the glare from the sky coming through the window to guide him. He located the toolbox and found a flashlight. He also found some candles and matches on top of the piano that was used during rehearsals.

"I think we should get out of here," Andre suggested, while walking back to her with the flashlight. He guided Tyler toward the front door but when he tried to open it, it was locked. Andre shook the doorknob back and forth trying to push open the door, but it wouldn't budge.

"What's wrong?" Tyler asked, confused because she couldn't get a plain view as to what Andre was doing, but it was clear the door wasn't opening.

"I don't know what the hell is wrong with this fucking door but the shit won't open," Andre growled.

"Is there another exit?"

"Unfortunately not," Andre revealed, not liking the idea of being trapped alone with Tyler.

"Andre, I'm so cold, what are we going to do?" The sweet sound of Tyler's voice was driving Andre crazy. She sounded like a lost little girl turning to him for all the answers.

"I saw some blankets and candles over by the piano; I'll get them for you." Tyler walked behind Andre craving to reach out to him. As they reached the top of the stage Andre handed the blankets to Tyler and then lit the candles. Tyler laid one blanket on the floor and sat down and then wrapped the other blanket around her body.

"How long do you think we're going to be stuck here?"

"I don't know. Why? Am I making you uncomfortable?"

"No, you're actually making me feel safe," Tyler said looking intensely into Andre's eyes. For the first time Andre couldn't resist and was unable to look away. Tyler was hypnotizing him with her passionate stare. He so badly wanted to take her in his arms right then but he still wasn't certain if he was picking up on the correct body language. But then Tyler gave him the signal that welcomed him. She stood up and slowly slipped out of her chiffon dress. The light from the candles was highlighting the silhouette of her perfect body. Andre lusted for her as the dress slowly revealed her round, delicious breasts and then her smooth, toned stomach and her luscious curved legs. Once the dress was resting at her feet and she slowly stepped out of it, Andre still couldn't move. He couldn't believe that the woman he had been fantasizing about for the last few months was actually giving herself to him. The rain was pouring down so hard, Andre almost couldn't hear the words that Tyler spoke so softly.

"Don't you want me?" Tyler asked, not feeling sure about herself. Andre was amazed that this exquisite creature was second-guessing her sex appeal. It made him want her all the more. Before Tyler could say another word, Andre put his finger to her soft lips, gesturing for her not to speak.

"Baby, I've never wanted anybody as much as I want you," Andre whispered in her ear as though the room was full of people and this was their little secret. Tyler felt chills going down her spine. Her inside was so wet, longing to feel his manhood. Wanting to savor every moment, Andre laid Tyler down on the blanket and followed every curve of her body. For the first time in his life he didn't want to rush and pleasure himself, he wanted to pleasure her. He wanted her to remember every detail of this night, he wanted to make her fall in love. Andre unbuttoned his shirt and then slid out of his pants and briefs. He caressed his hands up her smooth legs and when he reached her buttocks he pulled her forward and opened the gates to heaven. As Andre's tongue entered her, Tyler shivered from pure pleasure. As he brought her to the first orgasm, Tyler wrapped her legs tighter around Andre's neck, pulling him in even closer. She was hoping he would completely swallow her up. After pleasuring her to her second orgasm, he took the head of his well-endowed penis and stroked it up and down her clitoris. Andre felt so divine that Tyler would have bet her life that he sprinkled some magic potion on his penis to make her instantly fall in love. Because when Andre did finally enter her, Tyler knew there was no turning back. Her body now completely belonged to him.

Chantal was literally pulling out her hair. She had been trying to call Andre all night and his cell kept going straight to voice mail. He wasn't answering his home phone and torrid thoughts filled her head of what he might be doing. But Chantal actually hoped he was somewhere having a ménage or fucking some hoochie, anybody but Tyler Blake. The thought of the two of them being together was enough to make Chantal slit her wrists. She was so stressed, she was once again smoking a pack of Newports a day. The tears were now pouring down Chantal's face as she began embracing the truth; that with all her scheming, this time she had gone too far. Andre didn't want her anymore. He probably hadn't wanted her as his woman for a long time. For all these years she had been fooling herself to believe that if she stuck around long enough that Andre would marry her and they would live an ideal life as husband and wife. It seemed overnight all those dreams were crumbling right before her eyes. Right as Chantal was about to finish crying herself to sleep she heard a banging at her front door. She was about to call out to the nanny but quickly remembered that since Melanie had been with her parents for the last week the nanny hadn't been over. Chantal slowly walked toward the door as the banging got louder and louder. "Who is it?" Chantal asked through her stream of tears.

"Chantal, open up. It's me, Shari." Chantal quickly unlocked the door and was alarmed to see her best friend standing before her in worse condition than her.

"What happened to you?" Chantal asked as she grabbed Shari's arm and pulled her inside. Shari was shaking uncontrollably, all her makeup was smeared and her hair was disheveled, but even with all that going on Chantal managed to see the black eye that decorated Shari's face. Chantal continued to question Shari, who kept crying and hyperventilating. She sat Shari down on the couch and just held her for a few minutes until she pulled it together. "Shari, it's okay, I'm here. Everything will be all right."

"No, it's not, Chantal. This is the worst day of my life," Shari muttered.

"Talk to me, tell me what happened." Shari scooted out of Chantal's arms and sat in an upright position and began rocking herself back and forth. Her fingers were tapping each other and her face was blank. She looked like someone who had just escaped from the psychiatric ward.

"I spent last night at Chris's house and when I got home this afternoon I realized I had left my wallet at his house. I kept calling to tell him I was on my way over to get it but he wasn't answering any of his phones. I decided to just drive over to his crib and when I got there his car was in the driveway so I rang the doorbell. He didn't answer so I figured he was asleep or doing something and didn't hear me. Since I know where he keeps the spare key I let myself in." Before Shari could continue she once again burst into tears. Chantal thought that she pretty much had the rest of the story figured out and once again held her friend.

"Shari, you know how men are. They all cheat and that's why you can't go sneaking up on them because nine times out of ten you gonna catch them with the next bitch. It's going to be okay. Just go max out his credit cards and don't speak to him for a couple of weeks. That will teach him to be more discreet with his shit."

"It's so much worse than that," Shari babbled with a lost look on her face.

"What, he was with a couple of bitches?"

"No, it's worse than that. Take a look, you can see for yourself." Shari handed Chantal her cell phone. At first Chantal didn't understand why Chantal was handing her the phone until she saw the image on the screen.

"What!" Chantal screamed. "I know you didn't catch this nigga fucking some dudes! Girl, don't play with me like that!"

"A picture doesn't lie."

"You must be running a joke on me." Chantal still didn't want to believe what was staring her right in the face.

"I wish I was." Shari put her head down and raised her hands to her forehead as though fighting off a migraine. "Chantal, it was so sick. When I walked in the house I didn't see anybody but I heard the television. I followed the sound and then I heard other sounds, like moaning and grunting. When I finally reached the entertainment room I saw one guy on his hands and knees getting fucked in the ass, then the guy that was fucking him was getting fucked in the ass by Chris. Can you imagine seeing three big black men fucking each other? It was like a big black bus. Then on top of that, the other two guys were his teammates. I've seen them at practice before." Shari sat there shaking her head as if she was fighting to escape the nightmare she'd entered.

"Does Chris know you took this picture?"

"No, he was so caught up in his homo love train that he didn't even feel my presence until I started going upside his head."

"I can't believe this shit. I'm shocked right now and I didn't think too many things could shock me anymore. Who would have ever thought that fine-ass motherfucker was a dick lover? Now it make sense why when we were at that party all them motherfuckers was all huddled up together and they were keeping all the women behind the rope. I figured they just didn't want to be bothered with a whole bunch of gold-digging groupies. Them niggas just don't like pussy! I'm through right now. So what happened to your eye?"

"When I walked in on that bullshit I flipped out. I just ran up to the nigga and started punching him in his face, his back, just everywhere. I was kicking him with my stiletto boots just trying to beat that nigga's ass. When he finally managed to pull his dick out that other nigga's ass, he tried to grab my arms and calm me down. I told that motherfucker to let me go before I pulled out my razor and slit his throat. He was still cool and trying to calm me down until I told him I was going to tell everybody that he and his friends were nothing but hairy-ass fairies. That's when he lost it and punched me in the eye. Girl, I thought he was going to break my neck, so I bolted out of that house. Chris might have some sugar in his tank, but he punches like a straight up dude."

"Well, girl, did you even leave with what you came for, which was your wallet?" Chantal said with a slight smirk. Both women looked at each other and laughed in unison. They somehow were able to find a moment of laughter in the midst of Shari's heartache. "But, Shari, seriously, I'm so sorry."

"I feel so betrayed. He was so good to me and to Alex. I honestly thought he might be the one. That sick son of a bitch was probably lusting after my son."

"Girl, let's hope not. I hope he want them at least eighteen and older. But besides his preference for men, he's going to have to come out his pocket for punching you in your eye. Doesn't he know that's how you make your living, off of your pretty face? Fuck that, I'm getting the camera. After we take these photos, you will be meeting with an attorney friend of mine first thing tomorrow morning. If that nigga don't come off with no serious dough then you will be filing criminal charges. And you got this picture of him being caught in the act. Oh, yeah, he definitely fucked up in the game. He'll find his dirty secret splashed across every newspaper in America if he fuck around and don't meet our demands. Shit, this right here is that 'you better do what I want forever' type ammunition."

Chantal knew exactly what she would do once she downloaded the picture to her computer. She would put copies in the same safe that held T-Roc's tape. Chantal couldn't help but feel a stitch of excitement knowing she was building a collection against some wealthy and powerful men. "What about protection. Did you all use any?" Chantal asked with arms folded.

"Girl, praise the Lord that we did."

"Good, but we still going to the doctor after we leave the lawyer's office. You can never be too safe." For the first time Chantal wasn't thinking of her own drama, but instead she was concerned for Shari who was faced with a life-altering dilemma. As she took pictures of Shari's black eye she thought, for a brief moment, that maybe her life wasn't so bad after all.

"Tyler, I need to see you in my office ASAP!" Chrissie demanded.

"What's the problem?" Tyler asked, lying in bed with Andre. After the two first made love a few weeks ago they would sneak off as much as possible to be with one another. They were trying hard to keep their relationship under wraps, at least until the film finished shooting. Too much was riding on the movie and neither wanted to jeopardize the project.

"I don't want to talk about it over the phone so meet me at my office in an hour. Don't be late, Tyler. This is urgent." Chrissie hung up the phone. Tyler glided herself on top of Andre to have one last lovemaking session before she went to meet Chrissie.

When Tyler finally arrived at Chrissie's office two hours late, Chrissie was livid.

"You obviously didn't take my call seriously or were you so

caught up in fucking your leading man that you figured I could wait?" Chrissie's comment totally threw Tyler off. She stood there with her mouth wide open.

"What are you talking about, Chrissie? I'm confused right now."

"Tyler, you're talking to me—save the theatrics for the movie screen. Take a look at these and then start your monologue over again." Chrissie threw an envelope on her desk and pulled out the pictures of Tyler and Andre making love in the studio. Tyler was stunned.

"Where did you get these?" Tyler shouted, as if blaming Chrissie for their existence.

"Honey, I didn't take the pictures so don't yell at me," Chrissie hissed. "But I mean really, Tyler, on the stage at the studio? You could've at least gotten a room."

"Shut up. I'm not in the mood for your sarcasm. These pictures had to be taken the night of that terrible storm and Andre and I were locked inside for hours. That whole evening seemed bizarre, and now it makes sense. Somebody set us up."

"That's pretty obvious, Sherlock, the question is who," Chrissie wailed.

Tyler looked at Chrissie like she was one step from punching her in the mouth.

"Listen, smart-ass, this is the exact reason I had William hire you, for damage control purposes."

"Yeah, that's a given. But, damn, Tyler, you didn't say I would be putting out forest fires the minute I started the job. It seems like yesterday you told me you had the hots for this guy and now you're in a full-fledged lust affair. Maybe you need to slow down."

"This isn't a lust affair, Chrissie. I'm in love with him."

"I hate to break this to you, but sweetheart you definitely have Daddy issues. From the day I met you, you always get involved in these unhealthy relationships and you swear you're in love."

"This time is different."

"Different how, because it's a new man? This isn't about just having fun anymore, Tyler, we're talking about your career. William will hit the roof if he gets wind of this."

"I know. That's why Andre and I have been very discreet. We're not going public with our relationship until after the film has finished shooting."

"Obviously your plan isn't working. These photos landed on my desk. Who else's do you think they're on?"

"So you think I should come clean with William about my relationship with Andre?"

"Hell no! I'm going to get to the bottom of this and see what the person who sent these photos is after. I know I can't tell you to stop seeing Andre because you wouldn't listen anyway, but Tyler please be careful. Someone is out to get you and until we find out who and why you have to watch your back."

The minute Tyler left Chrissie's office, the only person she wanted to see or talk to was Andre. Although she knew she should've listened to Chrissie and put a little distance between them, her heart said otherwise. Tyler immediately jumped in her car and drove right back to whom she now considered the love of her life.

After Tyler stormed out of her office, Chrissie scanned the photos again. One photo was a close-up of the pair interlocked, with their eyes full of passion. There was no doubt in Chrissie's mind that the two were in love—it was written all over their faces. This was the sort of love that Tyler had always dreamed of having but she had never felt optimistic in her quest. Now that it seemed within reach, Chrissie just prayed that Tyler wouldn't destroy her life in a bid to hold on to it.

Tears on My Pillow

T-Roc had been putting his plan in motion the moment Chantal left New York to go back to Chicago a few weeks ago. She gave him the ammo necessary to know what direction to go in. Knowing that Andre had feelings for Tyler was just the type of information T-Roc needed to set the stage for a full-blown disaster.

"Did you deliver the package?" T-Roc asked the man he had hired to take the pictures of Tyler and Andre, and make sure they landed on Chrissie Ingram's desk.

"Yes sir, I made sure it was there to greet her first thing this morning," the man answered proudly.

"Wonderful, I'll handle everything from here. But still, watch Tyler. Any picture you can get with her and Andre in a compromising position is money in the bank."

T-Roc then placed his second call for the next step in his game plan. "Chantal baby, how are you?"

"T-Roc, I've left you over a million messages. Where have you been?" Chantal asked, frustrated that T-Roc was just now calling her back.

"I guess that means you missed me?" T-Roc stated confidently.

Chantal wasn't in the mood to toot T-Roc's horn. Yes, she enjoyed his company in New York and his sex game was crazy but it was what it was . . . a fuck. Her focus still remained on Andre and that's what she wanted to discuss.

"Of course you've crossed my mind, especially since you given me no clue as to what is going on."

"Baby, I apologize. I've been busy but I do have some news for you. But before we get to that, have you heard from Andre?"

"Only a couple of times, and it was primarily to see how Melanie is doing. So tell me what you know, T-Roc," she said eagerly.

"Well, pretty girl, I hate to break it to you but he's probably not calling because he is too busy romancing Tyler. My spies tell me they are pretty hot and heavy." Chantal felt as if T-Roc had just plunged a knife through her heart. It took her five minutes just to respond to T-Roc's statement.

"Chantal, are you there?" T-Roc asked, hoping she hadn't committed suicide with him on the phone.

"Yeah, I'm here. How long has this been going on?"

"For a few weeks now."

"Why are you just now telling me, T-Roc? I could've done something to try and stop it," Chantal said, sounding all choked up.

"I actually only just confirmed the information. I didn't want to tell you about rumors that may not be true. But, Chantal, whether I told you now or a few weeks ago there was nothing you could do to stop it. When two people are in love no one can keep them apart." T-Roc was purposely laying it on thick. He knew what a firecracker Chantal was and wanted to push every button precisely to send her postal. It also bruised his ego knowing that even though he put it down on Chantal she was still more concerned about mending her relationship with Andre.

"In love? You think they're in love?" Chantal repeated.

"Listen, pretty girl, I know you have a lot to digest but try to relax. It must be devastating to know that the man you were planning on marrying and spending the rest of your life with is now playing house with a Hollywood starlet. You're still young and you have a beautiful daughter who loves you. In time this pain will pass. And if you need a shoulder to cry on, I'm here," he added. "But Chantal, I'm late for a meeting. I just wanted to give you a call and let you know about Andre and Tyler before the media broke the news. Call me if you need me." When T-Roc hung up the phone he had a gigantic smile spread across his face. He was setting the ball in motion for Andre's downfall. Now all he had to do was let William catch Tyler and Andre in the act.

Chantal dropped the phone and couldn't even finish the French toast she was looking forward to eating just a few minutes ago. Her appetite was completely lost. For the last week her mind had been so focused on helping Shari through her traumatic experience that she didn't have much time to dwell on her dwindling relationship with Andre. Now with one phone call all that had changed. It seemed the strength that she had recently tapped into was completely sucked out by T-Roc. If he was right, and Tyler and Andre were in love, then that meant the end.

Tyler raced to Andre's house to share the conversation she had had with Chrissie. She hoped he could give some insight as to who would want to expose their relationship. It obviously wasn't the tabloids because the pictures would've already been on the front cover of every magazine weeks ago. Tyler knew whoever was behind it spent a lot of energy devising their plan, which made it that much scarier.

"Baby, what are you doing back here?" Andre asked Tyler as he let her into the house.

"Andre, someone is fucking with us."

"What are you talking about?" he asked seriously.

"Remember that night we went to the studio for the meeting and no one showed up but us?"

"How can I forget? That was the first night we made love."

"Yeah, and we thought it was a big coincidence, with the storm, the lights going out, and getting locked in the studio for all those hours. Well, of course no one can control mother nature so we can't blame anyone for the rain, but someone locked the door on purpose and set up the faulty meeting."

"How do you know?"

"The reason Chrissie was so frantic was because someone left pictures on her desk from that night when we were making love."

"What? Oh shit, do you have any idea who did it?"

"No I don't, but Andre, I'm worried."

"Baby, don't stress yourself, we'll figure something out."

"Figure out what? This is, like, out of our control."

"Listen to me," Andre said as he lifted up her chin so they were eye to eye. "I know I haven't said this, but I love you. I fell in love with you from the first moment I saw you. That may sound far-fetched to you, but it's true. Honestly I don't care who finds out about our relationship. What we share is way more important to me than some movie or acting career. We will get through this together, I promise."

"I don't know what I would do without you, I love you so much. Now that we're together I can't imagine us being apart."

"We won't be. I put that on my life." Andre lay Tyler down on the couch and they began making love. As they got lost in each other's embrace, they both thought this would last forever.

After throwing up the little bit of breakfast she did eat, Chantal was climbing the walls. She paced the floor back and forth for about an hour until she finally reached her breaking point. "Shari, I think I'm about to have a nervous breakdown," Chantal said timidly through the phone.

"What's wrong?"

"I just got off the phone with T-Roc. He told me Andre and Tyler are in love."

"What? Are you sure?" Shari reluctantly asked, concern for Chantal instantly setting in.

"He is positive they are seeing each other and with that being true I know Andre is probably in love. It was in his eyes last time I saw him, which was weeks ago. He hasn't even really called me. Shari, I feel like I can't breathe. The mere thought of Andre leaving me to be with someone else makes me feel like I have no reason to live."

"Chantal, don't say that please. You have so much to live for. You're an amazing friend. Look at everything you did for me regarding Chris. You hooked me up with that beast of an attorney and now my bank account is right. He even managed to have Chris set up a college fund for Alex. I couldn't have maneuvered any of that without you. You're my best friend, Chantal. I need you. I know you're hurting right now, but there are other men."

"Not for me. Andre is my life. Shari, I have to get him back. Tyler Blake will never love him the way that I do—no woman will."

"So what are you going to do, Chantal?"

"I have no choice but to go to LA and fight for my man."

"Then I'm going with you. But let's leave in a couple of days so I can get Alex situated. I want to be there for you like you were for me."

"Thanks, I appreciate your support but I need to do this on my own. I'll call you when I get there, though." When Chantal got off the phone with Shari she practiced the conversation she would have with Andre. She had to convince him that they belonged together and that some fling with his costar was meaningless. But no matter how many times Chantal went over the conversation in her head she couldn't fight the fact that she believed his relationship with Tyler was much more than a meaningless fling.

Shari was beyond worried about Chantal. She had never heard her best friend talk like that before. Chantal was the last person she would ever think would say she had no reason to live. It was freaking her out. Chantal was truly like a sister to Shari and she couldn't imagine her life without her. When Shari caught her boyfriend Chris doing the dirty deed with his male counterparts, Chantal was the first person she wanted to run to. Shari knew that Chantal would have all the answers and turn a negative situation into something positive. That was exactly what she did, too. Chantal nursed her broken heart back to health and made sure her pockets got laced for all her pain and suffering. There was no way Shari was going to let anything happen to her best friend.

T-Roc leaned his head back on the bed in his hotel suite as the blond beauty gave him the best head of his life. Her professional skills were so amazing T-Roc thought she should teach a class or at least give well-instructed pointers to the many women who couldn't get it right. T-Roc actually preferred a magnificent blow job over sex; he figured it was less risky, too.

"Oh baby, I'm about to cum," he moaned as he pulled on the woman's ringlets. As relaxed as he was, T-Roc lifted his head so he could watch the woman swallow all his cum, which turned him on more than anything. "You're unbelievable."

"I bet Tyler never gave you head like that," Chrissie remarked as she licked her lips.

"No, actually Tyler never gave me head. If I remember correctly she said that was only done strictly for her man, and as you know, we never got that far."

"You say that with disappointment in your voice."

"No sense in rehashing the past," T-Roc said, abruptly getting up from the bed.

"I guess having sex with Tyler's best friend must really boost your ego."

"Actually having sex with you is just a bonus. Your information is what makes you so invaluable."

"I still don't understand exactly what you're trying to accomplish by knowing Andre and Tyler are sleeping with one another. Why do you even care?"

"That's not for you to worry about. You just continue to do what I ask and funnel the information I need."

"I feel bad about deceiving Tyler. When I showed her those pictures you sent to me she was really upset."

"Excellent, that means what you said worked."

"What I said was for her to stay away from Andre and she basically refused. I think she's in love with him."

"I doubt it," he said with certainty. "But even if she thinks she's in love it won't last long. That relationship will end just like all her other ones. None of the men she gets involved with are right for her."

"So who is, you? Is this what your whole plan is all about, to get Tyler back? Are you using me so you can get her back in your bed?" Chrissie was now putting on her clothes, feeling cheapened by the idea of T-Roc still having feelings for her friend.

"What are you getting yourself all worked up for? Whatever my plans are for Tyler don't concern you. You and I enjoy each other's company. That's all that matters."

"No. Not if you're just using me until you can have the woman you really want."

"Everyone uses everyone, Chrissie. Stop acting like a dizzy blonde, it's not very flattering. You had no problem fucking me and discussing Tyler's personal business during pillow talk, so don't try to be morally correct all of a sudden. It's a little too late for that."

"Answer me this: Were you ever truly interested in me, or was

I just part of your well-orchestrated plan when you just happened to run into me at my favorite restaurant?"

"Does that even matter?"

"Yes. So answer the question. I want to know."

"Honestly, it was a setup but you're selling yourself way too short. You're great in bed and you know how to swallow me just right. I would've fucked you whether you knew Tyler or not, but because you do, it definitely made you more appealing."

"T-Roc, you are truly a cruel, heartless man. I can't believe I let you play me like the fool you must think I am. But we'll see who will have the last laugh," Chrissie said, picking up her purse to leave. Before she could exit, T-Roc grabbed her arm.

"Don't do anything stupid, Chrissie, like tell Tyler what we've been up to."

"You mean what *you've* been up to."

"However you want to state it is irrelevant to me, but what you say to Tyler is. It wouldn't be wise for you to cross me, Chrissie. I promise you I'll be your worst sort of enemy." The look in his eyes sent a bolt of fear through Chrissie's entire body. She'd heard that T-Roc was a ruthless businessman and she was well aware of the drama he put Tyler through when they dated, but this warning was more sinister.

"Get your hands off of me, T-Roc," she said, yanking her arm free. "Don't worry. Your little secret is safe with me, but don't count on me to pump any more information to you. I'm done."

"You're done when I say you're done. If I need to know something I will be calling you and you better answer your phone. I don't take kindly to being ignored. Now give me a kiss good-bye," he said as he gripped her face and gave her a hard peck on the lips. Chrissie stormed out in tears.

"Okay, that's a wrap for the day," William shouted out to the movie crew. As he gathered the staff to go over some last minute script revisions for tomorrow's schedule, Andre took advantage of the chaos to speak to Tyler.

"Meet me at the Beverly Hills Hotel in an hour. I got a bungalow for us," Andre whispered and then jetted off to his trailer. Tyler was excited about being alone with Andre since William had occupied all of her time for the last couple of days. It was becoming increasingly annoying spending time with William when all she could think about was Andre.

When Tyler arrived at the bungalow the room had flowers everywhere and a box was placed on the table with a card attached. The card read:

> *To the love of my life. It's finally complete with you in it.*
> *Love, Andre*

Tears instantly filled Tyler's eyes. But then when she opened the box her tears were replaced with a stunned scream. To her surprise, the most beautiful pink diamond she had ever seen greeted her. Tyler stood, frozen, admiring the gorgeous bauble and didn't realize Andre had walked in.

"Tyler, will you marry me?" Andre asked, now down on bended knee. Tyler was still standing with her mouth open, not acknowledging the reality of the situation.

"Is this really happening to me?" she asked, looking down at Andre who was the vision of the prince charming she had dreamed would someday sweep her off her feet.

"If you say 'yes' it will," he responded with a nervous chuckle. Although he knew in his heart that Tyler was in love with him, he wasn't confident that she would accept his proposal.

"Of course I'll marry you," Tyler gushed. Andre picked up the box and took out the pink sparkler and placed it on Tyler's finger. They both admired how beautiful the ring looked on her and when Tyler leaned down to kiss Andre she noticed a tear slowly running down his face. "Oh, Andre, I love you so much."

"Not as much as I love you," Andre declared. They began undressing each other with a level of intense obsession that neither had ever experienced. Andre lifted Tyler up and carried her over to the plush king-size bed. When he laid her down, he stood for a moment and stared. She looked more radiant than ever before. Her skin sparkled against the ivory silk sheets and her long wavy hair glowed as if dipped in the purest water. She was the epitome of perfection and Andre felt blessed that she would be his wife.

After Chrissie left, T-Roc waited patiently for an update regarding Tyler and Andre. This was more than business to him; he had an emotional investment. It was imperative for his scheme to go off without a hitch, especially since Chrissie was now catching feelings. The last thing he wanted or needed was for her to fly off the handle and have a "clear the conscience" moment with Tyler. Even with his threat he wasn't sure Chrissie was strong or wise enough to take his warning seriously. The sooner the bomb dropped the closer he would be to getting what he wanted.

When T-Roc's cell phone rang he immediately recognized the number of his hired help. "What's it looking like?" was T-Roc's phone greeting.

"I just got word that the lovebirds are shacked up in a bungalow at the Beverly Hills Hotel."

"Cool, is your informant working on the inside?"

"No doubt."

"This is beautiful." T-Roc laughed. "I need you to get moving on this. Get the special delivery to William Donovan from Tyler telling him to meet her at the location ASAP."

"Already done. I even put the key inside so there won't be any knocking. William Donovan will walk right in on Romeo and Juliet."

"See, that's why I fucks with you. You know how to handle your business."

"Just remember that when you send my next payment," the co-conspirator added before hanging up.

T-Roc sat back in the bed thrilled by the news. He was counting on all hell breaking loose shortly and William sending Andre packing, and then calling him, begging to have him replace Andre as Damian. Soon he would be the one playing Tyler's love interest and Andre would become a distant memory.

As Tyler straddled Andre, he couldn't seem to go deep enough. He wanted to go farther inside of her; although he was filling her up, she wanted even more of him. Tyler's head was tilted back as her body was engulfed in pleasure. Andre massaged her breasts while stroking her in that special spot that was sure to give her a powerful orgasm. They moved their bodies in unison as if they were one and within an instant climaxed and then collapsed in each other's arms.

"Hmm, that was wonderful," Tyler said under exhausted breath.

"Tell me about it. We keep going at it like this you'll be popping out a baby every year."

"No, I don't think so. I barely have a chance to spend quality time with Christian."

"Don't you think you should start making time? Kids grow up so fast."

"I know, but I want to provide him with a good life and you need a lot of money for that."

"Tyler, I have a lot of money. Actually more than I can spend in this lifetime. Whatever I have is yours. You're going to be my wife."

"That means so much to me, but I want my own money. I've been in relationships where the man controlled all the funds and it led to nothing but trouble."

"No, you were just involved with the wrong man. Our life together is going to be different, I promise you that." Tyler couldn't help but passionately kiss Andre with those words of security.

"So, this is why you haven't let me touch you in weeks. You were too busy fucking this piece of shit," William said. Tyler jumped up, stunned to find William positioned in front of their bed.

"William! What are you doing here?" Tyler shrieked, distress written on her face.

Andre remained calm in the bed and it was obvious he could care less about William's unexpected visit.

"Tyler, put your clothes on right now, we're leaving," William directed her as if she were his teenage daughter getting caught with a high school boyfriend. To Andre's surprise, Tyler jumped up and started putting on the slacks and blouse he had ripped off only an hour ago.

"What are you doing? Get back in this bed," Andre said with authority. Tyler looked at Andre with confusion. Her body wanted to snuggle next to his strong muscular body, but her head told her to do as William demanded.

"Do as I say, Tyler."

"Man, you need to step off. That's my fiancée you're trying to dictate to."

"Your what?" William laughed. "Mr. Jackson, I don't know what you think is going on between you and Tyler, but I can promise you she's no more your fiancée than I am." Andre leaped out of bed, immune to the fact that his manhood was swinging in front of William, and grabbed Tyler's hand.

"Do you see this two-million dollar ring on her finger? This is my future wife. Recognize," Andre said, full of confidence. Throughout this whole ordeal Tyler had only spoken a few words. The drama was playing out between the two men in her life and she was torn.

"Tyler, finish getting dressed. We're leaving," William announced matter-of-factly.

"Did you not hear what I just said or should I speak more clearly?" Andre retorted, becoming increasingly irritated with William's attitude.

"Yes, I heard you but you're obviously not hearing me. The

woman standing before you—I created her. Tyler might be in lust with you, hell she might even care about you, but if you ask her to choose, she will always choose me. I have given her the life she always wanted and she is not going to let her infatuation with you get in the way of that."

"Tyler, will you please tell him that we're in love and we're getting married?"

Tyler gazed down at the beautiful rock on her finger and reflected on how much she loved Andre. "William, I don't want to disappoint you, but I'm in love with Andre and I want to be with him. I do."

"My dear Tyler, you could never disappointment me, but you know your relationship with Andre could never work. He will eventually break your heart and of course you will then come back to me."

"Hold the fuck up," Andre said, interrupting William. "Tyler will be my wife and I will never break her heart. I love this woman more than I ever believed humanly possible. Don't try to throw salt in the game because you all fucked up that she chose me."

"Both of you please stop. Andre, I do love you and I want to be your wife but I need to leave with William."

"What for? You don't owe him anything!"

"Yes, I do. I owe him a lot. He deserves an explanation and I need to give him one, in private. Please do this for me and don't be upset." Andre could see the pleading look in Tyler's face and rationalized he should give in to her request. Tyler finished putting on her clothes and followed William out the door. For some reason Andre felt empty when Tyler left, as though she were walking out of his life forever. He brushed it off to just missing the love of his life.

THIRTEEN

Beautifully Broken

Andre arrived home still reeling over his encounter with William. "Who in the fuck does this guy think he is? Demanding Tyler to leave with him like she's his possession. I should've made her stay. But she did have a right to talk to him in private even though his punk-ass didn't deserve it." He continued to babble out loud until he walked into his living room and saw Chantal sitting on the couch. Next to William, she was the last person Andre wanted to see. Chantal almost seemed like a stranger to him. So much had changed since the last time he'd seen her and he was a different person. He was in love and engaged to another woman. In his heart there was no room for Chantal, and having her in his house seemed like an invasion of his privacy. "What are you doing here, Chantal?"

"Andre, you haven't seen me in over a month and that's the greeting I get?"

"How are you doing? Is everything all right with Melanie?" he said, trying to sound diplomatic.

"She's fine, besides the fact that she misses her daddy. I was hoping we could go on a family vacation or something, maybe after you finished the movie."

"Yeah, maybe," Andre said in an insincere tone. Chantal walked over toward him and reached out her arms for a hug and a kiss but Andre turned away. "Chantal, not right now."

"Then when, Andre? We haven't had sex in months. I know somebody has been keeping your bed warm."

"Chantal, don't start or you're—" Andre stopped midsentence.

"I'm going to what?"

"Make me say something that you don't want to hear. Or maybe I should just say it," Andre reasoned.

"That's okay," Chantal countered. "Whatever happened in the past can stay there. Let's start off fresh. All is forgiven between both of us."

"I can't do that. You need to know I met somebody, Chantal, and it's serious, very serious." This was the sort of conversation Chantal wanted to avoid. Andre being so direct caught her off guard because she was hoping he wouldn't want to discuss his infidelity, as in the past. For him to bring it to the open meant that what transpired was serious and he had no intentions of letting it end. Pure fear caused Chantal to immediately put her hands over her ears and begin shaking her head and screaming over and over again, "I don't want to hear this! I don't want to hear this!"

"Chantal, you have to hear this. You came all this way, and you need to leave knowing the truth." Andre's insistence was a clear warning that there would be no avoidance.

Chantal put her hands down and said solemnly, "What truth is that, Andre?"

"I'm in love with Tyler Blake and we're getting married."

"How can you be in love with her, when you are in love with

me?" she cried. "You promised we would get married and be to-gether forever."

"Chantal, I never promised you that. You knew that I never had any intentions of marrying you. Those were your hopes and dreams, not mine."

"You liar! You made me believe that if I just waited around and let you sow your wild oats that I would be the one. Well, I've waited patiently and I deserve to be Mrs. Andre Jackson."

"That's all you care about is a name. You don't even know what being a wife is all about. All you want to do is party with your girl-friends and get high. Most of the time you're not even functional enough to take care of our daughter. Do you really think I want someone like that as my wife?"

"Andre, most of the time I'm partying and getting high with you, so don't blame me. I just want you to be happy and if that means drinking and partying with you, then I don't mind."

"Yeah, Chantal, but that's the problem. We've been running the streets together for so long that I can't even take you seriously as someone I can make my wife. I want a woman with something go-ing on upstairs besides where the next party is at or what's the lat-est Christian Dior bag. But those are your priorities and I need more than that from a woman. It's cool if I'm just looking for a chick to have fun with but not when I'm trying to settle down."

"I can change. I can be whatever you want me to be. We can make this work," Chantal pleaded.

"It's too late. I'll always care about you, Chantal, because you're the mother of my daughter, but I'm in love with Tyler. I want her to be my wife and nothing is going to change that."

"You think that uppity bitch is so perfect. She's no angel, Andre. She might appear to be dainty and sweet but from what I hear she is cold as ice. She will never love you the way I do. I would give my life for you, Andre. Tyler Blake will always put Tyler first and you'll end up getting the short end of the stick. You deserve more than that."

"Chantal, I know you're hurt and I'm sorry. But you can't begin to understand my relationship with Tyler because it's beyond you. I need for you to just accept what I'm telling you and move on." Even with the pitiful look on Chantal's face it still didn't reveal the level of devastation that was buried underneath.

"Andre, I'm not going to lie and say I'm happy about any of this. I love you more than I love myself and knowing our relationship is over breaks my heart. But I want you to be happy, I do. If Tyler is the one that can do that, then so be it."

"I appreciate that, Chantal. Maybe in time we will all be able to get along."

"I would like that."

"I'm not trying to rush you off, but I have a few phone calls I need to make, so if you don't mind, can I walk you to the door?"

"Oh sure, but can I use the bathroom first to freshen up? I came straight here from the airport and I feel a little sticky."

"That's cool but try not to be too long because I'm not sure when Tyler is coming back. I don't want her to get the wrong impression."

"I totally understand. I'll be quick." On the way to the bathroom Chantal couldn't help but feel shortchanged by Andre's dismissive attitude. He was so concerned about what Tyler might think that he didn't even consider the fact that he had just dealt Chantal heartbreaking news and she was on the verge of losing it.

On the drive to Tyler's place, William didn't say a word. Tyler was actually relieved because she used the time to map out what she planned on saying to him. The minute they stepped foot inside Tyler went to the kitchen and poured herself a glass of champagne. She needed some sort of buzz for the conversation they were about to embark on. When she was on her second glass William finally initiated the discussion. "Tyler, you know you have to end this so-called relationship with Andre."

"I had a feeling you were going to say that, but, William, I can't. I truly love him and we're getting married."

"Tyler, you don't love this man. Six months ago you were positive you were in love with me. This is just a phase. It's not uncommon to fall in love with your costar. After the movie ends so will your infatuation with Andre."

"It's different between us, William. I've been involved in enough relationships to know when it's the real deal. This is the real deal, I promise."

"I was trying to reason with you, but obviously that's not going to work. Tyler, I've made you into the rising star you are now, and if you don't stop seeing Andre you will leave me no choice but to take it all away."

"Why would you do that to me? You know how hard I've worked in order to gain a position in this industry. I thought we were better than that."

"I did, too. That's why I'm asking you to end this. Tyler, I couldn't handle continuing a business relationship with you knowing you're involved with someone else."

"Let's say I did end my relationship with Andre? Eventually I'm going to end up with somebody."

"Why can't it be me? We're so good together."

"William, for one you're a married man, and two I'm not in love with you. I believe our love came from a mentor-student bond. But we don't have a romantic future together. It's time for us to recognize that."

"Well, then you need to decide what you want out of life. Do you once again want to stand in a man's shadow or do you want to stand on your own as a movie star? The decision is yours. But, Tyler, if you continue seeing Andre then I promise I will do everything possible to cut your career short in this business, starting with axing you from *Angel*."

"William, you can't mean that."

"Believe it or not I'm doing it for your own good. You're letting some grimy hip-hop mogul who isn't worthy of you come in and sell you a fantasy life and you're falling for it hook, line, and sinker. Haven't you learned anything from your past dysfunctional relationships?"

"Oh, and getting involved with a married man isn't a dysfunctional relationship?"

"At least I'm offering you something more than a ring and some half-ass financial security. I'm offering you something that is priceless, which is independence. None of these men want to give you that. They want to buy you as though you're their prized possession. You have so much more to offer than that. With your talent the opportunities are endless, and I discovered that. You're now asking me to sit back and watch you flush it down the toilet to become barefoot and pregnant."

"That's not going to happen. Andre is very supportive of my career," Tyler said half-heartedly. She reflected on the conversation they'd had a few hours ago when Andre told her she didn't have to work—she could stay home and make babies. She had to admit that a lot of what William was saying was true. Eventually Andre would try to get her to end the acting career that she had worked so hard for. She knew from her past experiences that one thing was for sure: nothing was guaranteed in love.

"You know that's a lie, Tyler. But I'm leaving the decision up to you. Either you can choose a life with a man you don't really even know, or you can trust me. I've delivered on every promise that I've made and I will make you the superstar that you've dreamed of becoming. But you're going to have to do it my way. That means severing any sort of romantic relationship with Andre Jackson."

"I need an ambulance now!" Andre bellowed to the 911 operator.

"Sir, calm down, what is the problem?"

"My ex slit her wrists. Yo, there's blood everywhere. Please get somebody here now— I don't want her to die."

"What's your name?"

"Andre."

"Andre, what part of the house are you in?"

"The bathroom," Andre said as he held Chantal, wishing she would open her eyes and say this was all a bad joke.

"Wrap a towel around the wound and apply pressure. Hold it there until the paramedics arrive," the operator directed.

"Okay, okay, but please tell them to hurry up. My baby can't die." Andre stared at Chantal looking so helpless and innocent just like their daughter, Melanie. The thought of her dying had tears rolling down his face. He blamed himself for Chantal's predicament. It never dawned on him how fragile she was. If she died, he would never forgive himself. Andre left the door unlocked for the paramedics and heard them as they came in the foyer.

"We're up here!" Andre yelled out to the paramedics.

As they took Chantal away, Andre refused to leave her side. He rode in the ambulance and all he could envision was Melanie's face and how devastated she would be if he told her Mommy was never coming back home. Andre began making a deal with God. "Dear God, if you let Chantal live I promise I'll be a better man and a better father. Please dear God, forgive me for my selfish ways and don't let Chantal pay for my mistakes."

They rushed Chantal in for emergency surgery and Andre couldn't stop pacing back and forth in the waiting room. When he heard his cell ringing he prayed it wasn't Melanie looking for her mother. When he realized it was Tyler, he felt instant relief. "Tyler, baby, I'm so glad you called," Andre said while breathing hard on the phone.

"Andre you sound terrible. Is everything okay?"

"No, I'm at Cedars-Sinai."

"What happened? We're you in a car accident?"

"No, it's worse. Chantal tried to commit suicide. She slit her wrists."

Tyler felt numb. She immediately felt that she was the cause. "Why did she do that?" Tyler asked, afraid to hear the answer.

"When I got home she was waiting for me and I told her we were getting married. She must have taken it harder than I thought. I went in my office and made a few phone calls while she used the bathroom. When I finished, she still hadn't come out and I wondered what was taking her so long. I knocked on the door and got no answer. When I opened it she was sprawled out on the floor and blood was everywhere. It was the scariest shit I've ever seen in my life."

"Baby, I'm so sorry. I feel responsible."

"It's not your fault. If anyone is to blame, it's me. I should've been more sensitive to the situation. I mean damn, she is the mother of my child. I treated her like she was just some random chick that meant nothing to me. If she dies, I don't think I could handle it, Tyler. I would feel as though I actually took the knife and slashed her wrist. I would've killed my daughter's mother."

"Don't say that, Andre. You're being too hard on yourself. I'm going to pray that she pulls through this."

"I appreciate that, baby. I see the doctor coming out. I'm going to talk to him and I'll be over there later on tonight." Andre hung up the phone and marched straight toward the doctor. "Hi, I'm Andre Jackson. I came in with Chantal Morgan. How is she?"

"Mr. Jackson, I'm Doctor Stein. We've basically performed a miracle on your friend. She is going to pull through."

Andre was so relieved that he grabbed the doctor and hugged him. "Oh, thank you so much! I'm so grateful that you saved Chantal's life. She's the mother of my beautiful daughter and I wouldn't have had the heart to tell my angel that her mother was dead. Because of you and God I no longer have to do that. Thank you." The doctor seemed a tad overwhelmed with Andre's speech but at the same time he admired his heartfelt declaration.

"I'm always happy to save a life, Mr. Jackson, especially one that seems so precious to you. You can go in and see her, but she's still out of it. Tomorrow morning she should be coherent."

Andre sat next to Chantal and held her limp hand. God had answered his prayers and he was determined to keep his word. Even though he still had every intention of marrying Tyler, he would help Chantal with whatever she wanted to do with her life. Whether it was opening up her own business or pursuing some other career, she would have his full support. Although Andre had already set up a healthy financial trust fund for his daughter, he would also provide one for Chantal, too. He figured since he couldn't give her what she really wanted, which was his last name, he could give her the next best thing, which was financial security.

When T-Roc got word that William was seen going into the bungalow and thirty minutes later leaving with Tyler, he was in high spirits. He would've given anything to have audio on the hysterics he knew must have taken place. He considered bugging the room but felt it was way too risky. His source also informed him that Chantal had made her way over to Andre's house. T-Roc was counting on Chantal to cause a huge confrontation that would send Andre into a state of uncontrollable madness. Once that happened, he planned to seize the opportunity and step into Andre's shoes.

William left Tyler's place, struggling with his thoughts. The walk to his car seemed much longer since he was breaking down the entire situation in his mind. He wanted to believe that the lecture he had given her regarding Andre would resonate, but he wasn't totally confident. Tyler seemed to genuinely love Andre and that scared him. William couldn't believe he missed the red flags that would've indicated that Tyler's heart was straying. When he walked into the bungalow and witnessed the two caught in their own ecstasy, William's first thought was to strangle the lovebirds.

But he knew no matter how physically fit he was, Andre's strength would've overpowered his. William never carried a weapon of any sort and when he surveyed the room there wasn't one in sight. He was actually happy because the rage that erupted inside of him when he saw the two made homicide plausible, which he knew he would have regretted later.

When William got back in the car he slammed the door and began pounding his fist against the steering wheel. He was normally so in control of his emotions, but grasping the severity of the potential catastrophe hit him like a ton of bricks. After sitting in his car for an hour outside of Tyler's house trying to get his anger under control, William finally started the ignition. As he backed out of the driveway he noticed the final light go off in the house. He hoped that Tyler had come to the right decision and planned on ending her relationship with Andre immediately. If she didn't, William would have to come up with a plan to break up the pair permanently.

Where Do Broken Hearts Go?

Andre sat with Chantal for almost four hours before deciding to head over to Tyler's place. He knew she would be asleep at this hour, but he yearned to be next to her and feel her love. After his agonizing ordeal with Chantal he desperately needed the positive energy that only Tyler could give him. He slowly walked up the stairs and turned on the light on the nightstand next to her bed. She was lying on top of the blankets, which enabled Andre to get a clear view of the white negligee that hugged her body. Her angelic face seemed at peace. Andre sat on the edge of the bed, wanting to watch her rest forever. He decided before lying down next to this pure-looking specimen he would take a long hot shower.

The hot water pouring down his body was rejuvenating. He felt this was a new beginning for him and Tyler. Now that their secret had been exposed there would be no need for the sneaking around that Andre never wanted anyway. From the moment he and Tyler made love he wanted to share his feelings with the world. Stealing kisses here and there and whisking off for discreet rendezvous made Andre feel as though they had something to be ashamed of when he knew they didn't. He sometimes privately wondered if Tyler was embarrassed about their relationship, but brushed it off as one of the side effects of being in love for the first time.

Andre felt he would no longer have to be weary of such insecurities anymore since he and Tyler were free to show their devotion to one another. Soon they would be husband and wife and no one could come between them. Andre crawled in bed next to Tyler and the instant his body touched her soft skin he became aroused.

"Baby, you're back," Tyler mumbled, still half asleep.

"Shh, don't say a word. I just want to lie inside of you all night and feel your warmth." With that Andre entered Tyler from the spooning position and rested his manhood inside what he considered his personal heaven.

Listening to the sounds of Maroon 5 and sipping a glass of merlot, Chrissie was up late finishing some marketing ideas to promote the movie *Angel* that she was presenting to William in the morning. Chrissie always found comfort in her work, which could be the perfect distraction for her often topsy-turvy personal life. If it wasn't for the high demands of her whirlwind job she probably would've joined a convent to escape her consistent bad luck with bedding the wrong men. When she began her relationship with T-Roc she thought her luck in love had finally taken a turn for the better. In her gut Chrissie knew it was naïve of her, but somehow she made herself believe that maybe T-Roc genuinely cared about her. After their altercation earlier that day she knew she was completely fooling herself. T-Roc couldn't care less about her or their relationship. What they shared wasn't even a relationship. He had used her and she had to admit she was a willing participant.

Since the time Tyler had first introduced her to T-Roc a few years ago, she secretly had a crush on the notorious bad boy. She never shared it with anyone, but the feelings were always there. When Tyler's relationship with T-Roc ended, she was thrilled. It gave her hope that maybe one day she would have a chance to score with the known ladies' man. A couple of weeks after coming back to LA to do the publicity for *Angel*, she bumped into T-Roc while leaving her favorite lunch spot, and butterflies ensued. The chance to fulfill her fantasies of being with him had finally presented itself.

That afternoon, after briefly chatting over a couple glasses of wine, the two went back to her apartment and embarked on the most mind-blowing sex of Chrissie's life. It was more pleasurable than anything she'd envisioned. But before her heat even had a chance to die down T-Roc was questioning her about Tyler. At first she figured it was his natural curiosity since he had dated her but then it became their whole topic of conversation. It came to the point that every time they had sex there seemed to be a third person sharing their bed: Tyler Blake. Chrissie tried to shake it off as paranoia until T-Roc asked her to help him trap Tyler and Andre in the studio together. At first Chrissie refused but when T-Roc cut her off and wouldn't see or talk to her, she buckled under the sexual pressure.

The next thing Chrissie knew she was caught up in a conspiracy and showing Tyler explicit photos of her and Andre and trying to place fear of exposure in her heart. Chrissie honestly felt terrible since she considered Tyler her best friend, but she also felt like she didn't have a choice. In her mind, Tyler had Andre and William as a crutch. All she had was T-Roc, and if she didn't help him he had no problem disregarding her. Never in a million years did she believe that her actions would help set in motion a series of tragic events.

When Chrissie heard her doorbell ringing she had no idea who could be coming over so late. She turned down the music and peeped out her blinds to see who the late-night visitor was. "What do you want?" she said, somewhat disgusted to see T-Roc's face.

"I've left you several messages this evening and you haven't returned one. You left me no choice but to come over to make sure you were okay," T-Roc said as he brushed past Chrissie and into her apartment.

"You don't care how I'm doing. You just want to make sure that I didn't blow your spot up to Tyler. No need to worry, your secret is safe with me. Plus, to tell on you would mean telling on me and I'm not sure Tyler would ever forgive me."

"Thanks for the brief insight inside your mind, but that's not why I'm here. My sources tell me that William walked in on the lovebirds this afternoon. I need a detailed account as to what happened."

"What makes you think I know?"

"Chrissie, don't make me ask you again." She stood ogling T-Roc for a moment, wondering to herself how much he already knew and what new information he needed from her.

"How did your sources know where Tyler and Andre would be, and how did they know William would find them? Unless of course you also set that up," Chrissie said shaking her head. "Does it ever stop with you? If William wasn't such a levelheaded man he could've gone off the deep end and caused a massacre in that bungalow."

"Can you skip the hypothetical and tell me what transpired?" T-Roc said, growing impatient.

"Tyler actually called me twice. First to tell me that after William caught her with Andre, they left together and he gave her an ultimatum. Either her career or Andre."

"Did she tell you what she was going to choose?"

"She was torn, especially since she accepted Andre's marriage proposal."

"What! She can't marry him!" T-Roc stated, unable to conceal his anger and jealousy.

"I know that would be devastating for you, T-Roc, but as I told you before, she's very much in love with him."

Trying to ignore her last comment T-Roc continued with his next question. "You said you spoke to her twice. What was the next conversation about?"

"That one was a lot more serious," Chrissie said sitting down on her couch. "Andre's ex-girlfriend came into town unexpectedly and he told her about his plans to marry Tyler. She lost it and tried to commit suicide. When I spoke to Tyler she said Andre had just told her they rushed Chantal in for emergency surgery. Tyler is torn up over the whole incident. She blames herself."

"Wow, I knew Chantal would flip out when she came to see Andre but never did I think she would try to take her own life," T-Roc said, taken aback by the news.

"You knew Chantal was coming to LA? I didn't know you guys were friends."

"We talk occasionally."

"It has to be a little more than that if you knew she was coming to see Andre. He didn't even know that."

"Listen, I placed a call to Chantal letting her know that Andre and Tyler's relationship was getting pretty hot and heavy. Of course, I didn't know at the time that the two were engaged or that he would confess that to Chantal. I simply wanted to ignite a fire under Chantal so she could cause a further dilemma for Andre."

"'A further dilemma'? You purposely sent Chantal over the edge so she would come to LA and wreak havoc. Now she's in the hospital clinging to her life."

"That wasn't my doing. If anyone is to blame for that, it's the selfish actions of Andre. He's so mesmerized with his Hollywood love affair with Tyler that he hasn't even considered the repercussions his behavior would have on the mother of his child. Andre knows how crazy Chantal is about him and that to learn he planned to marry another woman would make her lose her mind."

"However you want to spin this, T-Roc, you are still responsible. Maybe if Andre had more time he could've come up with an easier way to break the news to Chantal, but you left him no choice. Placing that phone call to Chantal set the wheels in motion for a disastrous encounter."

T-Roc knew Chrissie was right but mentally refused to accept responsibility. It was too much for him to bear. He never wanted anyone to die because of his vendetta against Andre, especially not Chantal. She was a mother and T-Roc found her offbeat behavior fascinating. Not to mention their lovemaking was incredible. If she died because of his petty bullshit, T-Roc knew he wouldn't be able to live with himself.

"Oh baby, I slept so good last night," Andre whispered in Tyler's ear.

"You seem much better today. I guess that means Chantal is going to pull through."

"Yes, indeed. God answered my prayers. If she'd died, that guilt would've eaten me alive. But she'll be okay. Once she's completely healed I want us to start planning our wedding. That ring is so stunning on your finger," he said, caressing her hand.

"Andre, we need to talk about the wedding," Tyler said, sliding her hand from his grasp.

"I know this whole Chantal episode put a damper on our engagement celebration but we'll get through it, just like we handled the William situation."

"That's what we need to talk about."

"William? Yeah, I'm sure he didn't take it well but in time he'll accept it. He doesn't have a choice."

"Well, he gave me a choice."

"Which was?"

"You or my career. He made it clear that if I chose you he would make sure I never worked again in this town."

"I know you told him to go to hell. You don't need that pompous motherfucker."

"Actually I do, Andre. William basically discovered me. If it wasn't for him I would still be in New Jersey trying to decide what I was going to do with the rest of my life."

"I understand that you have a certain amount of gratitude for the cat, but that doesn't mean you owe him your life. I told you before you don't have to struggle for financial security. I have plenty of money and you don't ever have to want for nothing in life."

"Don't you understand I like the struggle? I've wanted to be a movie star since I was a little girl. William is making that dream a reality. I can't give that up."

"But Tyler, we're in love."

"For now, but how long will that last? There are no guarantees with love."

"There is none in an acting career, either. You can be hot today and nobody can remember your name tomorrow."

"That might be true but if I'm going to gamble, I'm placing the money on me."

"I can't believe you're saying this shit. I finally find the woman that I want to spend the rest of my life with and you're telling me that your career is more important. Tyler, you can't be serious."

"Andre, I'm so deeply in love with you, but I worked too hard for my career to just let it end."

"So what are you saying, Tyler?"

"We can't see each other anymore."

"Don't do this. We belong together. Baby, I love you more than anything."

"Don't make this harder for me, Andre. Don't you think I feel torn? This isn't an easy decision."

"It seems pretty easy to me. I never thought there was anyone more emotionally detached than me, let alone a woman. I guess we learn something new every day."

"That's not fair, Andre. It's killing me inside to let you go but I know it's best for both of us. I mean the mother of your child tried to kill herself, that's crazy."

"Don't blame Chantal for this. Because of your own selfish reasons this relationship is over with. If this is what you want, then so be it."

As Andre was getting out of bed Tyler reached out for him. "Andre, can you please make love to me one last time?"

Andre gawked at Tyler with confusion. "You have to be the coldest woman I've ever met, and we both know I've been through a lot of women." Andre's words stung Tyler to the core. Andre didn't understand Tyler and it was too late to explain. The chill in the room was unbearable for her. She put on her silk robe and strolled downstairs while Andre got dressed. When Tyler heard the door slam, she buried her face on the sofa pillow and cried a river.

T-Roc barely got any sleep. When he left Chrissie's place he drove around for a couple of hours trying to gather his thoughts. He didn't admit it to Chrissie but he couldn't deny it to himself. He felt absolutely terrible about Chantal. The second he got in his car he called the hospital inquiring about her condition. He lied and told the on-duty nurse that he was Chantal's brother. Although she was reluctant to answer any of his questions, after T-Roc put on his undeniable charm she revealed that Chantal had a successful surgery and would make a full recovery. That relieved T-Roc of half his stress but he was also overwhelmed with the notion that Tyler and Andre were engaged. That wasn't part of his plan. If Tyler was truly in love she would choose to be with Andre and that would ruin all of T-Roc's hard work. The unknowing was driving him crazy so when his cell phone rang early the next morning, he believed his questions would finally be answered.

"Hello, can I speak to T-Roc?"

"This is him. Who's calling?" T-Roc asked, although he knew exactly who it was.

"This is William Donovan."

"Mr. Donovan, what can I do for you?" T-Roc asked, feeling optimistic that his scheme worked out as designed, since William was calling.

"Actually, I wanted to see how your schedule was looking. If you were still interested I wanted to know if you could take over the role of Damian. Things didn't work out with the other actor and of course you would be our ideal replacement. But for the record, you were always my first choice," William added.

"This is surprising, but yes I'm definitely interested."

"Wonderful. How soon can you get to LA?"

"I had to handle some business, so I'm actually already here."

"This is perfect. I'll have my assistant call you to get the address where you are staying so she can send you over the script. I'll place a call to your agent so we can get all the legalities worked out. It's great to have you on board, T-Roc."

"I appreciate that, William." T-Roc was once again feeling untouchable. The guilt from the role he played in Chantal's predicament was a distant memory. He was too busy caught up in being back on top and closer to reaching his goal.

William knew he might've been jumping the gun by offering the role of Damian to T-Roc. He hadn't spoken to Tyler and honestly had no idea what she decided to do, but he was following his gut. His instinct told him she would end her relationship with Andre because he really didn't leave her a choice. William knew the thirst Tyler had to be a superstar and he was the only one who could quench it. Most men couldn't handle a career-driven woman like Tyler because it could be overwhelming, but William welcomed it. He could relive his career once again through Tyler. The more William contemplated this, the more he believed Tyler would follow his request, and locking T-Roc down was the right thing to do.

When Chantal woke up in the morning she was grateful to be alive. Waking up in a hospital bed with tubes coming out of her made her suicide attempt a reality.

"How are you feeling this morning, Ms. Morgan?" Dr. Stein asked.

"Happy to be alive."

"Yes, you gave us quite a scare. But you're going to make a full recovery. I did want to briefly discuss something with you."

"It sounds serious."

"It is. Are you up to talking or would you like to discuss it later on?"

"Please, tell me."

"Chantal, I doubt you knew this because it was in the very early stages, but you were pregnant."

"Were?"

"Yes, I'm sorry to say, but you lost the baby. With all the blood you lost from the suicide attempt that baby just didn't survive."

Chantal swallowed hard, absorbing the information. It all made sense. She'd assumed the nausea and not being able to eat were due to her broken heart, but really it was because she was pregnant with T-Roc's baby.

"I'm assuming the father is Mr. Jackson. He hasn't wanted to leave your bedside. He obviously cares a great deal for you." If only that had been true, then Chantal could've used the loss of their baby as a tragedy for them to grieve together and reconnect. But since Andre hadn't touched Chantal in months, that wouldn't be possible.

"Yes, it was his baby. But Dr. Stein, I would prefer if you didn't mention anything to him about it. He already feels so guilty about my suicide attempt. If we told him now that I also lost our baby he would go over the edge."

"I totally understand, Chantal."

"Thank you. I will tell him about our loss once we get past this hurdle." Of course Chantal never intended to tell Andre a thing. If he knew that not only did she sleep with T-Roc, but had also gotten pregnant he wouldn't want her in his life, period. That was one secret she was taking to her grave.

Andre went straight from Tyler's house to the hospital. He so badly wanted to erase the conversation he'd just had with her and forget that he ever loved her. His stomach was in knots and the pain was excruciating. For the first time he knew how it felt to have a broken heart and pondered if this was his payback for all the hearts he shattered so freely.

Andre replayed his last conversation with Tyler. He was still in shock that she would choose her career over their love. He had her pegged all wrong. When he first laid eyes on her, Andre thought she was this delicate flower that needed constant nurturing in order to bloom, but there was nothing delicate about Tyler; when she broke if off with Andre it was as if her emotions were made of steel. Andre noticed Chantal's doctor approaching and wiped away the tear that escaped him.

"Dr. Stein, how is Chantal this morning?"

"Good morning, Mr. Jackson. Ms. Morgan will be very happy to see you. She's been asking for you all morning. Under the circumstances she's actually doing well. I believe she'll be able to go home in a few days."

"Great, I'll go see her now." Andre felt somewhat nervous about seeing Chantal. He wasn't sure what to say. When he walked in, her eyes were closed but she somehow felt Andre's presence and instantly opened them and greeted him with a smile.

"Andre, I've been asking for you all morning. I'm so glad you're here."

"Of course I'm here. Where else would I be?"

"I'm sorry for putting you through this. You must think I'm a coward."

"Why would you even think something like that, this wasn't your fault. If anyone is to blame, it's me. I've been so foul to you. I'm sorry. But I promise I'll make it up to you."

"Just being here is enough. Does Tyler know you're here?" she asked. Even in her fragile condition, Chantal found the strength to fish for answers.

"It's over between me and Tyler." Saying those words out loud almost made Andre choke, but he had to remain composed for Chantal's sake.

"Andre, what happened? Just yesterday you said you guys were getting married." It disgusted Andre even more that Chantal was lying in the hospital for nothing. He and Tyler weren't even going to walk down the aisle and that was the reason Chantal had slit her wrists in the first place. His anger brewed every time he thought about it.

"It's not important. What is important is that you get better soon. I want you to come home with me. The nanny is going to bring Melanie here in a few days and I want you all to stay for a while." Chantal's eyes lit up with the idea of the three of them being under the same roof as a family.

"You mean that, Andre?" Chantal asked, almost afraid to build up any sort of hope.

"With all my heart. This incident has opened my eyes up to so much. You and Melanie are my family and I have to take care of both of you. Not only financially but emotionally, too. Unfortunately, it took a tragedy like this to make me realize that."

"It's okay. But baby if you give us another try, I promise I'll be the woman that you want me to be."

"Chantal, don't think about that right now. Concentrate on coming home. I have some things I have to take care of but I'll be back later. Get some rest." Andre kissed Chantal on the forehead and decided his future was with her. Maybe he wasn't in love with Chantal the way he was with Tyler but it didn't matter. For the first time in his life he gave his heart and soul to a woman but she let him go. He knew Chantal would always choose him first. She was willing to end her life if he wasn't with her. That was deep, maybe a little crazy, but deep all the same. After he pledged his love for Tyler and even asked her to be his wife she disposed of him like he was nothing. Not only was that bad for his ego, it was devastating for his heart. He had to accept there was no future for him and Tyler and he needed to let it go.

It took every ounce of strength Tyler had to pull it together and meet with William. She cried for over an hour when Andre left and then called Chrissie to pour her heart out to her. Tyler felt she had made the wrong decision by letting Andre go and hoped that she would get the encouragement she needed from her best friend to get him back. Unfortunately, Chrissie told her just the opposite, partially because she honestly believed that Andre was carrying way too much extra baggage, and also she was following T-Roc's strict instructions.

Now Tyler had to deal with William. After pouring her heart out to Chrissie she called William to let him know that she followed through with his demands, but now that she was standing in front of him, it was much too soon for her to see his self-satisfied face.

"So you took care of it," William stated, not even bothering to look up at Tyler when she entered his office.

"Didn't we already discuss this?" Tyler said, taking a seat.

"Just refreshing my memory," William said sarcastically.

"As a matter of fact I did and he didn't take it very well, but then again neither did I."

"You'll be fine. I've already placed a call to T-Roc and he'll be replacing Andre."

"William, don't you think you're jumping the gun? Andre

might just want to finish the movie. He has invested a lot of time in the role."

"Oh, please, his ego won't let him. He's not professional enough to finish a job he was hired to do under these circumstances. Luckily, T-Roc is already here in LA. The script has been sent over and we will start shooting the new scenes first thing tomorrow morning. We will be working double-time to try to make our deadline. So I need you at your best."

"That's not a problem. I'll be on set first thing tomorrow morning, but for the record I think you're underestimating Andre. He takes the role in this movie very seriously. On that note, I'll see you tomorrow."

Before Tyler reached the door, William looked up and bellowed, "Tyler dear, try not to sleep with T-Roc, too."

"Don't worry, been there done that," she retorted before slamming the door. Tyler's debate with William had the exact effect on her that she wanted to avoid. She drove straight to the liquor store and got two bottles of champagne. Even though she had an early call in the morning she needed something to numb the pain. Champagne always did the trick, at least temporarily. Tyler wanted to stop replaying the final conversation she'd had with Andre. It kept repeating over and over again and she thought at any minute her brain was going to detonate.

William felt pleased with himself. He was able to get rid of Andre once and for all. He knew that right now Tyler was feeling depressed but he had no misgivings about what transpired. In his mind there wasn't any debate as to what had to be done. Andre had come this close to ruining everything William had planned for Tyler, but luckily he found out just in time. William still had no idea who sent him the letter with the room key attached, leading him to Andre and Tyler's hideaway. One day William hoped to personally thank the informant for exposing the love tryst before it got out of hand, leaving him rendered powerless over Tyler.

That night Tyler fell asleep with Sade's "No Ordinary Love" blaring from her speakers and an empty champagne bottle beside her bed. Although Tyler detested the idea of working with a slimeball like T-Roc, she was relieved that William was replacing Andre. To work with Andre day in and day out would be emotional torture, torture that her heart wouldn't be able to take.

Chrissie was livid when she got word from William that he was bringing T-Roc onboard to replace Andre. It was all making sense to her and she felt like a complete idiot. She knew T-Roc was somewhere gloating right now, but not without Chrissie giving him a piece of her mind.

"So I hear you're replacing Andre in the movie. You must be thrilled. I should've figured out that this was what your whole over-the-top plotting was about. You got the part now. You must laugh to yourself, saying, 'I sure took that dizzy white girl for a ride.' Well, I hope you're satisfied with yourself, T-Roc," Chrissie snarled, wanting to reach through the phone and rip his balls off.

"Chrissie, being dick whipped is color blind. You being white has nothing to do with it. So, no, I'm not laughing behind your back. My plan was to thank you with a gift to reflect my gratitude. I was thinking maybe I would let you pick out a car of your choice. Top of the line, fully loaded, only the best. It's the least I could do. Without your help none of this would've been possible."

"Save your token of appreciation. There is nothing you can buy me to give me back my self-respect. But I will tell you this, you might have your dream role but you'll never get Tyler back. I might have fallen for your calculated charms, but Tyler is im-

mune to your bullshit. The closest you'll get to a relationship is
through the make-believe love affair between the characters Angel and Damian." Chrissie slammed the phone down, reeling
inside. She prayed she was right and that Tyler wouldn't find
comfort in the arms of T-Roc. Due to Tyler's frail emotional state
Chrissie knew it was possible but hoped she would lean on
William instead.

At one point Chrissie had even fixed on telling Tyler the truth
about everything, including the role she played in the fiasco. Then
Chrissie reasoned that not only would Tyler hate her but she would
lose her job and T-Roc would make it his mission to make sure she
never worked on either coast again. She decided it was best to contain what she knew and just keep a close watch over any signs of a
developing romantic relationship between the two.

The alarm clock woke Tyler up bright and early. One of the reasons
she loved to get wasted off champagne was because she never came
to with a hangover. She still decided to gulp down a Red Bull to
give herself a boost of energy. Today she would be working with
T-Roc and she wasn't looking forward to that. T-Roc was the worst
kind of manipulator that Tyler had ever met. She knew he would
no doubt have a steadfast commitment toward his role but he
would try to undermine Tyler and everyone else at every given opportunity. It was all part of his divide-and-conquer routine. That
was his way of keeping some sort of control. Tyler wasn't mentally
up to playing the games that T-Roc was sure to bring, but with Andre out she had no choice. For extra focus Tyler grabbed one more
Red Bull before she hit the road.

When Tyler arrived, everyone was already on set. She zoomed in
on T-Roc who was sitting in Andre's chair as if he owned the place.

"Good morning, T-Roc."

"Good morning to you, pretty girl. I must say I'm pleased to be
working with you. I have no doubt we'll make history together."

T-Roc is still the same cocky, egotistical maniac he always was, Tyler thought to herself.

"I'm glad you're both here. I want you guys to go over this scene together while the crew is setting some things up," William said, pointing toward the highlighted part in the script.

"Is there a reason why someone is sitting in my chair?" Andre said as everyone turned and gaped at him with utter surprise.

"I was under the impression that you would no longer be playing the role of Damian," William said, feeling flustered by Andre's presence.

"What would give you that idea? We have a contract. Unless you've fired me and if so I would like to know why before I get my lawyer on the phone."

"As a matter of fact you *have* been fired, so you can leave now," T-Roc said boldly.

Andre ignored T-Roc's outburst and peered at William pulling his card.

"T-Roc, I apologize, there must have been some misunderstanding. I was under the misguided impression that Andre had quit. I was wrong," William said.

"Are you crazy? This is my role now. You called me and now you're letting this nigga punk you out? Fuck that!"

Andre stepped forward with hate in his eyes. "I suggest you have a seat, my man, because you're out of line."

"Make me sit down, bitch," T-Roc spit.

Right when Andre was about to lunge at T-Roc, the whole crew ran and stood between the two men, sensing an outright war was about to erupt.

"Everybody calm down. Let's take a thirty-minute break. T-Roc come with me so we can clear some things up." T-Roc followed William but not before sizing Andre up and mouthing, "This ain't over."

"Whenever you want it, son," Andre warned. He sat down in his chair and idly flipped through the script.

"I didn't think you were going to show up," Tyler stated.

"Oh, you thought I was going to let your sugar daddy run me off the movie?"

"He isn't my sugar daddy, and no, I didn't think you were going to let William run you off the movie. I figured you wouldn't want to work with me anymore."

"This is business and I always finish the job I'm hired to do. You're an excellent actress and we work well together. I'm not going to let our personal relationship interfere with that." Tyler looked down and saw her hands shaking. She realized she was the one who couldn't handle working with Andre.

"How's Chantal?" Tyler asked, trying to divert him from how uncomfortable she was.

"She's doing well. I'll be bringing her home in a couple of days."

"Home with you?"

"Yeah, do you have a problem with that?"

"So are you guys getting back together?"

"We've decided to give it another try. After the way everything went down, I came to the conclusion that Chantal and Melanie are my true family. I want to make things right for them."

"And that requires the two of you getting back together. I guess you've picked up the pieces pretty quickly," Tyler said, feinting for a drink.

"How's everything going over here?" William asked, sneaking up on them.

"Can you excuse me for a minute?" Tyler darted off to her trailer before she broke down in front of the men.

"What did you do to her?" William demanded to know.

"You mean what you did," Andre said accusingly. "What type of man makes a woman choose between her career and love? Only someone that is extremely insecure." Andre walked off and made his way to Tyler's trailer.

"Andre, leave," Tyler implored with tears streaming from her eyes. Andre became weak seeing his one true love in so much pain, but his anger held him together.

"You can't have it both ways, Tyler. Yesterday you ended our relationship like I meant nothing to you, and today you turn around and get upset because I'm getting back with Chantal."

"How can you just go from me to her? Why can't you just take a break for a minute?"

"Take a break for what? So I can mope around feeling sick over you? I refuse to do that." Tyler sniffled, trying to hold back her tears, but Andre was breaking her heart.

"I can't listen to this. You're killing me right now, Andre."

"Well, blame yourself because I wanted to give you everything but you chose William and your career." Andre tried to resist giving in to his heart but Tyler seemed so delicate, hovering in the corner. He relented and walked over and held her in a deep embrace and kissed the lips he missed so much. Tyler reciprocated the passion and they fell down on the couch giving in to their obsession. Right when Andre grabbed her buttocks and began removing her panties, Tyler jumped up.

"I can't do this. I've made my decision. I have to stick to it."

"You're so fucking confused, but I'm done playing these games with you. I'll see you on the set." Andre stormed out, furious with the mixed messages Tyler was sending. As Andre was walking out, William walked in.

"Tyler, pull it together. Your boyfriend is showing that he has more substance than I gave him credit for, so you need to carry yourself with some professionalism before you are blamed for the collapse of this movie," William threatened.

"'Collapse'!" Tyler echoed out loud. "What are you talking about? This movie is coming together as planned."

"For now, but if you have a nervous breakdown over some hiphop hustler turned wannabe actor, this movie will be a complete bust."

"I understand, William. I'm actually starting to understand a lot of things. Or maybe I'm finally accepting that when it comes to men and relationships, I'm a glutton for punishment. I've been through so much in the past but I continue to make the same stupid mistakes when it comes to love. First I fell for your pathetic married-man lines and now I'm in love with a man who has a crazy baby mama. I don't know what's wrong with me. Maybe I'm in love with love or maybe I love the drama that comes with such dysfunctional relationships. Or maybe I just need to see a therapist. Whatever it is, I will hold my own and finish this movie," Tyler stated, not appreciating the fact that William was implying that she was weak. She went over to the mirror, checked her reflection and exited the trailer, leaving William with a slight grin on his face. He knew exactly what to say to whip Tyler back into shape.

A few weeks had passed and Chantal had made a full recovery. Her wrists were still bandaged up, but that was a minor setback for the drama queen. She was enjoying the attention Andre was lavishing on her since he had brought her home from the hospital. She knew most of it came from the enormous guilt he harbored, but that didn't matter to her; she was willing to get it any way she could. In Chantal's mind she deserved every ounce of sympathy since her suicide attempt could've backfired. She thought about the night when Andre had given her the brutal news that he was marrying Tyler and her form of self-preservation had instantly kicked in.

After Andre had given her the brush-off and closed the door to the study, Chantal ventured off to the kitchen. She went through several utensils until coming upon the perfect knife. The fear of what she was about to do was making her stomach bubble but as she grasped tightly to the knife she honestly believed this extreme action was her only chance to save her now defunct relationship with Andre.

On her long walk upstairs to the bathroom, several times Chantal reconsidered the route she was about to take. Her biggest concern, besides accidentally cutting her wrists so deep that she might die from blood loss because Andre didn't come to the rescue in time, was the fact she had no sort of pills to medicate herself. She would be of clear mind as the edge of the knife ripped through each layer of skin and the blood splattered. Chantal wouldn't be able to find any comfort until her body lost enough blood to make her unconscious. When she had closed the bathroom door to begin her diabolical plan, Chantal felt it would all be worthwhile if Andre came back to her.

"Chantal, I was shook as shit when I heard about your suicide attempt," Shari sputtered nervously. "I knew you were bugging out over Andre and Tyler but I had no idea it was killing you like that."

"Neither did I until Andre told me he was going to marry that chick. Shari, my whole world crumbled instantly. I couldn't believe this bitch just came along and snatched my man up just like that. It reminded me of high school when the new girl comes along and all the niggas are checking for her. You expect for her to get all the attention for a couple of weeks maybe even a month if she's dope like that. But then you assume niggas will get tired of sweating her and she'll be old news especially if she ain't giving up the ass. That's what I figured would happen with Andre. He would be infatuated with the glamorous starlet for a minute but then realize he would never have her because her loyalty was with her creator William Donovan."

"Damn, so Andre and Tyler are getting married. How is she taking the fact that you're staying in his crib?"

"Actually, the engagement has been called off," Chantal said with a devilish grin.

"Excuse me?" Shari asked with eyes bugged out, feeling as if she missed a part to the story.

"I guess I did have the starlet figured correctly. I don't know all the details, but just from eavesdropping and the little that Andre has unwittingly revealed to me, Tyler *did* pick her creator over him."

Shari sat down on the white leather couch Chantal was cuddled up in. She moved one of Melanie's teddy bears and hovered close to Chantal as if about to get some top secret information. "What do you mean, Tyler picked the creator?" she said.

"You heard me," Chantal said, as she gingerly held the cup and sipped her hot tea.

"Andre must be devastated," Shari blurted out quickly, then, just as quickly realizing how those words must have crushed Chantal, said, "I'm sorry, Chantal. I didn't mean it like that."

"Yes, you did, but that's okay. He is devastated. He's trying to walk around here as if just a few weeks ago he didn't confess how deeply in love he was with Ms. Tyler Blake and he planned to make her his wife, but now the relationship is over. I even heard him crying a couple of times in his study. Of course, I didn't let him know that I heard him, but he really has it bad for that bitch."

"How do you know Tyler picked William Donovan over him?"

"One afternoon, when Andre thought I was sleeping, I over-heard him on the phone with his mother. He told her that William basically gave Tyler an ultimatum, either her movie career or him. The selfish bitch picked her movie career. I've been running through hoops trying to get Andre to marry me, but this snotty bitch comes along with her fake-ass innocence and he's rushing to get her down the aisle. But instead of her being grateful to catch a winner like Andre, she gives him his walking papers. That's an un-grateful bitch right there. Lucky for me her behavior has shown Andre that no one will ever be down for him like me. I almost fucked up and killed my ass trying to prove that shit."

"What you mean 'almost fucked up'?" Shari was now looking at Chantal like "bitch, you don't mean what I think you mean."

"Girl, you know damn well I don't want to die, but after Andre dropped that bomb on me I had no choice but to go hard. What's harder than slitting your wrists? I didn't mean to cut so deep though," Chantal added with a chuckle.

"Chantal, you're fucking crazy. I can't believe you faked trying to kill yourself over that nigga. But I guess that's better than really trying to kill yourself over him. I don't know, all this shit is sounding confusing to me. I'm just happy that Melanie still has her mom and you're alive and able to talk to me."

"Tell me about it. But I had to do it for my family. If Andre would've married that girl they would start their own family and Andre would soon forget about me and Melanie. My daughter deserves better than that and so do I. My only concern is that Andre was still going to marry that chick even after I slit my wrists. Yeah, he was promising that I would never have to want for nothing and he would finance whatever business I wanted to start, but he still was going to marry her. The only reason he's not is because she backed out."

"I know you're sick of me asking you this, but what are you going to do?" Shari questioned, totally enthralled in this real-life soap opera.

"Hope that Andre comes to his senses and realizes that Melanie and I are his family and he needs to go ahead and wife me."

Just as Shari was about to ask Chantal another million-dollar question, Andre walked in with a big Fred Segal box and laid it on the glass table.

"What's up, Shari?" Andre said as he walked around and kissed Chantal on the forehead.

"I'm good. How you doing, Mr. Hollywood?"

Andre smiled at the understated compliment Shari bestowed upon him about his budding career as an actor. "Just trying to maintain," he said.

"What's in the box?" Chantal asked, curiously hoping it was something expensive for her.

"Open it. I know how you love Fred Segal," Andre grinned. Chantal removed the top of the box and her eyes instantly beamed at the sight of the gorgeous fuchsia dress. Right beside the dress was another small box that obviously had a pair of shoes in it. The shoes were studded with fuchsia and clear-colored stones. Andre definitely had incredible taste.

"Andre, this is beautiful!" Chantal wailed.

"That shit is hot," Shari chimed in.

"I'm glad you like it, because I want you to wear it tonight to the Beverly Hills Hotel. The movie is about to wrap up and we're having this Hollywood shindig to celebrate."

"Andre, look at me. I need a pedicure, manicure, and my hair needs to be done. Not to mention the shit around my wrists," she complained.

"Don't worry about that little shit. I have someone coming over to take care of all that. You'll be the prettiest woman at the party." Chantal couldn't help but wonder if that meant Tyler wasn't coming. "As far as the packaging on your wrists, just cover it with love bracelets." Chantal instantly lit up at Andre's words. Maybe she did still have a chance to be Mrs. Andre Jackson.

When Chantal and Andre walked into the party at the Beverly Hills Hotel she immediately scoped the place to see if Tyler was in attendance. She breathed a sigh of relief when she didn't spot her, but part of her was disappointed because she wanted the home-wrecker to know she and Andre were back together. Andre led Chantal to her seat and introduced her to everyone they came in contact with. The studio heads and crew from the movie set were congratulating Andre on the fantastic job he did on the film. Some went so far as to say that Denzel Washington needed to watch his back because everyone would be banging down Andre's door once the movie was released. Andre took it all in stride. He tried to remain cool about the compliments but on the inside he was hoping he would one day have half the acting career of Denzel Washington.

Just as everyone was sitting down and getting comfortable, the room seemed to freeze and everyone's eyes shifted in one direction, including Andre's. Chantal slowly turned around in her seat to see what had everyone in the room so mesmerized. To her utter disgust, Tyler made her movie star entrance in a form-fitting pastel pink satin dress with William Donovan trailing behind her like she was the queen of the world. Photographers were snapping her picture and she was posing and eating it up like this was what she was born to do. To make matters worse, one of the movie executives came over and told Andre he wanted him to go take some pictures with Tyler for the press. Andre seemed reluctant, but it was more out of anger for Tyler showing up with William than anything else. Chantal sat in her seat burning up inside. *Look at that bitch cheesing all in the cameras with my man. I want to slit her throat.* Chantal thought. *Unfortunately, going to jail isn't an option.*

"You look beautiful tonight," Andre whispered in Tyler's ear as they posed for the photographers.

"I'm sure your date wouldn't appreciate you saying that to me," she said burning with jealousy after noticing Chantal.

"Yeah, well, William looks as if he's about to have a heart attack if I stand any closer to you."

"Then I guess you better move," Tyler barked as she gave one last fake smile to the paparazzi and strolled off with William.

From the short distance it looked as if some heated words were exchanged between Andre and Tyler, but Chantal couldn't get a clear read. It was obvious to her and she assumed everyone else in the room that their body language ignited sexual chemistry. When Andre eventually made it back to the table, he didn't even acknowledge the fact that she had to witness him posing with Tyler. He was still fuming over whatever words he had exchanged with his ex. Then to add fuel to the fire, William and Tyler sat straight across from Andre and Chantal, but no one made eye contact. It didn't matter, though, because Chantal was burning a black hole through Tyler's sensuous pink dress and everyone's tension levels were at an all-time high.

"Can you pass me a napkin?" Tyler said demurely. Both William and Andre instinctively reached for the same napkin, with William beating Andre to the prize. William smiled as he handed

Tyler the napkin and Andre felt embarrassed that he reacted as if Tyler were his date. To further Andre's repulsion, William played with Tyler's hair before planting an intense kiss on the luscious lips he'd briefly owned. Chantal actually felt empathy for Andre and the obvious pain he was in, seeing Tyler and William so happy together.

"Andre, it's okay, I'm here for you," Chantal whispered in his ear, while gently patting his stiff arm. As William and Tyler continued making out at the dinner table like two teenagers at a drive-in movie, Andre abruptly stood up.

"Can I please have everyone's attention? I have an announcement to make," Andre called out, looking around, making sure all eyes were on him. Andre didn't begin his speech until his and Tyler's eyes were fully connected. A slight glaze of sweat appeared on Chantal's forehead and she shifted her body back and forth due to the anxiety that encompassed her from not knowing what Andre was about to say. "As you all know, I'm truly grateful for the opportunity I was given by getting the part of Damian. Breaking into film isn't easy but to get a starring role in a major movie and to act alongside such a talented cast my first time out is unbelievable. I hope that I've done the part justice and hope this is just the beginning of many more roles to come." Everyone began to applaud, assuming Andre was finished with his speech.

"That was beautiful, baby," Chantal said, relieved that he didn't make an ass of himself.

"Thank you everyone, but I'm not finished yet." The guests looked around at each other, wondering what else the up-and-coming actor had to say. "Through my many struggles and the journey that has gotten me to the place that I am right now, one woman—besides my mother—has always remained by my side." Andre gently grabbed Chantal's hand. "Chantal, please stand up. I want everyone to see the most beautiful woman in the world." Chantal bashfully smiled because for the first time in her life she was overwhelmed by Andre's attention. Then, to her amazement, the words she longed to hear for so long flooded the ultra-exclusive crowd. "Chantal, will you marry me?"

Tyler's champagne glass sounded like an explosion as it hit the floor. William grabbed her arm under the table and hissed, "Pull it together."

"Baby, are you going to answer me, or are you going to embarrass me in front of all these people?"

"Of course I'll marry you!" Chantal screamed, not caring how she got the proposal as long as it came. Andre lifted her up and gave her a long, lingering kiss in front of the ecstatic crowd. Everyone stood up in a loud chorus of applause. William lifted Tyler up by her right arm to direct her to applaud with the rest of the guests.

The live band once again began playing music and the room filled with idle conversation. Many people came up to congratulate Andre and his blushing fiancé. Tyler desperately wanted to run to the ladies' room and vomit but opted to guzzle down five glasses of champagne back to back instead.

"Andre, do you know how happy you've made me? I can't believe I will finally be Mrs. Andre Jackson. Wait until Melanie hears the news—she will be the happiest little girl in the world."

"Melanie will be happy," Andre repeated, as he nodded his head in agreement. As Chantal rambled on about all the plans she would start first thing tomorrow morning for their wedding, Andre stared at Tyler who was now completely drunk. Although he knew his marriage proposal to Chantal ignited Tyler's drunken stupor, that wasn't the reaction he'd hoped for. He envisioned her standing up and confessing her undying love for him and then maybe tossing a drink in his face for proposing to another woman. Then Chantal and Tyler would get in a heated argument and both ladies would ask him to choose. He would look lovingly into Tyler's eyes and tell her she was the only woman for him. They would exit together leaving William to lick his wounds. But now Andre was engaged to a woman he wasn't in love with and William would be the one to nurse Tyler back to glory. "Let's go home and celebrate."

Chantal jumped up, anxious to be with her future husband. She hoped they would finally make love again since it had been months since she had felt Andre inside of her. As the couple exited the party, Tyler reached across the table and grabbed Andre's still full glass of champagne and drank it in what seemed like one gulp.

Tyler sat back in her drunken state, watching the newly engaged couple leave the party. Her heart wanted to flood the table with tears but even in her dismal trance she knew that was impossible, mainly because William would never let her live it down. He would scold her for the lack of self-control she exhibited.

"William, I'm awfully tired. Can you take me home?" Tyler was standing up to leave before even giving William an opportunity to answer. She knew he would and if he didn't, she would simply hop in one of the many limos parked outside. Tyler sauntered toward the exit with William in pursuit. By the balancing act Tyler was doing on her heels, William could clearly see she was one misstep from an embarrassing fall.

"Tyler, wait a minute," William said as reached out to grab her arm. "Listen, I know you're upset but slow down. The last thing you need is for the paparazzi to snap a picture of you falling on your ass because you're drunk and angry," he whispered calmly in Tyler's ear.

"Fine, I'll slow down. Just please get me home."

On the drive home Tyler drifted off into her own world. Her heart was gasping for air but there was nothing Tyler could do. The tears silently rolled down Tyler's face, but that didn't stop William from feeling her pain. But how couldn't he, it was dominating the air.

"I know you don't want to hear this, but you made the right decision. Right now your heart is telling you otherwise but trust in time you will see that I'm right."

"I have serious reservations about that. You have no idea how my heart was just ripped out of me when Andre asked Chantal to marry him. He doesn't love her. He loves me and I love him."

"Whether that is true or not doesn't really matter. Chantal is the type of woman Andre needs to be with, not you. You're too good for him. Andre would only be able to give you small doses of happiness and nothing lasting."

"How do you know, William? Maybe Andre and I are meant to be. Did you ever consider that?"

"No, because you're not. If I honestly believed he was the right man for you, I would give you my blessings, but he's not. Look how he hurt you tonight and asked Chantal to marry him in front of you and everyone else."

"He did that out of anger," Tyler said, defending Andre's actions.

"Exactly, that is a perfect example of his immaturity. Do you really want to give your heart and life to a man that childish?"

"I don't know why I'm having this discussion with you, William, because there is no way you can remain impartial. You blame Andre for our relationship ending, but it wasn't his fault."

"To say that I don't have any hostility towards Andre would be a lie, but it still doesn't change anything I just said. Tyler, I do love you, I'll always love you and because of that I want what is best for you. If you were to marry Andre it would be one heartbreak after another. You know why I know"—there was a short pause as William turned and looked at Tyler—"because I used to be Andre Jackson."

Tyler digested what William said. There were a lot of similarities in Andre's and William's personalities. Maybe that was one of the reasons she felt so close to Andre, because he was a younger more exciting version of her mentor. William turned out to be an incredible man but what demons did he have to fight to get there? She was beginning to understand that William was trying to protect her from having to ever find out.

"Thank you," Tyler said as William pulled up to her house.

"For the ride or the advice?" he asked teasingly.

"Both."

"Do you want me to walk you in? You still seem a tad bit out of it."

"I am, but I'll be okay."

"Are you sure? You don't have to worry about me trying to seduce you."

"I know, William. I'm fine, I'll see you tomorrow."

"Get some rest, you have an early call in the morning. Don't be late."

"Yes, captain," Tyler said as she saluted him. William waved good-bye hoping that his starlet would soon get Andre out of her system.

"Oh, Andre, I missed having your dick inside of me. Baby, you feel so good. I'll never let you go."

"Oh, Tyler, baby, I'll never let you go, either," Andre moaned.

"What the fuck did you call me?" Chantal screeched. Andre's dick instantly lost all life as Chantal jumped up from riding him and he opened his eyes to the daggers in hers. "I know you didn't call me that bitch's name. Are you so far gone that you still thinking about her while you in this good-ass pussy?"

"Well, I see your ego is still intact," Andre huffed as he turned his body in the opposite direction of Chantal.

"Oh, please, Andre. You just proposed to me in front of a room full of people but now you're calling out the next bitch's name. How am I supposed to take it?"

"Chantal, what do you want me to say? That I'm over Tyler? Well, I'm not. I don't know if I ever will be. But what can I do? She chose her career over me and I have to accept that."

"So what was that whole speech about tonight?"

"Honestly, I was pissed watching William all over Tyler. I wanted to hurt her," he said nonchalantly.

"So you basically used me to get back at her. That's cold, Andre. I thought we were better than that. Don't you understand how much I love you? I would do anything to make you happy. I can be a good wife to you."

"You still want to marry me?" he asked as he rose up in the bed.

"Of course I do. There is no other man for me. You are the father of my child and the love of my life."

"But Chantal, I'm in love with someone else. My heart will never belong to you."

"You say that now, but I have enough love for both of us. Eventually you will realize that I'm the woman for you. You'll see, Andre, Tyler will never appreciate you the way that I do. I'll always be in your corner and I will be the woman that you want me to be."

Andre knew that wasn't the case, because Chantal would never be Tyler. But he did have love for Chantal and if he couldn't have the woman he truly wanted why not have the one who truly wanted him. Andre went to sleep that night feeling empty and alone. With everything he had learned in life, no one ever taught him how to mend a broken heart.

The nonstop phone ringing jarred Tyler out of her much-needed sleep. Not only was her head banging but she still had on the clothes and makeup from the night before. She couldn't even say hello as she held the phone to her ear.

"Tyler, can you hear me?" Chrissie bellowed through the phone. She could hear breathing on the other end but preferred the sound of Tyler's voice. "Tyler, if that's you, wake up."

"I'm up, what is it?" Tyler slurred.

"First of all, you were supposed to be on set an hour ago. No one has been able to get you on the phone. I heard about Andre's announcement last night and I hope that's not why you're still passed out in bed," Chrissie stated, as though she were a teacher scolding her student. By this time Tyler managed to carry the phone into the bathroom and put a wet, cold towel on her face. Half of her clogged-up makeup was removed by Chrissie's last sentence.

"Actually, I came on my period early this morning and I had terrible cramps. I took some pain medicine and it knocked me out. I apologize. Tell the crew I will be there shortly." Before Chrissie could ask another question, Tyler hung up the phone. She didn't want Chrissie to mess up her off-the-top-of-her-head lie by drilling her.

The last thing she wanted to hear was a lecture from Chrissie about forgetting Andre and being more professional. She had no idea how this whole situation was eating her up inside. Watching the man you love propose to another woman had to be the worst punishment in the world. Even the coldest woman would defrost watching a spectacle like that. Tyler decided to take her time getting to the set in order to get her mind right. She got in the shower and let the hot water seduce her body. As she lathered every curve, Tyler reflected on the last time Andre made love to her and how incredible he felt. She couldn't believe she was giving all that up, but then reasoned that men were the biggest gamble in life. She couldn't afford to take that type of chance especially with all her dreams within reach. After her long shower Tyler took her time applying her makeup. Normally she would arrive on set bare-faced since the makeup artist would do her up, but she wanted to arrive looking like a star. She slicked her hair back in an elegant pony tail and put on a pair of low waist Stella McCartney cream pants with a low-cut fitted cashmere sweater. With a pair of Fendi stiletto boots and matching bag, she knew Andre would lose his mind when she strutted past him.

"Tyler will be here shortly," William announced to the irritated cast and crew.

People were whispering to each other, wondering what was delaying the usually prompt star. As the chatter continued, to everyone's surprise Tyler entered like Miami sunshine on a rather gloomy day. Her body seemed to glide in the fitted pants and all eyes were on her.

"Good morning all, please forgive me for my tardiness," Tyler said, sounding cheerful.

"Don't worry. We're just glad you're here," one crew member said with a bit of flirtation, although he had been cursing her out to a coworker less than ten minutes before. Tyler strutted past Andre and walked straight up to William. From the angle Andre was watching they seemed to be flirting with one another and it was driving him crazy. Unable to contain his anger he stormed over to Tyler, grabbed her arm and took her into his trailer. It all happened so unexpectedly, William was too stunned to react. By the time he did, Andre's door was locked and instead of making a scene, William thought it best to let them talk in private.

"What the hell is wrong with you?" Andre asked with rage escaping on every breath he took.

"There is nothing wrong with me. You seem to be the one with the problem. You have a lot of nerve whisking me off to your trailer against my will, especially since you're now an engaged man."

"I didn't think you noticed, the way you were wasted last night."

"I wasn't wasted," Tyler said on the defense.

"Whatever, Tyler. Are you back fucking William?"

"Are you back fucking Chantal?" she said, throwing the question right back in his face. There was a long silence on Andre's part before finally answering.

"Not really."

"What type of answer is not really? Either you're fucking her or you're not."

"Listen, I'm the one asking you the question," Andre reminded her.

"It's none of your business."

Andre stepped closer to Tyler and tightly held her chin with her head titled up. "It is my business and I want to know."

Tyler felt a sense of power knowing that Andre still cared if William was sharing her bed. She purposely had a meaningless make-out session with William last night to infuriate Andre. Tyler was so enraged that he was carrying on with Chantal and wanted him to be just as disgusted at the thought that she was back tangling with William. But she couldn't decide whether to tell him the truth or see how enraged with jealousy he would be if she lied and said they were still lovers. To her surprise and disappointment she wouldn't have the chance to find out.

"You're right, it isn't my business," Andre said as he turned to walk away.

"Andre, wait, don't you want to hear what I have to say?"

"It doesn't matter. I'm sorry for treating you as if you still belonged to me. Whatever your relationship is with William, it is your business. I've moved on and you've been moved on. I guess it's time for me to let go."

Tyler so badly wanted to reach out to Andre and admit how deeply in love she was with him, but something held her back. She agonized as Andre walked out of the trailer, leaving her crushed. It took all Tyler's will power not to run out of her trailer and beg Andre to come back. But the words that William spoke to her last night lingered in her head. Maybe Andre would break her heart, and Tyler feared that more than anything else.

After Tyler shot her last scenes, she grabbed her belongings and dashed off, not even bothering to say good-bye to the cast and crew. Before she could find seclusion in her car she bumped into a familiar face.

"Hello, T-Roc, I'm surprised to see you."

"I actually have a late meeting with someone who works here."

"Oh, well, I won't hold you up."

"Wait, I have a few minutes to spare," T-Roc said, wanting to share a few minutes with the distraught-looking Tyler.

"Well, I don't—I have to go."

"Tyler, stop," T-Roc said with authority. To her surprise, but not his, she did. For a brief moment it was like they were back in time when T-Roc had a strong, sickening hold on her.

"What is it?" she asked in an uneasy voice. T-Roc could see the discomfort in her eyes, but he couldn't resist toying with her mind.

"You seem upset, Tyler, and I want to know what's wrong," T-Roc said as he stepped closer to Tyler. She observed the diamond studs that sparkled from each ear, the perfectly smooth and groomed face, his charcoal cashmere turtleneck, tailored black slacks, and loafers. His eyes and smile reflected sincerity, but Tyler knew better. There was nothing sincere about T-Roc and when you put your guard down he would swallow you up like the snake that he was.

"I'm fine, T-Roc, but even if I wasn't it's none of your business." Tyler began to pick up her stride and walk off, but T-Roc seized her arm.

"Don't ever turn your back on me, Tyler. When I first saw you again at William's party, you didn't acknowledge me but I let that slide. I know you were the reason I didn't get the part and I let that slide, too. I know you are going through some emotional turmoil right now, so I'm going to excuse you getting sweet with the tongue, but that's your third and final pass."

"You don't know anything about what I'm going through, T-Roc."

"I know a lot more than you think," he said, staring so hard Tyler got light-headed.

"Regardless, I don't have to explain anything to you. The hold you once had over me, T-Roc, is long gone. It died when your venom caused your cousin to throw me down the stairs and I lost my baby. Do you know how different my life would be right now?"

"Yeah, I would be a father and you would be my wife."

"T-Roc, that baby wasn't yours. It was Ian's, and you refused to let us be happy together."

"In your heart you know that baby was mine." Tyler turned her head, unable to look T-Roc in the face. She didn't want him to see the tears that were welling up in her eyes. "But you're right, your life would be so much different. You wouldn't be the movie star you are now. I remember how desperately you wanted your independence, free to make your own decisions and have your own money. This is the life you said you wanted so many years ago. Is it everything you dreamed it would be, or are you still that lost little girl in search of love?" T-Roc could feel Tyler's entire body shaking. He always knew what buttons to push to mentally crush her.

"Why do you do this to me?" Tyler asked with the sound of defeat in her voice.

"Do what? Make you think?"

"T-Roc, I can't do this with you. If an ounce of compassion runs through your blood just let me go home, please."

T-Roc hated to let go but he released Tyler from his grip. He didn't need her to answer his question anyway. Tyler was lost but he still planned on being the man to save her. The first thing he had to do was dig deep in Andre's closet and find out what skeletons he had buried. There was no way a man that powerful didn't have a couple of dead bodies lying around somewhere. After Andre got the better of him by keeping his role as Damian, T-Roc was more determined than ever to bring Andre down. He would dig so deep and leave no rock unturned.

That night Tyler went home and drowned her sorrows in a magnum of Dom P. Luckily it was the last day of shooting so she didn't have to be on set early the next morning. She took the phone off the hook, put on her favorite Sade mourning CD, and lay on her couch and passed out.

On his way home Andre stopped by Harry Winston and picked out a beautiful engagement ring for Chantal, just the sort of obscene rock that she would adore. When Andre slid it on Chantal's slender finger, she immediately got on the phone and called all her friends and some people that she hadn't spoken to in years. Andre left Chantal to brag and walked into his study and locked the door so he could be left alone with his thoughts. He wanted to dream about Tyler one last time before he totally tried to erase her from his heart. If only it was that easy to let go of love.

FIFTEEN

Magic Stick

It had only been a few weeks since she became officially engaged to Andre but it seemed like a lifetime to Chantal. The fairy tale she envisioned as a little girl was no longer a fantasy. She occasionally pinched herself to make sure it was real. Chantal even had to admit that in her wildest dreams, marrying a man like Andre Jackson seemed a bit out of reach. After accepting that the proposal and ring were the real deal, she tried to delete Tyler Blake from her mind. She kept a close watch on Andre and from what she observed he wasn't in touch with her opponent, which relieved a ton of stress. For the first time Chantal felt secure enough to relish in all her glory.

"Girl, I can't believe you did it. You got that motherfucker to finally marry yo ass. Work it bitch," Shari popped as she gave Chantal a pound.

"Persistence is the key."

"Yeah, and slitting your wrists also helps," Shari said sarcastically.

"Yeah, in my yet to be released book titled 'How to Bag Your Millionaire Man,' I'm going to put that in the desperate measure chapter. I mean, fuck it, I did what I had to do."

"You're not the least bit worried that Andre might go running back to Tyler?"

"I'm not gonna lie. At first it would be the last thing I would think about before I went to sleep, and the first thing I thought about when I woke up in the morning. But after drilling Andre, he reassured me that it's over between him and Tyler."

"Excuse me? Andre reassured you? Come again?"

"Yeah, we had a long discussion. He still has feelings for home-girl, but he knows his future is with me. She is so caught up in all that Hollywood bullshit that she ain't paying Andre no mind. It's her loss and my gain."

"Hmm, so it don't bother you that you're second choice?" Shari asked.

"Girl, hell no! I rather come in second to an official chick like Tyler Blake than some bum groupie bitch. It's actually rather good for my ego. If she would've married him, my ass would be sick. Seeing their pictures splashed across all the magazines and on the television, they would replace the void left by P. Diddy and J-Lo. At least now I know he ain't going anywhere, because if he can't be with her then he'll definitely be with me. I'm more secure than ever. I am praying William Donovan will get a divorce and marry Tyler, and then I can really breathe." Chantal started spitting the hook to the Young Jeezy song as Shari watched and then joined in, pretending to be a backup dancer in a video.

"Work it, Shari, I'ma tell Andre to hook you up in 50 Cent's next video," Chantal said, half-laughing.

"Video, oh please. 50 is cool and I love all his songs, but I no longer need to do insignificant things like that thanks to the Chris Duncan fund," Shari bragged with pure confidence. Both women jammed and bounced their hips off one another as if the actual Jeezy record were blasting on the radio.

"Damn, ya having a straight up party up in here except there is no music and nobody but the two of you are in attendance," Andre said, eyeing Chantal and Shari in confusion.

"Baby, we just tripping. Actually Shari came over to start helping me with our wedding plans." Chantal nudged Shari discreetly who was unaware of her plans but knew to go along with it.

"Yeah, we're trying to decide the location and color scheme for the wedding," Shari added proudly.

"Don't you think it's a little too soon to be making wedding plans?" he asked, looking uncomfortable with the realization that he would soon be tying the knot.

"No, I was hoping we could have a Christmas wedding," Chantal revealed for the first time.

"But it's the beginning of November—that's next month. We need more time to prepare. I'm sure you want a top-of-the line ceremony," Andre reasoned, trying to stall the inevitable.

"And I will. I already contacted the hottest wedding planner in LA and told her you would have no problem paying extra to make sure we have the most beautiful wedding, although we working on limited time. At first she acted high post but once I dropped your name she got her shit together quickly."

"This all seems a little rushed to me, Chantal. Maybe you should slow it down a little."

"Andre, I can't. I already told my family and informed Melanie. She was the one that actually gave me the idea. When I asked her what she wanted for Christmas she said for Mommy and Daddy to get married." Chantal knew that was the clincher right there. Andre's back was against the wall. After the emotional roller coaster Melanie had been on, there was no way he would disappoint her.

"Well, I guess we're having a Christmas wedding," Andre said reluctantly. "I can't let down my sweet little angel." Chantal winked at Shari, letting her know that she knew exactly how to push her man's buttons.

"I'm going to let you ladies continue on with your planning. I have some phone calls to make," Andre said, exiting the room.

Chantal waited to make sure Andre was nowhere in sight when she started jumping up and down.

"Shari, I wasn't sure if I was pushing too hard with the Christmas wedding, but it damn sure worked out," Chantal gasped with excitement.

"I know. When you said that shit I thought Andre was going to be like 'hell no,' but he gave in a lot easier than I expected."

"I knew once I dropped Melanie's name, he would give in. If that hadn't worked, I was going to send Melanie in here with those big crocodile tears in her eyes to plead my case."

"You should be ashamed of yourself using that sweet little girl to do your dirty work," Shari said smiling, although she was serious. But Shari knew Chantal long enough to know she had no shame when it came to getting what she wanted.

Tyler's world was crashing down all around her. Her breakup with Andre had hit her harder than she anticipated. William had been relentless in his pursuit to rekindle the love affair with his star pupil but soon realized that she needed more time to mend her broken heart. He hoped that once she started working on a new film project she would snap out of the depressed mood she seemed stuck in. William was sure that Tyler would pull it together, but Chrissie wasn't as confident. Every time she would call or visit Tyler she seemed to be in a drunken state. Chrissie was determined to snap her out of her downward spiral.

"Tyler, it's not even two o'clock in the afternoon and you're drinking. That's not a good look," Chrissie remarked.

"Chrissie, please, it's only champagne. It's harmless. Some cultures can't start their day without having a drink."

"Yeah, you're talking about that culture called drunk. I know a few of those. I'm hoping that I don't have to add you to that list."

"You're so cynical. I'm just trying to relax. I recently finished a grueling movie schedule and in a few weeks I start another one. Can't a girl have a couple of glasses of champagne to clear her mind?"

"It depends what you're trying to clear. If it's a certain man, I hate to break it to you but no amount of liquor will erase that memory." Tyler sat on her couch, flipping through the latest edition of *Cosmo* with Angelina Jolie on the cover, trying in vain to act as if she didn't hear a word Chrissie said. A frustrated Chrissie walked over and snatched the magazine from Tyler's hands.

"What is that all about?" Tyler squealed, irritated by Chrissie's obvious attempt to butt into her personal feelings.

"Because you're using that damn magazine as some sort of block so you don't have to pay attention to me." Tyler took a deep breath and rolled her eyes, letting Chrissie know she wasn't amused by her therapy session.

"What do you want me to say, Chrissie? That I'm using alcohol as a crutch because I'm not with the man that I love?"

"Is that what's going on?" Tyler reached for her glass, trying to avoid answering the question, but Chrissie ripped it from her hands. "No more until we finish our conversation," Chrissie said with authority.

"Fine!" Tyler was tired of fighting with Chrissie and figured the sooner they had their talk the sooner she could resume drowning her sorrows in the two cold bottles she had waiting in her refrigerator.

"Wonderful. So I guess you're not taking this whole wedding thing very well?"

"That's a dumb question. That's the best you could come up with?" Tyler remarked as she fidgeted with her velour jogging pants.

"No need to get smart. I thought we would start with the basics and work our way up to the more complex topics," Chrissie said candidly.

"Listen, Chrissie, when you're trying to nurse a broken heart there is no such thing as basic, everything is complex. Do you want to know what I ask myself every day? Is it worth it? The fame, the money, is it all worth losing love for? I don't know. At one point in my life I would've said without a doubt, because the only love I knew that was guaranteed was the love from my son. Now, I don't have a clue. Part of me wants to run to Andre and say I'll give it all up for you so we can be together but then to do that means I would make myself naked and vulnerable for him to break my heart. The funny thing is after Brian I didn't think I had anything left inside of me to break but I was wrong. Every day I'm not with Andre my stomach literally hurts. The only thing that numbs the pain temporarily is this glass of champagne. Without it, I'd probably be somewhere drowning in tears."

"Then go to him. Give up everything you worked so hard for in order to secure independence and freedom to be with Andre Jackson. A man that obviously has an extremely unstable fiancée, is a notorious womanizer, and you haven't even known for a year. If that's the man you want to gamble your and your son's future on, then I'll be the maid of honor." Tyler turned her head, disgusted by Chrissie's lack of understanding of her pain. "I know you think I'm being insensitive," she said, as if reading Tyler's mind. "But I know what you've been through in your prior relationships and how far you've come. I don't want to see you throw it all away on a man that doesn't deserve you."

"But maybe it will be different between us."

"Tyler, do you really want to take that chance? It's nice to see that you're still optimistic in love but I don't think Andre is the one you need to take that chance with."

"Maybe you're right, but it hurts so bad." To break the somber mood, Chrissie broke into a horrible rendition of Whitney Houston's "Why Does It Hurt So Bad."

Tyler couldn't help but crack a smile. "Chrissie, you sound like a straight-up clown. Let's get the hell up outta this house and go shopping."

"That's the Tyler I know and love." Both women grabbed their purses and headed out the door.

As Andre entered William's office building he looked down at his watch, hoping he was making perfect time. He figured William was out on one of his power lunches and he would handle his business with William's assistant and be in and out without even running into his Achilles heel.

"Hi Stacey, I'm stopping by to sign that paperwork my agent insisted was so important," Andre said derisively, since his agent always acted as if everything was an emergency.

"Yes, Mr. Jackson, let me get them for you." The receptionist left her desk and disappeared into William Donovan's office to retrieve the documents. "Mr. Jackson, Mr. Donovan has the paperwork. He said to please come into his office to go over a couple of minor details." Andre let out a loud sigh, revealing his annoyance at having a one-on-one encounter with his adversary.

"Hi William, I'm in a rush so exactly what do we need to go over?"

William stood up from his chair, walked around his desk and directly toward Andre. Andre instantly shifted his body in defense mode, wondering if William was about to tackle him like a football player. To his surprise and relief, William glided past him and shut the door. Although Andre knew he could handle any sort of physical altercation with William, he wasn't in the mood for an afternoon brawl.

"I don't like to discuss any sort of business with the door open," William explained, as he walked back to his desk.

"No problem, but can we speed this up because as I said I'm in a rush."

"Of course. Feel free to read over the papers and just sign where you see the 'X.' "

Andre dissected every sentence in the document and he noted in his mind that everything was just as his agent stipulated, so he had no idea what William needed to discuss. "Everything seems in order, so I'll just sign on the dotted line and be out."

"Actually, I wanted to discuss the press junket that I'm having Chrissie set up for you to promote the movie. Here is the initial draft for the dates and locations." William handed Andre the paper and could see the frown on his face. "Is there a problem with the dates, Andre?"

"Not the dates but the location. All these press junkets are taking place overseas. I was under the impression that Tyler and I would do the press junkets together here and then go overseas."

"We thought it would be more productive and cost efficient if we had Tyler doing the press here and you doing them overseas."

"You mean *you* thought," Andre said disparagingly. "You're still determined to keep me and Tyler apart."

William let out a small but detectable chuckle. "Keep you apart? If I'm not mistaken, Andre, you're due for a wedding soon. I don't have to try and do anything."

"Then why can't Tyler and I do the press junkets together? It makes better sense."

"I explained that to you, so please let Chrissie know if those dates work for you. I know you're in a hurry so I won't keep you any longer." William put his head down and started going through some other materials, giving Andre the sign that their conversation was over. But Andre was far from done.

"You may think that because you pushed Tyler in a corner and she chose her career over me that it means she also chose you, but you're wrong. Tyler wants independence but she doesn't want you. You'll never have her heart. Whether she knows it or not, she'll always love me and one day she will come back."

"Do you hear yourself, Mr. Andre Jackson? You're engaged to the mother of your child and talking about another woman coming back to you. Come back to what? A man that is tied down to a whole other life. Tyler is a star. She deserves better than that. I don't need you anywhere around her, poisoning her with that garbage."

"You're one to talk. You're a married man. You think Tyler needs to be with an over-the-hill egotistical actor who is having an ongoing midlife crisis? So you have no right to judge me or my situation."

"I'm only married on paper. My marriage has been over for a very long time. In another year my youngest child will be off to college and I will be getting a divorce. Once that happens, I have every intention on marrying Tyler. I promise you, she will be my wife. I have everything to offer her and you have nothing. After this movie Tyler will be a superstar, and she doesn't need to be caught up in your baby mama fiasco. The woman damn near killed herself trying to win you back. Nobody has time for that bullshit."

Andre's natural reaction was to punch William for making light of Chantal's near-death experience, but something in him knew that her suicide attempt was nothing more than a well-thought-out scheme to win him back. Deep down inside he harbored resentment toward her because he believed that Chantal's actions played a part in the demise of his relationship with Tyler.

"Understand something, William. It's none of your business what happened with Chantal."

"Yeah, but it is my business what happens to Tyler and that is my only concern. Personally I wish you and your ready-made family would go somewhere and never come back, but unfortunately I have no control over that. But I do have control over Tyler's career and I guarantee you'll never do another movie with her again."

"You pompous son of a bitch! I may not have Tyler, but neither will you. If she does marry you, it will be out of pity. So know one thing, when you're inside of her, she is wishing it is me." Andre stormed out and slammed the door so hard one of William's million-dollar paintings fell to the floor. Luckily, it was carpeted.

When Andre reached his car he started the ignition and the Ja Rule song "New York" was blasting from his radio. He didn't turn it down but instead got pumped up over the song about his hometown. "I need to get the fuck out of this bullshit Hollywood town and take my ass back to New York. That's where all the real niggas at. Motherfuckers out here don't appreciate no real nigga, they just want a house nigga that know they place. I'm done with all this. I'm taking it back to New York." Andre slammed on the gas and speeded home.

By the time Andre reached the front door, his anger over the conversation with William was still brewing. He wanted to put his fist through the wall but when he saw Chantal lying on the couch looking through bridal magazines he decided to take his frustrations out in another way. Without saying a word he lifted Chantal off the couch and pushed her up against the wall. He ripped off her lace boy shorts and thrust his dick inside of her from the back. He grabbed her hair and pulled it back as he pounded Chantal, making it nearly impossible for her to keep her balance. Her legs were becoming weak and her knees began to buckle under the intense pain but Andre wouldn't let go. Instead he pounded harder and Chantal had no choice but to scream for him to stop. "Andre, please stop, you're hurting me." But still Andre didn't say a word. He threw Chantal down on the floor and held her head down with her on hands and knees, as he continued twisting her back out. Chantal was still in pain but was now in a more comfortable position and she began enjoying the intensity of the sex act. Her moans of pleasure became louder and louder, and Andre was actually pissed that she was now enjoying what was supposed to be a punishment. He put all his body weight into two last strokes and then grabbed Chantal's hair, slid out and squirted in her mouth. Like the good whore Andre gave her credit for being, she swallowed all his cum like a champion. Before Chantal could finish tasting the last of Andre's semen, he had walked off and went straight in the shower. When she followed behind him, still in "ah" of the dick down he just put on her, he locked the bathroom door. It wasn't until then that Chantal realized that it wasn't a fuck of love or lust, but a fuck of hate.

When Andre woke up the next morning Chantal was sitting in the bed once again going through the bridal magazines. He couldn't believe that in just a few weeks she would be his wife. A woman that he didn't respect or even love for that matter. But if he couldn't marry the woman that had his heart then why not marry the woman who had his child? At least with Chantal she knew he would be fucking around and was used to it. The only woman he could imagine being true to was Tyler, and she made it clear they would never be together, so why keep torturing himself? But as he looked at Chantal he couldn't help but wonder if it was possible to turn a hooker into a housewife.

"Good morning, baby," Chantal beamed as she realized Andre was now up. "I was trying to get some ideas for the bridesmaids' dresses. Baby, the dress that has been designed for me is off the hook but I can't have my bridesmaids upstaging me, so I'm coming up with what I want them to wear. What do you think about this?" she asked, showing Andre a picture of a matronly dress.

"It's cool," he stated, not even glancing at the photo. "You need to pack your bags because we're going back to New York today."

"What, going back to New York? Baby, I have a wedding to plan," Chantal said in a panic-stricken voice.

"You can plan it in New York. We can have a nice wedding there."

"Hell, no, Andre. I've already hired a wedding planner and everything is underway. We are having our wedding in Beverly Hills. It is too late to make any changes and I'm not postponing this wedding." Andre could hear the determination in Chantal's voice. He couldn't believe that less than three months ago he gave a beautiful pink diamond ring to the love of his life and now he was marrying the baby mama from hell. He was almost tempted to elope with Chantal and get the whole thing over with, since their marriage would be no more sacred than Britney Spears's Las Vegas wedding to Jason Alexander, but he knew Chantal wasn't having it. This was her moment to floss in front of all her chickenhead friends and family members. The only joy Andre could imagine was the happiness the wedding would bring to Melanie.

"Fine, Chantal, we can have the wedding here, but as soon as we say 'I do,' we're out." The moment Andre left the room Chantal got on the phone with Shari.

"Girl, when are you getting here? You was supposed to be back in LA two days ago."

"Chantal, I told you that I had to make some babysitting arrangements for Alex. My mother has been straight tripping about keeping him. You know she think I'm rich now since I bought my new crib with some of Chris's money. Now she saying she needs to be paid for watching her own damn grandson. Mind you she doesn't even work. She would be sitting up in her house regardless if Alex was there or not."

"So what you doing? Trying to hire a nanny or something?"

"Nah, negotiating the price with my mama. At the end of the day she is blood and she'll look after him better than a stranger would."

Chantal let out a heavy sigh. "You and yo mama is crazy. But besides all that, I need you here with me."

"I should be there tomorrow morning. I'm working out the last few details because my mother wants a separate payment for transportation. Because of these outrageous gas prices she feels that's a whole other bill. With everything she's putting me through, I'm thinking maybe she should have negotiated my pay-off from Chris. I would've probably got an island out the deal."

"Girl, I still got those disgusting pictures of him locked away, so if you need that island, it's still up for negotiation." They both laughed. "But, Shari, I really need you," Chantal pleaded sincerely.

"What's the problem? You about to be Mrs. Andre Jackson. You should be on cloud nine right now."

"Andre is having seconds thoughts. I think it's finally hitting him that we're about to be married. He even tried to get me to go back to New York today, saying we could have our wedding there. I shut that down on the spot, but the point is I know he doesn't want to marry me."

"Then maybe you should cancel the wedding, Chantal. You don't want to marry a man who doesn't want to marry you."

Chantal looked at the receiver with eyes twitching. She knew Shari didn't say what she thought she heard. "Excuse me, Shari, I think we have a bad reception because I thought I heard something like 'cancel the wedding.' But that couldn't have come from you?"

"Stop tripping, Chantal, I'm dead-ass serious. This whole housewife lifestyle you're longing for may not be all what you imagined it would be. Sometimes you have to know when to let go."

"I know you mean well, but this is it for me. I was so desperate to hold on to Andre I had to plot a fake suicide attempt. You know I could've really killed myself behind that shit. Luckily, Andre found me in time. The ugly scars I have on my wrists was all in the name of love. Andre is everything to me. He might be reluctant right now about marrying me, but I'll be such a wonderful wife that he'll forget about his initial hesitation. The important thing is making sure I get him down the aisle. That's why I need you here, Shari. I'm more confident when I know you're watching my back."

"You don't ever have to worry about that, Chantal. If you're determined to marry Andre then I will do whatever you need to make that happen."

"I knew you wouldn't let me down, Shari, so get yo ass here." They both laughed and Chantal instantly felt better.

T-Roc was still heated about how close he had come to getting everything he wanted, and then Andre came in and took it all away. He had his spies working overtime trying to find some explosive dirt on Andre. After his run-in with Tyler there was no question in his mind that his hold on her was intact. T-Roc felt he and Tyler would be together now if he had gotten the part in *Angel*. William apologized profusely for the mix-up but that wasn't enough. He was losing ground at making a romantic connection with Tyler. The only solace he found was in the fact that Andre's relationship with her was history. T-Roc's expectations were unbroken. William promised to cast him in his next movie starring Tyler, which would begin filming in the next few months. He wanted to make sure there were no obstacles this time, and decided it would be in his best interest to keep Chrissie as an ally.

"What do you want?" Chrissie asked nastily, even though she was secretly happy to see T-Roc.

"You," he answered as he pulled out the flowers he was holding behind his back. Chrissie unintentionally let a huge smile spread across her face. She didn't want to let on how much she missed the man who had humiliated her so. As Chrissie let T-Roc in and he handed her the bouquet, it dawned on her that no one had given her flowers in so long and she wondered if she even had a vase to put them in. Her next dilemma was figuring out what T-Roc was up to.

"Chrissie, I know how upset you are at me, but I was hoping we could call a truce."

"Truce, that's what the roses are for?"

"That, and because I miss you." Chrissie eyed T-Roc suspiciously. He knew that he would have to lay on the charm thick in order to regain her confidence. "Listen, Chrissie, I want to come clean to you about a few things."

"What has brought about this sudden urge to purge yourself?"

"Shame," he stated. Chrissie didn't even know that was an emotion T-Roc was capable of feeling. "Chrissie, I was wrong for the way I treated you. You're a wonderful woman and you deserve so much better than the way I've behaved towards you." T-Roc then lowered his head as if he was too embarrassed and ashamed to look at her. His little charade was essentially working. Chrissie was being taken in by his so-called profession of the truth.

"T-Roc, why did you use me and humiliate me the way that you did?"

"I don't know if you know how everything went down with me and Tyler in the past, but after it ended she left me crushed. I was never given the opportunity to express my feelings to her. Then when I ran into her after so long she didn't even acknowledge me in front of her so-called mentor, the almighty William Donovan. Tyler had once again shitted on me. When I had the chance to break into movies and star opposite her I thought this was my opportunity to prove she made a mistake by breaking things off with me. But once again Tyler had the last laugh. The part of Damian should've been mine. Andre couldn't have been better than me, but I know Tyler vetoed it. Chrissie, all I wanted was to seize my opening and because it wasn't given to me I decided to take it. Since you were the closest person to Tyler, I used you to get what I wanted," he admitted, now standing face-to-face with Chrissie.

"Seize what opening? Winning Tyler back or grasping on to your dream role?"

"I don't want Tyler back," T-Roc lied. "We had our moment but she is way too screwed up for me. I wish her well but I have no interest in revisiting the past. All I wanted was my chance to break into film, which I doubt will even happen."

"That's not true, T-Roc. William told me himself that you were talented. You will have your moment to shine on the big screen."

"William did promise to cast me in his next movie starring opposite Tyler, but I have my misgivings that she will let that happen."

"What do you mean?"

"What do you think I mean, Chrissie? As soon as William presents the idea to her she will immediately shut it down. I know there are other movies but William is the hottest director right now, and to star in a movie of his would give me the stamp of approval needed to be taken seriously in this business." Chrissie stood, nodding her head, understanding and agreeing with what T-Roc was saying. He knew that his victim act was paying off.

"I tell you what, T-Roc. I'll have a conversation with Tyler, you know, put in a good word for you."

"You would do that for me, Chrissie?" he asked, pretending to sound shocked.

"Of course, everyone deserves to pursue their dreams, including gazillionaires like yourself," she said, laughing.

"Chrissie, you're the best." T-Roc slowly moved in and gently slid his tongue into Chrissie's inviting mouth. Her body melted in his arms in anticipation of the foreplay to come. "I'm so sorry, I shouldn't have kissed you," T-Roc said as he stepped away from Chrissie.

"No, don't be sorry."

"I am. After the way I treated you I'm sure you never want me to touch you again. Please forgive me. You just looked so beautiful standing there. You know how much I love the way your curls frame your face," T-Roc said, as he stroked her cheek. Chrissie rubbed the side of her face against his hand, loving his touch.

"It's really okay. Your lips, your touch made me realize just how much I miss you."

"I feel the exact same way, but I'm no good for you. I have to stop being selfish and do the right thing for once in my life. That means no matter how much it's killing me, I have to give you up." T-Roc was now beginning to believe his own lie-filled sermon. "Chrissie, I hope we can at least still be friends. You're the most amazing woman I've ever met."

"Of course we can be friends, but I want so much more. You're too hard on yourself T-Roc. Everyone makes mistakes. We can make this work."

"I want to believe you, but I have so much growing up to do. If and when we can ever have a real relationship I want to come at you correct. Until then, I'm just grateful that you're willing to be my friend." T-Roc gave Chrissie a soft peck on the lips and left.

A tear rolled down Chrissie's face as she stood there for a few minutes thinking that T-Roc was the most incredible man she had ever met and the best lover.

Down the Aisle

Tyler sat in William's office, dreading the idea of discussing any business with him this early in the morning. She wished she could crawl back in bed and sleep all her pain away. "You know how I hate morning meetings, but yet that seems to be when they are all scheduled," Tyler complained.

"It is part of the business, so get used to it darling," William said with an irritating grin on his face, one she was seriously considering smacking off. But soon she would be away from him and all the other Hollywood honchos. Tyler was leaving in a couple days to take a much-needed two-week vacation at the exclusive island of Mustique. By the time she returned, she would've missed the well-publicized wedding of Andre Jackson and Chantal Morgan and hopefully the honeymoon. Ideally, she wanted to be home right now, packing for her adventure, instead of discussing work with William.

"William, you know I'm leaving in a couple of days. Can't we discuss business when I get back? I'll be well rested and more inclined to listen to any new movie ideas."

"Listen kiddo, we have to keep you working so you can continue to afford vacations like the one you're about to take. Besides the projects you already have lined up, I want you to read a script that I specifically wrote for you and T-Roc. This vehicle is an urban version of *Pretty Woman*."

"Why are you writing a movie for T-Roc?"

"Because he is actually a damn good actor and I worked out something with his agent after we had to renege on our agreement, when Andre decided to complete *Angel*. I want to start filming in the summer after you've completed your next movie. We're expecting this film to take you way over the top."

"I'm sure T-Roc is pleased with this, but you're going to have to find yourself a new leading lady. I'm not doing a movie with T-Roc," Tyler said defiantly.

"Why not?"

"Where do I start? For one T-Roc's ego wouldn't allow for anyone else to be on the screen with him."

"You were going to work with him on *Angel*."

"Yeah, because we were desperate and I really didn't have a choice."

"You don't have a choice this time, either," William said sharply.

"Excuse me, I don't think I heard you correctly," Tyler responded with a clear threat in her voice.

William could sense his approach wasn't working and opted to go another route. "Tyler, listen, you don't have to do anything you don't want. This script is just so damn good and no one can play the part but you. Just please read over it and if you don't want T-Roc, we'll consider someone else. I know you'll be excited about the concept."

"That sounds fine to me, I'll read the script—" Before Tyler could complete her sentence she let out a deep breath and put her hand to her head as if in pain.

"Are you okay, Tyler?" William asked, full of concern.

"Yeah, I just felt a little dizzy for a minute. See, I told you I need a vacation. All this work and no sleep is throwing my whole body out of whack."

"Darling, take the script with you, or better yet I can bring it with me when I join you on vacation."

"Cute, William, you know I need this time to be alone. That means no visitors, including you. I will take the script and read it between massages and facials." Tyler grabbed the papers and gave William a kiss on the cheek before leaving. While walking to her car she couldn't help but take note of how light-headed she felt.

Chantal was beyond psyched about her pending marriage. For the last few weeks she and Shari had gone over every detail and in a very short time she had planned a magnificent wedding. Now it all came down to her and the perfect accessory.

"You look fierce in that dress," Shari said as she held up the long train on Chantal's custom-designed Vera Wang wedding gown.

"Isn't it beautiful? I feel like a princess." Chantal did a slight turn in the floor-length, three-sided mirror, relishing her beauty. "In a couple of days I will be Mrs. Andre Jackson. All my hard work is finally going to pay off. I will be in that elite crew of women who turned being a jump-off, then baby mama to full-fledged wife. I must say I'm very proud of myself."

"Yeah, Chantal, you went from being hooker to housewife. I have to give you props. Honestly, I didn't think it was possible, but once again you have proven me and everybody else wrong. Let's all bow down to the Queen." Shari got on bended knee as if bowing down to Chantal.

"Girl, stand up, before we read in *Us Weekly* that I'm some sort of tyrant that makes her friends bow down and worship her."

"Well, isn't that what you want? To be the queen of the world?"

"Of course, but that's our secret," Chantal squealed as she ran her hands down her beaded dress.

"So what's up with Andre's bachelor party? Are all his boys flying in for one last big blast before he is no longer a single man?"

"Believe it or not, Andre isn't having a big blowout. I think a couple of his friends are taking him out for dinner and drinks, nothing too spectacular."

"What? Party boy Andre is playing low? Surprise, surprise, maybe this whole family thing is mellowing him out."

"I hope so. After the wedding me, him, and Melanie are going to Fiji for our honeymoon and family vacation. Maybe we can start working on a little brother for Melanie."

"That's a perfect idea. My mother always told me that when your child turns three or four it's time to start working on the next one. Men start losing interest around that age and you have to pop out another one to keep the momentum going. Andre will definitely be a happy camper if you give him a little man."

"My sentiments exactly. I have the million-dollar daughter. Now it's time to give him the future billion-dollar son," she said with a mischievous smile while taking off her wedding dress.

"Don't take off your dress just yet. I want to take a good look at you before you become Mrs. Andre Jackson." Both ladies turned around at the exact time to see who was invading their privacy.

"What are you doing here?" Chantal asked in a stunned tone.

"I wanted to personally congratulate you on your victory and thank you," T-Roc said, clapping his hands. "You truly are a fighter, Chantal. Who knew with all of your scheming that you would finally get the brass ring?"

"T-Roc, are you here to congratulate me or threaten to expose some of the secrets we share?"

"Chantal, I'm on your side. Plus why do I need to tell Andre what he already knows about you? That you're a lying, manipulative, but very resourceful woman, all the qualities that I admire in the opposite sex. Besides, you're doing me a favor."

"What favor is that?"

"Marrying Andre, of course. With him out the way I have a chance with Tyler."

"What is it with you men and this Tyler Blake bitch? She's totally overrated, you know."

"My beautiful Chantal, you'll never understand, but then again why should you, you're not a man. But don't worry your pretty head. You just make sure you get Andre down that aisle. It would be a shame if you slit your wrists in vain." Chantal wasn't sure if she wanted to cry or throw her shoe so the heel would land directly in T-Roc's evil eyes. The one thing she was sure of was that making the porno tape of T-Roc was the best decision she had ever made. Chantal had a feeling that in the future she would have to use her weapon to keep him on a short leash. But now wasn't the time to let all be known.

"Thanks for the visit, T-Roc. I would invite you to the wedding but I'm afraid if you came no one else would show up. You're more than welcome to send a gift though. You know my taste in presents, six figures and up."

"Once again, congratulations. I truly wish you the best, Chantal. By the way I've already given you a gift. If it wasn't for me, none of this would be possible." T-Roc disappeared just as quickly as he showed up.

"What did he mean by that?" Chantal asked Shari as if she knew the answer.

"I don't know. I'm still in awe that the infamous T-Roc was right in front of my face a minute ago. He looks even better in person."

"Just remember the most evil things come in the most beautiful packages." Chantal couldn't help but turn and admire herself in the mirror.

As the big day neared, Andre's nerves were getting the best of him. From the moment he proposed till now all seemed like a nightmarish blur. He never expected that his split-second of payback against Tyler would turn into a lifelong commitment with Chantal.

"Man, I can't believe you really about to get married. I never thought I would see you walking down the aisle," Andre's best man, Kenny, said, shaking his head in denial.

"Who you telling? I still wouldn't be convinced if it wasn't for all these damn high-ass bills for this wedding that keeps coming to me. Chantal sure can break the bank. She spent a hundred grand on her wedding dress alone."

"The shit made of diamonds or something? Man, what have you gotten yourself into with that broad?"

"I'm trying to figure it out myself. Chantal was definitely not the woman I imagined marrying. When I first told my mom she actually hung up on me. When I called her back she said whoever the impostor was on the other end of the phone she was going to call the police if they didn't stop calling. When I told her to stop playing and that it was her son, she barked that there was no way she raised an idiot and whatever bad drugs I was on I had to stop taking them immediately."

"Your mom came at you like that?"

"Damn sure did, and she wasn't playing. She swears up and down that Chantal must have put some sort of voodoo on me because there is no way I could want to marry a woman like her. But it has nothing to do with voodoo. Between you and me, I asked Chantal to marry me out of spite."

"Spite, what you mean?"

"I was at the wrap party with Chantal, and Tyler sashayed in there with that asshole William Donovan. They were going at each other like I wasn't even in the room. Honestly, man, if I had a gun I would've put a bullet through both of their heads. Since I couldn't shoot her with a gun I shot her with my mouth. When I proposed to Chantal I saw death across Tyler's face, and for that moment I felt vindicated. Unfortunately, the very next moment I wanted to take the whole thing back, but it was too late."

"Man it ain't never too late to change your mind, especially when it comes to standing before God and everyone else vowing to dedicate the rest of your life to someone. You better cancel this shit now before it blows up in your face."

"I already tried, but Chantal being the talented schemer she is has made this wedding front-page news. And besides that, Melanie's heart is set that her mommy and daddy marry; it would crush her if I backed out now."

"It's going to break your heart waking up every day with a woman you don't love. Are you sure there is no chance for you and Tyler?"

"Positive. I practically begged her to take me back but she refused. She is so dedicated to her career and William knows that. He dangled that over her head to do exactly what he wanted her to do. It makes me sick every time I think about it. Do you know he is planning on getting a divorce next year and then marrying Tyler?" Andre's whole face wrinkled up in agony as he spoke those words. "I have to get the fuck out of this town because these people are on a whole other level with they bullshit. At least in my world when they come at you, you see them coming. These cold motherfuckers out here come from the back and fuck you straight in the ass with no lubricant or nothing, just straight raw dawg. All us industry cats running around like we gangsters; up here in Hollywood is where the real gangsters reside. You feel me?"

"Damn nigga, they got you out your element. It's definitely time to get back to New York where your people at. Don't get me wrong, I can definitely see you and Tyler as this Hollywood power couple but you don't need all this stress. If shorty wants to be a part of this fake-ass bullshit then let her live. Chantal may be a little over the top but she does have your seed and she definitely will always have your back. You never know, she might surprise us all and make one hell of a housewife, but this Hollywood shit is dead. You don't need them. Your paper is long."

Andre listened intently to every word that was coming out of Kenny's mouth but the point was being lost in translation. His mind and heart were somewhere else. He thought that by now the pain of losing Tyler would've passed and it wouldn't hurt so badly. He reflected on a conversation he had with his father when he was twenty-one and sowing his wild oats. His father had looked at him seriously and said, "Son, I know you're out here enjoying all these ladies and breaking hearts along the way, but remember something. One day you will meet a woman that you'll fall deeply in love with and when you do, it will be the most powerful feeling in the world. The love you will have for her will be ten times greater than all the love she has for you, and the reason being is because God made man first. So watch yourself because all the hearts you break combined still won't be able to touch the pain you will feel after that one woman breaks yours." After Andre's father made that statement he laughed for an hour straight. He never believed that any woman would ever have his heart and surely not break it. Now, here he was, a broken man. Marrying a woman he didn't even love, let alone like, all to prove something. Andre had made his bed, now he had to lie in it.

"You look pale. Is everything okay?" Chrissie asked while helping Tyler pack for her trip.

"I think I'm coming down with the flu or something. I'm going to take some medicine before I leave. I'll be fine."

"What time is your flight?"

"First thing in the morning. I was actually supposed to leave today but I had a last minute emergency that I needed to handle."

Chrissie paused for a moment and observed her best friend. It was killing her that Tyler was in so much pain. Even though she was trying to remain stoic, the heartache was clearly written on her face. "It must be difficult knowing that Andre's wedding is tomorrow. You're handling it well," Chrissie said, while rubbing Tyler's back, trying to comfort her.

"You have no idea, Chrissie. I'll just be happy when it's all over with," she said, knowing that even then the throbbing of her heart wouldn't ease; if anything it would intensify. The reality of them being married would make everything official and there would be no turning back.

"Honey, it will be soon. When you get back, Andre will be a distant memory. You'll be back to work on a new movie and you won't have time to even think about Andre Jackson. You'll be fine, I promise."

"I hope so, but I'm not really looking forward to work, either."

"Why? You love doing movies."

"The other day when I was in William's office he gave me a script to look over. It's a vehicle that he wants me and T-Roc to do together, as if I would ever do a movie with T-Roc."

"For a minute he was going to replace Andre in *Angel.*"

"As I explained to William, we didn't have any other options. I wasn't about to let the movie go down the toilet because of my disgust for T-Roc. This is different. We can find someone else to star opposite me. If not, William can get himself a new leading lady."

"You don't mean that—you love working with William."

"I do, but not enough to deal with that narcissistic T-Roc."

"Tyler, I think you're being too hard on T-Roc. I don't think he's a bad as you think."

"Excuse me?" Tyler spit out, surprised Chrissie was defending him, especially since she knew their past.

"All I'm saying is that everyone deserves a second chance, Tyler."

"How can you defend that monster?"

"His cousin Ian who threw you down the stairs while you were pregnant is the monster, not T-Roc. You should stop blaming him for that."

"How can I not? If it wasn't for T-Roc trying to do everything in his power to destroy my relationship with Ian, none of that would've happened. I shouldn't have to explain any of this to you, Chrissie you were there. You know how T-Roc almost ruined my life."

"I'm sorry, Tyler. T-Roc did put you through a lot but we al make mistakes, even you. For the short period of time I spent with T-Roc when we thought he would replace Andre, he seemed like a different person."

"Different how?"

"More grounded and compassionate."

"You got all that from a couple of conversations with T-Roc' Well, no one ever disputed that he is charming as hell. Once you get past all that charm, if you look a little closer you'll see the devi horns sprouting from his head."

"Sweetie, listen, I know you're already feeling bad over Andre and I don't want to upset you any further. All I ask is that you do me a favor."

"Anything. You're my best friend."

"Just consider giving T-Roc a chance. William really believes in him and you even said he was a good actor."

"Fine, Chrissie, I'll consider doing this movie with T-Roc bu why do you care so much? It's not like T-Roc is a friend of yours,' Tyler said, confused by Chrissie's request.

"I just know how it feels to want something and not be given the opportunity to have it. Acting seems to be important to T-Ro and it wouldn't be fair for you to take his chance away from him Tyler."

"Maybe you're right. I've never thought about it like that before William gave me my big break. Why shouldn't T-Roc have his?"

"I knew you would understand, Tyler, that's what makes you so special. You know I want to stay and talk but I have a meeting that can't wait. Are you going to be okay? I can come back after finish up."

"No, I'll be fine. I'm going to take a long hot shower and turn in early. I don't want to oversleep and miss my flight. I'll call you when I get there. Thanks for all your support, Chrissie." The two women locked in a deep embrace before Chrissie walked out of the bedroom, giving Tyler the opportunity to check on what had been occupying her mind after Chrissie showed up unexpectedly. When she finally heard her front door slam she ran in the bathroom and picked up her pregnancy test. Like she expected, she was with child. She had to be at least three months pregnant since that was the last time she had sex with Andre or any man for that matter. She couldn't believe she was carrying Andre's baby. Between work and all the other stress in her life she didn't even notice that she hadn't had a period in months. Tyler wanted to be happy that she was carrying the child of the man that she loved, but that same man was engaged and due to walk down the aisle in less than twenty-four hours. She sat on her bed and studied the test as if the blue line would somehow disappear if she stared long enough. But then she had to admit to herself that she didn't want it to change. Inside she was bubbling over with joy at the thought of having a baby with Andre. She was in love with him and having his child would only validate that.

As much as Tyler wanted to believe that Andre would be happy about the baby, she was far from sure. She had treated him badly, and dismissed him as if she could care less. He called her cold and heartless and maybe he still felt that way. But Tyler decided she wouldn't know for sure unless she went to him and told him she still loved him. If he reciprocated the feelings, only then would she tell him about the baby she was carrying. If he turned her away then she would have an abortion and he would never know about it. The last thing Tyler wanted was for Andre to take her back out of pity or obligation because she was pregnant. Either they would be together out of true love or they wouldn't be to-gether at all.

Chantal was standing in the doorway tapping her foot, becoming impatient with Shari. She was in the final stages of becoming Mrs.

Andre Jackson and her diva instincts were in full swing. "Shari, you ready? All the girls are at the hotel waiting for us."

"Chantal, can you wait a minute? I'm trying to get all your shit together since we're not coming back here tonight. Next time you walk through these doors you'll be Chantal Jackson."

Chantal looked around the master bedroom smiling about how far she had come in life. No longer would Andre be twisting her out on the Frette sheets as his baby mama/girlfriend—she would now be his wife. To Chantal that made all the difference in the world. She could now hold her head up high because she had come full circle.

"Chantal, I said 'Can you please grab this bag before everything falls out?'" Shari screamed. "What are you daydreaming about?"

"I'm sorry, girl, my mind was somewhere else."

"All right cool, that's obvious but can you get the bag?" Chantal grabbed the bag as she and Shari headed downstairs. From the top of the winding staircase, Chantal could see her future husband talking to his best man, Kenny. Chantal couldn't help but to chuckle at the sight of Kenny. He was the same guy who used to play her to the left, like he was better than her because he was a Harvard graduate and some big-time lawyer.

Chantal never forgot when she overheard Andre telling Kenny she was pregnant and he said, "You can't make every pretty bitch your baby mother. The dumb ones like Chantal you have to fuck them and send them home. The last thing you want is to get jammed up with a chick who believes having a master's degree in fucking and sucking is the only form of education necessary to achieve great career heights." *Well, look at me now—who is the dumb fuck? Surely not me. This time tomorrow you'll be calling me Mrs. Jackson. So take that you bitch-ass nigga,* Chantal said to herself.

"Hi, baby," Chantal cooed as she gave Andre a kiss on the lips. "Hello, Kenny, it's so nice to see you again," she lied and said. "You remember my friend Shari." Kenny nodded his head yes and shook Shari's hand.

"So you're on the way to the hotel?" Andre asked, trying to break up the tension in the room.

"Yeah, all my ladies are waiting for me in the penthouse suite. All of us are going to get pampered, so I'll be looking flawless for my new husband on our wedding day. What you getting into tonight?"

"Just the bed. I want to be well rested for our big day. Is Melanie staying with you tonight or is she still with your parents?"

"With my parents—their room is right down the hall from mine. Wait till you see our little angel all done up. She's going to look beautiful, just like her mother." Andre smiled, remembering that being modest was never one of Chantal's strong points. Shari and Chantal said their good-byes and left to get spoiled on Andre's tab.

"Man, that Chantal is something else. She hasn't changed a bit," Kenny said as he walked over to the bar and poured himself a drink.

"You don't have to tell me, but if you can't beat them join 'em."

"You up to hitting a strip club for old times' sake?"

"Nah, man, I'm going to bed," Andre said as he lay back on the couch.

"You serious? I thought you said that shit to appease Chantal. Your last night of being a single man you want to spend it in the bed asleep? You better get out this house and get your rocks off in peace one last time."

"Maybe I'm getting old, but I have no interest. I'm going to cook myself a delicious meal and then chill out. You're welcome to join me."

"Negro please, I'm single and horny. Working sixty-hour weeks, I never have an opportunity to do me, or get done. I'm about to go out here and find me a fine-ass beach bunny and get some. Hopefully, I'll get so lucky that next time you see me we'll be at the altar."

"I feel you. Try not to have too much fun. I would hate to lose my best friend the night before my wedding."

After Kenny left, Andre sat in front of the fireplace reflecting on his life and what his future would be like. He was so lost in his thoughts that he almost didn't hear the front doorbell. Just as he was about to call out to his maid he realized he'd let her go home early today. He couldn't imagine who was ringing his doorbell at this time of night but figured it was probably a defeated Kenny coming back home.

"Back already?" Andre said as he opened the front door. His heart instantly felt as if it was about to jump out of his chest and the palms of his hands became sweaty.

"No, I've actually been gone for quite a while," Tyler said with a nervous smile spread across her face. Part of her wanted to turn around, scared of the rejection that Andre might greet her with, but it was too late.

"Tyler, what are you doing here?"

"Do you want me to leave?" she asked, wanting to get the dismissal over with.

"No, I'm just surprised to see you. Please come in." Andre let Tyler inside and couldn't decide whether he should have the conversation right there in the foyer or invite her to have a seat in the living room. He decided to let her set the pace.

"Do you have a minute to talk, or am I intruding?"

"Actually I'm home alone. Would you like to have a seat?"

"Thank you, that would be nice." Tyler could now feel a light layer of sweat engulfing her body and hoped her nervousness wasn't being detected by Andre.

"Would you like a glass of champagne? I know it's your favorite," Andre offered, starting to warm up to the idea of having Tyler close to him after so many months.

"No thank you, I'll have a glass of mineral water." Andre was surprised by Tyler's request but granted it all the same. "I know you're probably wondering why I'm here, especially since tomorrow is your wedding day, but I had to get a few things off my chest before . . ." Tyler paused, not able to get her thoughts together.

"Before what, Tyler?"

"Maybe I shouldn't have come, Andre. This feels all wrong." As Tyler stood up to leave, Andre gently put his hand on her arm.

"Don't leave. I want to hear what you came to say."

"That's the thing I don't remember. Maybe I'm just nervous or scared, but everything I practiced to say has left my mind."

"Well, maybe you shouldn't try to remember and just speak from your heart." Tyler gazed down at the marble floor trying to muster up the strength to let down her guard and pour her heart out to Andre. She knew this would be her last chance to get the love of her life back, but fear was clouding her judgment. Tyler reasoned this wasn't the moment to waver on her decision and to go full-speed ahead. Tyler locked eyes with Andre before she slowly spoke her words. His almond-shaped eyes were drawing her in and all she wanted to do was touch his smooth chocolate skin.

"Andre, I don't want to let you go. I've been miserable since the day you left my life and my heart yearns for you to come back to me." Tyler couldn't believe that she had put her feelings out in the open that way; now Andre had all the power to either embrace her or discard her. He began walking back and forth digesting what she just said. He almost wanted to ask her to repeat her words just to make sure he heard her correctly. Andre was now feeling hot and restless in his button-up shirt. He didn't know if it was discomfort or lust but rationalized it was a combination of both. But he needed to stay calm because he still felt he needed to play his cards close to his chest. He wasn't sure if Tyler just wanted to see if she could still get him back the day before his wedding or if she was she being sincere.

"I'm a little shocked by what you just said. You say your heart yearns for me to come back to you, but you're the one who left me. I tried to get you back not once, not twice, but numerous times. You shut me down at every turn. I thought you were the one I would be walking down the aisle with but you chose your career over me. Now, you tell me that you still love me and you want me back. How am I supposed to believe you? This could be you just having a moment of weakness, and tomorrow you can put that same wall back up between us."

"I know you have no reason to believe that my feelings are sincere, but look in my eyes. These eyes are full of love and it's only for you. I was scared of love for so long and the pain that it brings, but I don't want to live in fear anymore. The idea of letting some other woman marry the man that I truly believe is my soul mate is too much for me to bear. I wouldn't have been able to live with myself if I didn't at least try to get you back."

"Tyler, everything you're saying is what I wanted to hear for so long." Andre looked up at the vaulted ceilings clenching his fist. "Why now, the day before my wedding, would you come here and put all this on me? If I had my way we would be married right now and you would be pregnant with my child, but that's not the case. My family, friends, and most importantly, my daughter is expecting me to marry Chantal tomorrow. If it wasn't for the fact I would crush Melanie's heart, I would run off with you right now, Tyler, but honestly I don't trust you. I don't trust you with my heart or my love."

"I know I don't have anyone to blame for that but myself, but Andre I do love you and I always will. I hope that you will be happy and maybe one day you'll forgive me for messing everything up between us." Tyler turned and walked away, devastated by Andre's rebuff. She knew the odds were stacked against her when she decided to divulge all of her feelings to him, but actually facing the rejection head on was killing her inside. As Tyler reached to open the door she felt Andre's strong hand on her shoulder.

"Can you promise that you'll be in this with me to the very end, no turning your back on me to chase a bigger dream?"

Tyler turned to Andre with big tears in her eyes. "You are my biggest dream," she whispered, choking back tears. Andre's long arms wrapped around Tyler's petite body and he lifted her up and carried her back in the living room where he placed her on the fur rug in front of the fireplace. He pulled her white winter cashmere sweater over her head and ran his fingers over her full breasts firmly cupped in her satin bra. With ease he pulled off her boots and jeans and freed the silky skin he had craved to touch again for so long. Andre swiftly stepped out of his clothes to glide inside of the woman he desired to make love to. Once his penis entered her wetness, they rocked back and forth in a steady rhythm that only lovers that were made for each other could do.

"I'll never let you go again. I belong to you."

"Oh baby, I wouldn't let you go even if you wanted to." Andre felt as if he couldn't go deep enough as Tyler's juices consumed his very being. He knew this was the woman he was destined to spend the rest of his life with.

Chantal was standing in the building that represented her new future. Everything that happened in the past was of no consequence. Today was the beginning of the rest of her life. Growing up in the projects of Southside Chicago, where she stood right now was said to be the impossible. There always seemed to be limits put upon her dreams. While most of her homegirls' biggest ambitions were to date the local drug dealer, Chantal had always wanted more. She came into the world believing she was special and deserved the best in life. When her friends would brag about a new pair of shoes some guy bought them, Chantal felt a guy should buy her the whole store. It wasn't just because she was the prettiest girl in her neighborhood and school, but she was more beautiful than any star on television and she didn't have their money to buy the illusion. Her beauty was God-given and her mother always told her how blessed she was. She stressed the importance of not using her looks for evil, which she considered to be for selfish material gain. That never sat right with Chantal; she often said to her mother, "What was the sense of God blessing me with such a gorgeous face and body if I can't use it to my advantage?"

Chantal thought back to how her mother read the Bible every morning at the breakfast table. Up until the very end, Mrs. Morgan continued to try and instill morals into her willful daughter. She would bribe Chantal to go to church every Sunday by promising her a new outfit or buying her something that she knew they couldn't afford. But one day that was no longer enough for Chantal and she ended that abruptly. Mrs. Morgan knocked on Chantal's bedroom door and she was just lying in bed staring at the wall. First her mother thought she wasn't feeling well until Chantal said, "Why should I waste my time and best clothes to go to a place where I'll never meet my husband. Plus people that go to church are the biggest sinners anyway." With that, Chantal put the covers over her face and waited for her mother to close the door. From that day on Chantal went into full-blown rebellion.

Chantal had made it clear to her parents that her sole goal in life was to marry a rich powerful man who would spoil her like the star she was supposed to be. She was tired of seeing her parents struggle all their lives barely making ends meet. It seemed like yesterday that she was sitting on the school bus admiring a picture of a very wealthy mogul whose face was splashed across the front cover of a magazine with the headline KING OF NEW YORK. That photo and inside story was her motivation to leave the hood behind and seek the jet-set life she craved.

The road Chantal traveled to get here definitely wasn't an easy one. When she arrived in New York with the $7,000 she stole from her mother, she soon realized that would only get her so far. After renting a hole in the wall room on a weekly basis she immediately started hitting the club scene in the heart of the city. One night while seductively gyrating in the middle of the dance floor she caught the eye of a well-known video music director. He promised that if she listened to his advice he would make her a music video queen. Even then Chantal thought prancing around in videos was beneath her, but she knew it would get her within touching distance of all the music bigwigs. In her mind she felt that was all she needed; once the music industry honchos got an eyeful of her, one of them was bound to put a huge rock on her finger. The next day she called the director and he kept his word. Now seven years later she was about to marry the most powerful man in the music industry. Who said that dreams never come true?

"Chantal, I can't believe today is the big day! Girl, I'm about to start crying like I'm getting married," Shari said under sniffles, bringing Chantal out of her deep thoughts of the past.

"Shari, this has to be the happiest day of my life. All my dreams are about to come true. If someone would have told me ten years ago that I would be getting married at a church on Rodeo Drive in Beverly Hills I would've burst out laughing, but look at me. Today that is exactly what is about to happen. I have my best friend by my side, my beautiful little girl, and the man I love. My parents might have thought I was a major screwup but I've made them proud. I've landed the biggest catch of them all."

"Yeah, you have." Shari nodded in agreement. Both women looked around at the thousands of flowers and the beautifully decorated church. It was of the caliber to make even Star Jones second-guess her wedding planner. "Listen, Cinderella, it's time for us to get you dressed and ready for the momentous occasion. In a couple of hours this church will be filled to capacity and it will be your moment to shine."

Kenny entered Andre's house close to ten o'clock in the morning still replaying his late-night rendezvous with two buxom twins. Although they wanted to keep the party going, and so did he, Kenny was determined to be at his best friend's side for his wedding day. Right when he was about to skip up the stairs and take a quick shower he was startled when he saw what looked like two bodies wrapped around each other in the living room. As he walked closer, trying to focus on the image, he felt arousal at the outline of a woman's glistening body peeking from the blanket.

He still couldn't see her face but soon realized that the well-defined man's body was no other than Andre's. Kenny couldn't help but say out loud, "That's my man. You decided to get some before taking the plunge." Kenny's thunderous mouth instantly woke up Andre and he saw that Tyler was still sleep.

"Man, keep it down!" Andre demanded, while making sure the blanket covered Tyler's naked body, and he grabbed his boxer shorts.

"Who is that?" Kenny asked, trying to get a better view of the sleeping woman. Andre grabbed Kenny's arm and led him into his study. Andre didn't say another word until they reached the destination and he closed the door behind them. "Man, you still didn't answer my question. Who is that fine piece of ass lying on your living room floor?" Andre gave Kenny an intense glare that sent chills down his spine. "Did I say something wrong?" Kenny said, feeling uncomfortable with the look Andre was giving him.

"That woman you're talking about is my future wife."

"What? I know the pussy might have been good but damn, man. Your future wife is waiting for you at the church." Andre wanted to punch Kenny in his mouth because he felt as if he was disrespecting Tyler in some way, but then he also knew that Kenny thought the woman in his living room was just some random chick.

"Listen, Kenny, that woman in the living room is Tyler."

"Tyler Blake, the movie star? Stop playing, man." Kenny made a gesture as if he was about to leave the study and go back to the living room to drool over the sleeping starlet.

"Where the fuck do you think you're going?" Andre asked, stunned by Kenny's actions.

"I have to go see for myself. There is no way that Tyler Blake is lying on your living room floor butt-ass naked." Andre grabbed Kenny's arm with serious intent.

"Man, if you don't stop saying her name in the same sentence as some disrespectable shit we gon have a problem. No, my fault, you're going to have a problem," he warned.

"My bad—I didn't realize. I'm just so amped right now. I know you said you dated her but I must have never told you that I have a crush on her." Andre rolled his eyes and started shaking his head, not believing that his childhood best friend was acting like a straight-up groupie right now.

"I more than dated her, Kenny. If you get your head out your ass you'll remember that just last night I told you I had asked her to marry me."

"Yeah, you did tell me that. I guess I have selective amnesia. Now I can't even fantasize about her no more. So what now, you guys are back together? When did all this happen?"

"It's a long complicated story, but the point is we're in love and we're getting married."

"What about Chantal? You know I'm not a big fan of hers but man she is going to be devastated."

"I know, and Melanie she's going to take it really hard. But I have the chance to be with the woman I truly love. This is the rest of my life we're talking about." Andre sat on top of his cherry wood desk and stared at the picture of him with Chantal and Melanie. They did look picture-perfect but his heart wasn't there; it belonged to Tyler. Deep down inside, Andre believed in the future he could make Melanie understand that she would always be his angel but things just didn't work out between her parents.

"I totally understand. I didn't think you should've gotten engaged to Chantal in the first place. The timing is just so bad. You actually are going to leave that girl at the altar?"

"I'm so torn right now, Kenny, but I do know I won't be marrying Chantal today or any other day. I need to ask you to do me a favor and step up to the plate."

"Hell no! Don't even ask me to do what I know you're about to say." Kenny had his hands up in defensive mode, waving them, saying, "No."

"Don't make me beg, but I will. Kenny there is no way I can go to that church and confront Chantal. It would hurt her more coming from me. All her friends and family will see me leave and wonder what happened. All the paparazzi that are surrounding the church, it will turn into a circus out there. Please, man, do this for me. I'm going to write a letter that will be here waiting for her when she returns."

"Where are you going?"

"Tyler was supposed to leave for the island of Mustique this morning. I'm going to go with her and we'll take a later flight. By the time Chantal gets here, we'll be gone. My letter will fully explain everything. She and Shari can take the trip to Fiji, and hopefully by the time they return, Chantal won't be so angry."

"Andre, I don't know, this is the same chick that slit her wrists trying to win you back. She may wig out on me and beat me with her shoe or something."

"Kenny, stop playing," Andre said, annoyed by his comment.

"I'm not playing. Something ain't quite right with that chick."

"Listen, go to the church and ask to speak to Chantal in private. Tell her that I sent you because it would hurt too bad to see the disappointment on her face but that I'm not ready to get married. Let her know that I have explained everything in a letter that I left on the nightstand in the bedroom. If she asks where I am, tell her that I got on a flight this morning and would call her later to see how she is doing. But no matter how angry she gets or even if she curses you out, Kenny, do not be cruel to her." Kenny stood in the middle of the study, speechless. He was the same defense attorney who cut prosecution witnesses to shreds on the witness stand, but to have to break the heart of a would-be blushing bride was more than he could stomach.

Chantal stood in the mirror, admiring what a vision of perfection she was. She had never seen a more gorgeous bride. With her full spread in *InStyle* magazine she would be the envy of all grown women and little girls everywhere. Chantal's chic chignon hair-style and super-sized diamond earrings perfectly complemented her white strapless gown that clasped every curve in her hour-glass figure. Chantal's stylist came over and made the final touches to her makeup and it was show time.

"Chantal, are you ready?" Shari asked, as she grabbed her best friend's delicate hand.

"Definitely," Chantal said with pure confidence.

"Before we go out there and you face all those people I want to tell you something. Chantal, I truly love you. You're the sister I never had. To see you standing here looking like a princess is un-believable. We've been through so much together and I know you truly love Andre and that you're going to make him a wonderful wife. We joke a lot about landing that one sponsor who will change our life forever, but I know you and I know your heart. Andre is the only man that you've ever given your heart to and one day he'll re-alize just how lucky he is to have a gem like you." The two women held each other in a deep embrace, not noticing that Kenny was standing in the entrance of the door.

"Excuse me, I'm sorry to interrupt but can I speak to Chantal alone for a minute?"

"What's up, Kenny? Don't tell me that Andre is running late. Everyone is waiting for us."

"Can I speak to you alone, Chantal?" he repeated, not cracking a smile. Shari could sense that something was wrong but remained unruffled for Chantal.

"Whatever you have to tell me you can say it in front of Shari. She's family."

"I'd much rather tell you in private."

"Chantal, it's not a problem, I'll be right outside," Shari said, making her way to the door.

"No, you stay right here, Shari. I want you to hear what Kenny has to say." Kenny glanced at Shari and then back at Chantal. He so wanted to get the whole thing over with that he wasn't about to go back and forth about if Shari was staying or not. Plus, he figured she would need her girlfriend to console her after the news he was about to break.

"I'm going to come right out with it, Chantal: Andre won't be showing up here today. He can't go through with the wedding," Kenny stated matter-of-factly.

"There must be some mistake. You never liked me, Kenny, and now you're trying to ruin my wedding day. But this isn't funny. There are hundreds of people waiting for me to walk down the aisle. Andre would never leave me standing at the altar." The shivering of Chantal's lips and the twitching of what seemed to be her entire face made Shari and Kenny stand there frozen.

"Chantal, calm down. Andre sent me because he didn't want to see the pain in your face when he broke your heart. He explained everything in a letter that is waiting at home for you."

"A letter, a fucking letter! This isn't happening to me! Andre loves me, he really does. We belong together. No one will ever love Andre the way that I do. He has to marry me. What will I tell Melanie?" Chantal was now sitting on the floor, rocking back and forth. Shari ran to her side and laid her head on Chantal's shoulder, trying to carry some of her pain. At that moment Kenny had not only broken Chantal's heart but Shari's, too.

"Chantal, I'm so sorry," Kenny said sincerely.

"Where is he, Kenny? Tell me where Andre is."

"He took a flight out early this morning. He said he would call you later to make sure you're all right." Before Kenny could say another word, Chantal scurried past him with vengeance in her eyes.

As T-Roc drove down Sunset Boulevard he got the call he'd been waiting for. "Hello. Tell me something good."

"How about I tell you something great," his most trusted informant replied.

"That's even better."

"Meet me at our usual spot in an hour."

"What for? You can't tell me over the phone?"

"The skeleton we hoped to drag out of the closet on your enemy Andre turned out to be a full-fledged grave. This information is so explosive I have to see the expression on your face when I reveal all."

"Say no more. I'm on the way." T-Roc made a U-turn in the middle of the street, smiling at the thought of finally bringing Andre down once and for all.

SEVENTEEN

Sweet Dreams

Tyler finally believed that her heart was at peace. For so long, true love eluded her and she was suppressing the pink inside-out of fear that she would once again be left blindsided by a man's deception. But her love for Andre and his love for her was the key that unlocked all of her inhibitions.

"I can't believe I'm here with you right now. I feel like the luckiest girl in the world," Tyler beamed, as she hugged and kissed Andre.

"You are the luckiest girl and I'm the luckiest guy," he said, rubbing the tip of his nose against the tip of hers. "Although I would love to sit here and debate who is luckier, we need to get dressed and catch this flight. I can't wait to get you on that island and make love to you every day and every night. Not only do I want to make love, but I'm hoping that we'll make a baby. Does that sound like a plan to you?"

"Actually that doesn't sound like a plan at all," Tyler said shifting her body on the couch so her back was now turned away from Andre.

"Tyler, please don't tell me that you want to wait to have kids because of your career? I thought we were past all of that," he said, grabbing her arm so they would be face-to-face. Tyler was trying to hold back the grin that was about to escape, before answering his question.

"No, the reason why we don't have to plan is because we're already pregnant." Tyler stood for a minute absorbing the shocked look on Andre's face. While he sat with his mouth agape she continued, "I knew that when I came over here last night, but I didn't want you to take me back because of a baby. I wanted you to take me back for me, for the love we share for one another."

After finally getting over the initial shock, he said, "You must be at least three months pregnant. I can't believe this. Not only are you going to be my wife but you're also going to be the mother of my child." Andre rubbed Tyler's stomach, overjoyed that he would once again be a father, but this time by a woman he would spend the rest of his life with.

"Andre, this all seems like a dream to me. It's like I don't want to wake up because I'm afraid it won't be real."

"Baby, you don't have to be afraid, this is not a dream. This is about two people who belong together. I promise you that I will spend the rest of my life making you the happiest woman in the world." Andre went in his pants pocket and pulled out the pink diamond engagement ring that Tyler had given back to him what seemed like a lifetime ago. He slid the sparkler on her long slender finger and in both of their hearts they felt like husband and wife.

After making love and then taking a long hot shower and then making love again, the lovebirds were ready to catch their flight to Mustique. Andre and Tyler walked hand-and-hand out the door oblivious to their surroundings because they were so caught up in their love.

Chantal was contaminated with hatred when she bolted out the church and jumped in her Benz. As she sped off, the paparazzi went ballistic coming up with scenarios as to why the bride-to-be stormed out the church like a bat out of hell and where she was off to on her wedding day. Chantal kept replaying the words that Kenny said to her. *Andre isn't going to marry you.* It was suffocating her brain. All she could think about was getting home and reading the letter that he left. There had to be an explanation for all this, and some sort of clue as to how she could get him back. As Chantal pulled up to the driveway she slowed down when she saw what was supposed to have been her future husband lovingly embracing her archenemy. She sat in her car from a distance studying the couple as if they were strangers. The man was standing on the front door steps kissing the woman and running his fingers through her long dark hair. The woman jumped up and wrapped her legs around the man's waist and he twirled her around as if they were new young lovers. They laughed and smiled at one another as if they were the only two people in the world, as if no one else existed or mattered. Chantal couldn't help but wish it were her.

Shari seized Kenny's arm as he was turning to leave. "Wait a minute, Kenny. I want you to tell me what's really going on with Andre."

"No disrespect, Shari, but I explained everything that needed to be said to Chantal. I'm done here."

"How can you come and wreck a woman's world and then say you're done? I know you're not that cold, maybe Andre but not you."

"You don't even know me, so you can't say what type of man I am."

"I know that you were the one who had enough balls to break the news to Chantal, instead of Andre's coward ass doing it."

"I know the whole situation is a little fucked up, but Andre means well."

"A little! He left the mother of his child at the church on their wedding day. That is more than a little fucked up. Now I have to go out there and explain to hundreds of people and a sweet innocent little girl why her parents aren't getting married today. Now I want some answers." Kenny put his head down and turned his back, leaving Shari to answer her own questions.

Reality returned and Chantal comprehended that the couple weren't strangers but the love of her life Andre and the love of his life, Tyler Blake. She looked down at her $100,000 custom-made Vera Wang wedding gown and the diamond-studded Manolo that was placed firmly on the brakes. Her fresh French-manicured hands were gripping the steering wheel to her silver CL600 Coupe. It all made sense now. Andre wasn't marrying her because his heart belonged to a woman who didn't deserve him. No matter how hard Chantal tried, Andre couldn't accept as true that her mentality had gone from hooker to housewife. Instead, he chose a woman who didn't truly love him at all. But there was no way that Tyler Blake would steal her thunder. Andre and Chantal had exchanged vows and it was until death do them part. Chantal lifted one Manolo off the brake and pressed the other on the gas.

Tyler was the first to notice the silver Benz racing toward them. She had a flashback to when she was a teenager in Georgia and everything went in slow motion as Trey, the abusive boyfriend she dated in high school, blew his brains out. Tyler's body once again froze, and as the sound of the engine got closer and louder, Andre slowly turned his head and locked eyes with the deranged Chantal, and all Tyler could let out was, "Andre look out!"

CPSIA information can be obtained
at www.ICGtesting.com
Printed in the USA
LVHW031926110321
681237LV00005B/101

9 780312 354084